Lazarus Rising

Anthony D. Flores

Dedication

I dedicate this novel to my stepfather, Jack, who despite everything I put my entire family through, has always been there for me. Thank you for contributing to my education by buying all my school books. This work of fiction is just a small part of what your investment has produced. I love you and cherish our time together.

Part One

In the Beginning...

*"The people never give up their liberties
but under some delusion."*
—Edmund Burke, 1784

1

September 11th, 2016.

The sun shined brightly down on the harbor in Dana Point. The morning fog had dissipated, yet the air still had a chill to it. Power boats slowly made their way in carrying drunk tourists and locals disguised as fishermen. Seagulls dipped and floated and searched for food from high above. Abigail Payne stood between two trees; her long, auburn hair lifted slightly from the wind. Through her cheap, oversized sunglasses she could see the coast of San Clemente as a small crowd began to make its way to the front of a short stage.

But her thoughts weren't on the beauty or activities going on around her. She could barely smell the salt from the ocean. For most Americans, it was the fifteenth anniversary of a horrible act that led to a decade of war. That wasn't the case for Abigail. Since her mom was visiting the World Trade Center when the planes hit, that horrendous act was much more personal.

"Hey." She turned and smiled, recognizing the voice of her father. "Happy birthday, baby girl." He took her in his arms and squeezed her tall gangling body. Since Abigail had moved out two years ago and started college they had only seen each other a handful of times.

"It's not until tomorrow," she told him.

"I can't believe it, my little girl is twenty-one!" he said, with a grin on his face.

Abigail shook her head. She could see tears begin to form in his eyes. Her birthdays were always bitter sweet. She knew he did his best to separate their horror on 9/11 from

7

the celebration of each birthday, but they both realized years ago it just wasn't possible.

"Jack?" it was a woman's voice.

"Hey, honey, I want you to meet my daughter." Abigail could hear the stumble in his voice. She backed off and stared at him with dagger-filled eyes.

"Abby, this is Karen. Karen and I—well, we've kind of been dating for a while now," he said wearing a nervous smile.

"Nice to meet you, Abby," Karen said, extending her hand.

She shook her hand. "It's Abigail," she barked. Karen apologized as the three of them stood frozen in the uncomfortable moment of silence.

"Welcome ladies and gentlemen," a voiced echoed from the speakers on the temporary stage. "It is my pleasure to introduce the Congressman from the 47th district, Forrest Vance." The speakers squealed; the applause was sparse and lethargic.

"Good afternoon, and welcome to the families of the victims of that tragic event fifteen years ago. Your sacrifice is not forgotten." Vance's voice had the sound of defeat. He had been serving in the House for the past twelve years, but the new Congressional lines left little hope for a Democrat even of his stature to win reelection. He thundered on playing to the few fans he had in the crowd. He needed a miracle to win...or a deal with the devil.

Abigail could only hear the troubling voices in her head.

"And I say to you that it is *my* job to fight. Fight for better jobs, better pay, and for the small business owner. I have spent my life fighting for the little guy. So remember, on November 8th, to cast your vote for Forrest Vance. God bless you, and God Bless America!" He finished with the typical hands in the air hoping to ignite the crowd.

Once again the applause fell flat.

Abigail fumed. Karen wanted to run. Jack Payne prayed.

"Nothing more dangerous than a man with nothing to lose," Jack said breaking the silence. Karen put her hand on his back and rubbed.

Abigail closed her eyes praying for calm. She opened them and looked away from her father. The withdrawn faces of the crowd told her everything she needed to know about Vance; his political career was over. She couldn't pinpoint it, but there was something about this man that told her he had bigger problems: it was in his voice, in his demeanor, in his very *soul*.

"Dad," she started abruptly, "can I speak to you?" Abby turned to him refusing to make eye contact with *her*. The two of them walked over behind a tree. In the distance she could see a mother and father sitting at a picnic table. A white cloth covered it and two kids, a boy and a girl, chased each other around in a circle as the mom placed bowls of food strategically from the cooler. Abigail's hands turned to fists. She quickly turned and faced her father with cold, piercing eyes.

"Look—"

"Stop! I don't want to hear it," she yelled. Abigail huffed as her body fell limp. In a quiet yet stern tone she continued, "I can't believe you brought her here to meet on this day. On this day! What—what were you thinking? What about mom?" She put her hand up letting Jack know that she wasn't finished. Deep in the back of her mind she knew at some point her father would find someone. She understood how ridiculous she was being after fifteen years. The idea that her father would have to become some monk or remain celibate for the rest of his life was unfair. But this...this person didn't look right for him. This Karen woman had auburn hair, obviously dyed to look like her mother's. She probably was just a dumb blonde. Abigail noticed that she stood taller than most women and carried herself like she was important. She wasn't fat, but Abigail knew in a few years she would be.

She folded her arms across her white blouse suddenly realizing she had nothing more to say. "Well?" she asked.

"Abs, please, I know this isn't easy, I know—I realize the timing is bad, it's just that, well, we don't see each other that often and—"

"Hi folks, how you doing?" It was Vance. Both Jack

and Abigail turned and shook his hand. "You must be the famous Jack Payne. I've heard so much about you; thank God there's people like you in our government."

"Thank you, Congressman. This is my daughter, Abby."

"You know, your dad is a hero." Abigail smiled and shook her head. She looked over at her father and wished this Karen thing hadn't hit such a nerve. After the attacks and mom's funeral, Jack had joined a Special Forces group that Abigail never knew much about. After five years of running around stopping terrorists, one day he just quit. There was no explanation. Abigail came to the conclusion that her father finally realized he couldn't kill enough of them to bring Elizabeth back.

"Congressman," Jack said as he led Vance over to meet his girlfriend, "allow me to introduce you to my friend, Karen." Abigail had to get away. She made it to her car before she turned around. There stood her father searching the area for her. His favorite, collared white shirt with the faded palm tree waved in the wind. Their eyes met.

"Abs!" he yelled.

She looked down and opened the car door. She paused and contemplated a final look but knew if she glanced at her father again she wouldn't be able to leave. The engine of her 1990s Mustang roared. Tears dropped off her face like a November rain as she slipped on her seatbelt. She put the car in gear and drove off past her father where he still stood on the side of the road. She turned and crossed the bridge to the mainland side of the harbor.

***

Congressman Vance had moved on in a vain effort to shake everybody's hand that day. He caught a glimpse of a family torn apart by death and confusion, and cracked a smile. *Misery loves company,* his mom told him when he was just a boy. Deep down Vance knew it was his mother who had made him successful. Still, he hated her.

***

Karen walked over to Jack. "Honey, you alright?" she asked. He shook his head.

"Did you tell her? Did you tell her about the baby?"

2

"Mr. Parker, the bottom line is I need your support," Vance said. The living room had a lingering Lysol smell. Congressman Vance sat at the kitchen table with Lazarus' parents, Barry and Lucille Parker. The table had a dark, redwood finish with four chairs that stood as tall as barstools. The kitchen island had a stainless steel sink in it and was quite big compared to the other rooms of the house. Off to Vance's right was the living room. A large flat screen TV hung in front of a black leather couch and a La-Z-Boy chair Lazarus was only allowed to use when his father wasn't home.

"Well," Vance got up out of the chair, "I won't take up any more of your Saturday."

Lazarus still had his mind on the man that was waiting for the Congressman, standing at the front door. How cool it must be to have someone wait on you hand and foot. For as long as Lazarus could remember he loved politics and all the bling that went with it. He listened in awe to what Vance had said about the real needs in this country and how the Republicans were out to get people like the Parkers. When Vance talked about how difficult it was for "us regular folks—*he knew Vance meant black folks*—to get jobs," Lazarus could relate. Nobody would hire him. He was seventeen now and looking to buy his own wheels. The chances of his mom and dad buying him a car were slim to none, and slim had already left town.

The family walked Vance to the door and Lazarus opened it. Vance shook his parents' hands then said, "As for you," he put out his hand to Lazarus, "you let me know when you're ready to join the campaign. I have a feeling you'd be my ticket to Washington." Vance turned and walked out towards the black Mercedes with the man standing at the door.

Barry Parker looked over at his wife, Lucille. "Son-ova-bitch doesn't even *buy* American." He closed the door and walked back into the kitchen.

"Yeah, but Dad, he's looking out for us," Lazarus said.

"He's a politician, son. He only came here today because we're black and your mom votes Democrat. I doubt he even knows that I'm a registered Republican."

"Well, what about his voting record? He talked about that and how he's trying to get us more jobs." Lazarus had followed his father all the way to the recliner. His father was looking for some relaxation and a chance to watch his Bruins play.

"Son, if any of them, including this Vance character, is really looking out for us than why have things stayed so bad? Why can't anyone get a job?"

"The government needs to do more. It's that simple. Us African-Americans have to stick together—"

"Who taught you we're from Africa? I'm an American," Barry exclaimed, "don't let these people separate us. No matter what your beliefs, color, sex, any of that, we are *all* Americans. As long as we allow those in Washington to keep us apart, they will continue to do as they please."

Lazarus huffed and made gestures with his hands expressing how "old" his father sounded.

"And as for that government you're so in love with, remember it's the same one that called a black man a slave. Don't look to the government to solve your problems," his father finished. Barry picked up the remote and turned on the television.

"But...but, Dad." Lazarus wanted to continue the discussion, but his father was done. He stood there for a minute hoping his father would reengage. His dad leaned back and melted into the chair. His bald head formed beads of sweat after seeing the score of the football game. Lazarus folded his arms and looked over to his mom for help. She just shrugged.

"Son, if you want to sit down and watch some football

with your dear old dad, great, but the discussion is over."

Lazarus threw his arms in the air and expressed his disappointment with a heavy sigh. He stomped off into his bedroom and slammed the door shut.

"I don't know what to do about that son of yours," Barry told his wife.

"Very funny. That stubbornness is all Parker," she said.

***

Outside Congressman Vance and his right hand man, Phillip Shaw, stepped into the back of the Mercedes. The stale stench of cigar smoke still lingered from the past weekend trip to Palm Desert.

"So what do you think, sir, do you have their vote?" Phillip asked.

"They're black, those people always vote Democrat." Vance looked over with a devious smile. "What I really need is their money."

3

Rain had poured down on most of Orange County on that late October day. Forrest Vance sat behind the driver in his black Mercedes smoking a cigarette. His window was cracked just an inch but the water still found its way in. The sounds and screeches of the windshield wipers mixed with the continuous pounding of raindrops played the unfamiliar tune of defeat. The three men in the car didn't say a word; they didn't have to; Vance would lose his seat in a landslide.

The trio was driving back to Vance's home in Mission Viejo. It was just past 7 p.m. and they were on the 5 freeway going north, stuck in yet another traffic jam. Two hours ago they were in a potential donor's home giving the usual kitchen table talk Vance had perfected years ago when the news began to air. The usual cute stories of dog saving man or man saving dog were given their 22 seconds followed by local and national sports, and finally culminating with the—why do we even have it—weather report for Orange County. Of course, right in the middle, as promised by that anchor with the fake hair, a different district would be highlighted each night before the election. Tonight it was district 47s turn.

"Incumbent Congressman Forrest Vance has slipped in the poles to twenty-seven percent," the TV news anchor explained.

Vance did his best to keep his chin up. He had to keep rolling with his usual spiel about jobs and what his victory would mean to the future, but it was no use. The Simpson family, although stanch Democrats and loaded, were not in the business of throwing money away. They gave Vance the 'we gave a small fortune to help that lady senator get her seat back' speech and wished him the best of luck. He didn't even get dinner out of the meeting.

Kill your opponent…

And so he got back into the car with his tail between his legs and began the long journey home to his wife. He called to let her know he was running a little late with the traffic, but there was no answer. Since the party choose to allow the redrawn districts that basically ended his career—*the Speaker won't even talk to you*—he had been left on his own. The relationship with Victoria had become even more strained than it was before. Something Vance once thought was not possible.

He threw the cigarette out the window, rolled the window up, glared down at the floor, and realized he never should have picked a trophy wife. Once the power and money were gone, she would be, too.

Vance began to wonder what went wrong. And when. He got into politics to help others. He was an idealist hoping to make changes for a better world. Maybe it is true that people go to Washington to change it, but instead Washington changes them. The power had consumed him, and then when some slick veteran member took him by the hand and taught him the ropes he went along for the ride.

Vance sat in the car realizing he never once—*so what*— cared what he was doing didn't help anyone. He looked around at some who slept in their offices and lived by what they believed in—worked hard to pass legislation they thought would benefit the people. *Their chumps*— Yeah, but who's the chump now?

The traffic moved a few more inches then started to race by on Vance's side. He stared out the window and watched as each person stared right at him, not even watching the road. Out the back window from all sides every eye was on him. From Phillip's side, who sat right next to him he could see the lady in the car next to them—staring at him. Two small children plastered their faces against the rear window of the car in front of her; just glaring at him. Phillip turned and stared back. In the rearview mirror the driver stared. Eyes from everywhere pierced Vance's very soul.

Kill your opponent…

Vance put his head down and closed his eyes. He covered his ears with his hands, wanting to keep out the noise in his head. The car began to speed up.

"So that's what was holding us up," Phillip said.

Vance sat back up and peeked in every direction. Nothing. No one was staring anymore. *Did that just happen? Or had he imagined it?*

An accident was being moved on to the shoulder of the freeway. The ambulance's flashing lights made Vance dizzy. He put his hand up to his forehead and checked to see if he had a fever. It was hot, sweaty and pulsating with each beat of his heart. There was a stale stench in the air. One of the stretchers being loaded into the ambulance had a body that was completely covered. Vance shook his head knowing that meant the person was dead. But he no feeling of loss or empathy. He felt hollow inside.

The two EMTs that were about to load the stretcher into the vehicle stopped what they were doing and ran over to the other victim. Vance kept his eyes on the dead. The body lifted itself up and lowered the sheet. The man's forehead was torn to shreds and covered in blood. The whites of his eyes had been filled with streaks of red as he stared right at the Congressman.

"Kill your opponent," the body said. Vance could hear the man's voice as if he was sitting right next to him.

He screamed.

"Sir, are you alright?" Phillip asked with concern.

Vance glanced back to the ambulance. Everything was normal. "I'm fine, Phillip. It's nothing. I just need some sleep."

***

The black Mercedes pulled into the sloping driveway of the two-story, five bedroom house on Tiagua Road. The Vances had moved in just after the redistricting in 2015. The rain had stopped finally. It was the only thing all day that seemed to go Vance's way. The house sat consumed in darkness except for one lone flickering light coming from the master bedroom.

Phillip opened the door for the Congressman. Vance could smell the freshness in the air that always lingered after a storm.

Parked on the street in front of their house was an old 80s Corvette. The gold paint that once shined now had a dull glow.

"Damn it," shrieked Vance. He shook his head and looked up at his trusted friend that had become his right hand man for the past decade.

Phillip shrugged and smiled.

It took Vance by surprise.

"Perhaps you need to teach her a lesson, sir," he said.

The Congressman moved around Phillip and headed for his front door. Looking back, both his assistant and the driver nodded, then grinned.

Vance opened the door and stepped in. Outside the rain began to fall once again. Thunder shook the very foundation of the house and Vance almost lost his balance. He wanted so bad to sit down and cry, or run for his very life, or—*kill her*—lie down and sleep for eternity. But something deep down inside compelled him to walk up the stairs.

Each step Forrest Vance took was another step to knowing what he already knew. He hated her; he hated himself. The desire to make her pay was strong. The need to feel sorry for himself was stronger.

Down the hall Vance could see the bedroom door was open. The usually sweet scent of sex consumed the entire floor. There was nothing sweet about it to Vance. He gently stepped towards the door—*kill her*—wanting to catch them in the act, and then hoping this was all some twisted nightmare. The floor creaked beneath him.

"Oh shit, I think he's home," she whispered.

Vance stepped into the room and watched two naked bodies scrambling for cover. "What the hell is going on here?" His words cracked and stumbled with each crazy emotion. He wanted to wish all this pain away. The young man with his wife was just a teenager. He fell over trying to put on his underwear. The kid grabbed his pants and shirt and shoes and ran past the Congressman with panic stricken eyes.

WHY DIDN'T YOU KILL HIM? The voice was loud in his head.

Vance realized he would be completely justified had he killed the little shit. His wife sat back on the bed and lit a cigarette. Vance knew it was the right thing to kill her as well. But instead he stood frozen in fear.

She put her back against the headboard and laid on top of the bed without a stitch of clothing on. She laughed at him. Laughed.

"You're so pathetic. That little boy did more for me tonight than you have during our entire marriage." She pointed at him. "Loser."

"I can't be—"

"Believe *what?* That I married you for love? You promised the White House, remember? Shit, I would've settled for Secretary of State or some lowly cabinet position but now, huh, now what?" She took a drag from her smoke and exhaled. "You're a loser, that's all you are. Twenty-seven percent of the vote? *Hell*, I'm not even going to vote for you."

Forrest wanted to choke the life out of the woman. The muscles in his arms tensed up and his face turned red. He began to breath heavy and closed his eyes. The voices in his head all shouted at once. The hatred in his heart settled down long enough for him to decide she wasn't even worth it. The one coherent thought said he wouldn't get away with killing her.

You coward.

"What is a loser like you going to do about it?" she asked.

He turned and walked away. He just couldn't do it. He didn't have it in him.

***

Election night, November 8th, 2016. Congressman (soon to be former) Forrest Vance sat in front of the TV in the Casablanca Inn in San Clemente, California. Just him and

Phillip. He knew he couldn't be with her tonight. The 32 inch flat screen clearly spouted out whatever version the two sides of the aisle were trying to convey to the American public. Phillip continued to switch between MSNBC and FOX NEWS and CNN waiting to hear who would announce first who the new president-elect would be. The race for the 47th district between incumbent Forrest Vance and some slick newcomer in the Republican Party Willy Tills had been over months ago.

YOU SHOULD HAVE KILLED YOUR OPPONENT.

Vance picked up his cell phone and called *her*.

No answer.

The blood in his veins began to boil. He went over and opened the window. The sound of waves crashing down on the beach was once something that had soothed Vance and could calm him down, no matter what the disturbance. That was no longer the case.

"We can now tell you, wait— is it official? Yes? Ladies and gentlemen your new president is Jefferson Smith from Tenneessee," the news anchor said.

The new president's picture came on the screen with the words 'president-elect' under it. The picture showed a man in his mid-forties with perfect, wavy dirty blonde hair and a JFK smile. His charcoal black suit and red tie was typical politician. On his left collar was the flag lapel everyone had to wear nowadays.

"Those bastards even won the White House," Vance said shaking his head. "It's hot in here."

"Did she answer her phone?"

"Huh? No," Forrest answered.

"You know what *that* means, right?" Phillip asked.

Vance nodded. "I got to get out of here. It's too hot, I'm going home." Vance circled the room, picking up this and that looking for his keys. Phillip stopped him, grabbed his hand, placed the keys and softly rolled Vance's fingers around them.

Phillip smiled, "Call if you need me."

The Congressman started the engine and grabbed the steering wheel with both hands. He needed to get home and—*teach her a lesson*—let her know that he was leaving her. With the end of his political career he could move on and lead a simpler life.

He put the car in reverse and headed towards the freeway.

The night was surprisingly warm for this time of year. The moonlight had a silvery coating to it. He raced the black Mercedes down the fast lane. As he passed each car on the road—and strangely there was hardly any traffic on the streets—*they* stared at him like they did *that* night. But this time it was different. This time he wasn't scared, nor did he give it a second thought. Vance's mind was consumed with the conversation—*kill her*—playing out in his imagination. The car seemed to be driving itself.

He peered down at the speedometer: *100*. "Gotta keep two hands on the wheel," he said, grimaced and stomped on the gas.

In front of him all the vehicles moved to the sides and let the great Forrest Vance pass, unimpeded by anything but his own interfering thoughts. The idea that he wouldn't go through with—*killing her*—leaving her started to creep in. He wanted to push down more on the gas but his foot was on the floor.

I have to get there NOW!

Vance closed his eyes briefly. When he opened them, he had pulled into his driveway. The driver's side door opened. There was that constant *ding* sound coming from the car. He stepped out of the vehicle and with care closed the door, shutting off the light and ding.

"I'm just going to—*kill her*—talk with her, reason with her, tell her how much I care," he whispered to himself on the way up to the front door.

This is YOUR house!

The door made a creepy sound as he made his way in. Vance headed for the kitchen first. The smell of sex filled the entire house. Again. Vance grabbed the butcher knife off the wall magnet and headed upstairs to the master bedroom. He held the knife just to—*kill*—scare her—and—*kill*—him. He wasn't quiet about it this time and could hear the usual rustle and bustle of two people caught. On the second floor of the house Vance walked briskly towards the bedroom. Out popped a man in his mid-forties that reminded Vance of the new president.

Kill them.

He flashed the butcher knife. "GET BACK IN THERE," he said in a voice that came from someplace deep in the darkness of his soul.

The man dropped to his knees and started to wail. His butt huggers were inside out.

Pathetic, Vance thought. As he stormed by the man, he grabbed a handful of the bastard's hair and dragged him back into the bedroom.

"Really, loser? What are you going to do, make us dinner?" she said.

Once again she was completely naked, smoking a cigarette, and sitting at the head of the bed. "We've been in this position before, only this time you're pretending you're going to do something about it, huh?"

Vance dropped the knife down to his side. The air had been drained from his lungs. His shoulders hunched over.

The man picked himself up and started to put on his pants.

"You were right, he is a loser," the man said.

KILL THEM!

All Vance could see was red. The slashing and hacking and screaming lasted a lifetime. The blood on the walls painted pictures in his mind of a brilliant future without *her*. When she finally stopped screaming he was thankful, but at the same time longed to hear more. After bashing the bastard's brains in with the butt of the butcher knife, he liked the expression on his face so much that he laid the man on the ground with the utmost care. His wife was not so lucky. Her once model-like body was stacked in a pile.

When Vance had finished the deed he walked over to the turntable she had bought him for Christmas last year and turned it on. From the speakers blared "The Marriage of Figaro," by Mozart. He waltzed around the room conducting the orchestra. He allowed the music to flow through his body as he performed for the first time for a *not so* live audience.

"I always wanted to do that for you, honey," he said pulling his phone out, looking at his dead wife. Under contacts he found 'Phillip Shaw' and pushed the green 'Call' button.

"Hello former Congressman Vance," Phillip answered. "How can I help you?"

"I have a small problem you need to take care of for me." He knew Phillip was the man for the job—he didn't know why. A voice or a thought, or some outside force pushed, prodded, and coaxed Vance to make the call.

"I was hoping that's why you called. Just stay put, I'll take care of everything. Including the resurrection of your political career."

4

Lazarus Parker trudged up Alicia Parkway and headed right for the small strip mall. The past couple years had not been kind to the businesses here. *For Lease* signs appeared in seven out of the ten storefronts. All that remained was an Irish pub that had been there since Mission Viejo had become a city, an attorney's office, and the newly opened headquarters for the 2018 campaign to elect Forrest Vance.

He folded his arms to keep out the cold. *I wouldn't need a jacket if I had a car.* Moving briskly along the sidewalk the argument between him and his dad continued in his head; what he *should* have said; what he *meant* to say, and better ways to *say it* invaded his mind.

Although the sun shined bright, it was the wind that kept the temperature low. Packs of vehicles filled the congested parkway creating as much noise pollution as air pollution. People in a hurry to go nowhere on that early, Saturday afternoon appeared light years away from humanity. Lazarus felt sorry for them. Their lives were meaningless. They all looked miserable just waiting for someone or something to save them from themselves.

Leaders like Forrest Vance were the answer. People couldn't be trusted to do what was in their best interest. The best evidence Lazarus had was the inexplicable election of a reactionary like the idiot President Jefferson Smith. Didn't they realize only the rich would benefit when a Republican was in office?

Barry Parker disagreed. Lazarus thought it was funny how uninformed old people really were. The country was inherently racist and unfair, and guys like Vance were there to help balance that out. His dad said the opposite was true. That it's actually racist to think blacks and Mexicans and other minorities can only succeed with the help of the government. Of course, he grew up privileged, in the middle class, and owned a business. He made *his* money off the backs of others.

"And still," Lazarus whispered under his breath, "he wants me to work for a car."

The bell rang when he opened the door. Lazarus rubbed both arms vigorously hoping the friction would start a fire, or at the very least warm him up. Boxes were stacked everywhere. A lone brown desk sat in front of a hallway leading to the back of the store. A wiry, black kiosk stood empty. A few stacks of flyers designed to 'get the word out' about Vance sat on the desk next to a silver lamp not yet plugged in.

"Good afternoon, can I help you?" a man said coming from the back of the room.

"Yeah, I saw you were looking for help in the paper today," Lazarus answered.

"We certainly could use someone to pass out flyers and get the word out to the younger kids, son," the man said smugly.

"I'm not some snot nose little shit. I've met Mr. Vance before and believe in his vision; don't jerk my chain, mister. And don't call me *son*."

"Sorry, usually kids your age—"

"Are what? Stupid? Screw you, man."

"Maybe you should leave," the man said, remaining calm.

Lazarus turned around and headed out the door, the bell sounding once more. "Whatever."

"Wait," said a familiar voice behind Lazarus. "Young man, come back here."

The calming tone stopped Lazarus in his tracks. Slowly he turned back around and saw Forrest Vance moving towards him.

"Your name is Lazarus, right? I remember meeting you with your parents, the Parkers, a couple of years ago."

"That's right, and you told me to come help you when I was old enough." He motioned to the man standing behind him. "But this—"*dickhead*, that was the word he wanted to use, "this—guy—"

"Please, I'm sorry for the misunderstanding. This is Phillip Shaw, and despite his poor first impression I couldn't breathe without him." Vance stepped to the side so the two men could shake hands.

Lazarus had a funny feeling about this guy. He had a unibrow. A friend once told him that a unibrow was a sign of evil. Certainly he didn't think this man was evil, but ever since his buddy told him that anytime he saw one he couldn't help but think about it. Despite the silly adage about the unibrow, Lazarus felt uneasy around him. Still, he offered his hand and made peace.

"Pleased to meet you. Hope there's no hard feelings. I'm willing to let bygones be bygones."

"Come on back and we'll discuss what role you can play for my campaign," Vance said. The two of them disappeared into the back room.

For the next hour or so Lazarus learned about the vision. There was a certain charisma circling Vance and Lazarus was consumed by it. He realized there was a certain amount of bullshit that went with being a politician, but instantly he trusted this man. They engaged in a conversation like they had been friends for years.

"So, how are we going to win this time?" Lazarus asked. "You're still way behind in the polls, Mr. Vance."

"You leave that to me," he said. "Here is a package that I would like you to deliver to Willy Tills." He handed Lazarus an orange envelope sealed. Based on the bulk of it, there was a number of CDs inside.

Lazarus gave him a strange look. "You mean, your opponent?"

"That's correct," he grinned. Vance handed him a piece of paper with an address on it and a set of keys. "Take my car."

***

The envelope was delivered without incident. Lazarus drove back to the storefront in silence since the noise in his head was so loud. On his way over to Congressman Tills' home he fought with himself to keep from opening it up. He imagined what must be in that package. *Had the Congressman had an affair? Did he misuse government funds? Perhaps he killed a man.*

Lazarus had been taken aback when it was the actual Congressman himself that answered the door. He figured all these damn politicians had maids and butlers and were born with a silver spoon in their mouth. Especially those Republicans. His father continued to point to the fact that Lincoln was the one who freed the slaves; he was a Republican. But also a dictator—the benevolent one as those who wanted to give him a pass would call him.

Lazarus loved to remind his father about all the 'crimes' Lincoln committed against his so-called beloved Constitution. In his eyes, the Constitution was nothing more than a slave document.

Tills took the papers and nodded. Lazarus grimaced knowing Vance had him cold on something. The grim look was worth the price of admission once he was able to tell the Congressman who the package came from. He didn't wait to see him open it. That moment of uncomfortableness was too much to bear.

Lazarus hit the steering wheel of the jet black four-door Cadillac. He would've kicked himself for not looking at the papers, if it was at all possible. He pulled into the parking lot, jumped out, and headed for the door. The bell rang but no one was there to greet him.

"Mr. Vance? Are you here?" he said. Slowly, like he was in some teenage horror movie, he walked down the hall peeking into each of the three rooms. Nothing.

A large, white door was built into the floor at the back of the store. The padlock was off to the side. Lazarus looked down the hall and back at the door. He shrugged and pulled it open. A narrow staircase led down.

A basement? In California? A light flickered from whatever was down there. His heart beat faster and it was hard to breathe.

"Screw it," he said nervously. He exhaled and stepped

down into the jumping light below. He couldn't hear any voices, but there was movement. With caution, he made his way down trying to wish away each creak of the wood beneath his feet.

Still, no one was there to stop him.

He made it all the way down and looked into a large room that felt like one of those bars in a fantasy novel. Lazarus wondered if he would run into an elf or halfling. He stayed low, hoping not to be seen. Splinter-filled picnic tables were everywhere. Teenagers not much younger than him sat four on each side. A man in a white coat paced the room, watching his helpers place bottles of a red liquid on each table.

Lazarus began to bite his nails and do the occasional hand through his receding hairline. Each kid was given a shot glass.

An underground bar for teenagers? Lazarus thought to himself.

At each of the twelve tables one teenager poured the red stuff into the eight shot glasses. There was not one who hesitated to drink it. The room filled with chatter and many of them grabbed for the bottle to have another.

"Stop!" yelled the thin, balding man in the white coat. His accent was Middle Eastern. Silence covered the room, but the red stuff was gone. Lazarus could hear the man mumble to himself.

"Hey!" a voice cried from behind him.

Startled, Lazarus stood up. It was Phillip. "What the hell are you doing? Get up here."

Once they both were upstairs Phillip grabbed the door and started to close it. A number of screams escaped, but then went silent once the door slammed shut. The latch and lock were put in place.

"What is going on down there?" Lazarus asked.

"We've rented the space. Campaigns are expensive; we need all the money we can get." It was Vance. He walked towards Lazarus and put his arm around him. "Did you deliver the package?"

Lazarus nodded.

"The doctor down there will pay you good money to be part of his experiments," Phillip told him.

"What kind of—"

"Never mind that," Vance started, giving Phillip a nasty look, "that's certainly not for a smart boy like you."

Lazarus hated being called 'boy.' It was a black thing. Plus, he was no longer a boy. That was something his father would call him when he got in trouble. But for some reason it was okay coming from Vance. He smiled and tried to forget about what was going on below.

By the time Lazarus arrived at home, both his parents were there. He felt comfort in the usual routine. His dad sat in his black, leather La-Z-Boy watching the news and his mom was in the kitchen preparing dinner.

"Hi Mom," he said giving her a kiss on the cheek. She gave that smile all moms do when their child shows any type of affection. Thankfulness. He went over and flopped onto the couch.

"Hey Dad, I was—"

"Shhh, hold on," his father said as he sat up.

"This is a Fox News Alert. We are now going to take you to California where first term Congressman Willy Tills has called a press conference," a sexy blonde behind the news desk announced.

The scene was the beautiful earth tone colored house Lazarus had visited earlier that afternoon. On the porch stood the Congressman, his wife and their two young children; all of them had a look of terror. Lazarus grinned knowing this was going to be good. How sweet it was that he was able to be the one that delivered the crushing blow. Finally, he would learn what this weasel was really like; what those papers said about this sorry excuse for a man. And yet, deep down in the very core of Lazarus' soul he felt—dirty.

"My fellow Americans, I come to you today to expose a crime. I have in my hands—" he stopped. Tills began to rifle through the papers in front of him. "What is…this?"

Lazarus and his father watched the man turn completely white. The Congressman looked straight into the camera—

right into the very depths of Lazarus. Sweat poured off his clean shaven face and in an instant his blonde hair was soaked. They watched as he began to shake. He tried to speak, but couldn't. From his pocket he pulled out a .38. His head began to shake back and forth. The Congressman's eyes bulged out. And then, as if he finally gained control of himself, he said, "God, please," and put the gun to his temple and fired.

The television screen went black.

5

"I want to thank each and every one of you for making this moment possible," the newly elected Congressman from California's 47ᵗʰ district said to the crowd. The large meeting room at the St. Regis Monarch in Dana Point held almost 200 people. As those in the room partied hard on this election night, in the background three different televisions broadcasted Fox News, CNN, and MSNBC simultaneously. It was 8 p.m. on the West Coast and all three networks had just announced Forrest Vance winner of his race. A race that saw the incumbent take his own life in front of his wife and children just ten months prior.

The Republicans had acted fast and did get another man's name on the ballot, but the attempt to hold this seat in a district that usually would be an easy win ended up being futile. Vance immediately soared in the polls by his actions towards the two small children and Mrs. Tills. He visited them on a regular basis; they were even incorporated into his campaign. The widow, with her son and daughter by her side, made a number of speeches honoring Vance and what he did for their family. The talk in political circles praised the brilliance of a man thought dead in the world of politics.

Vance thundered away at the business-as-usual attitude in the Capitol and how he planned to fight it. All of his words fell on deaf ears, yet at each one of his pauses the applause roared. The speech could've been in German for all they cared. Each and every one of them would've fallen on a sword for him. There was a love and dedication for Vance in the eyes of almost all who attended. A blind allegiance. Lazarus found it odd, but didn't care since Vance had come through for him, too.

Mrs. Tills and her two children sat in the front row off

to the right. She held on to her two children as if letting go would mean they would be lost forever. For a woman in her late thirties she looked tired, worn out. Her face was withdrawn. Over the past ten months she had lost over forty pounds. She used the sleeve of her white blouse to wipe away the tears that had formed.

"How are you doing, Mrs. Tills," Lazarus asked with concern. He sat next to the boy and hoped the right words would come to him.

The words didn't thunder as they once did from the stage. Vance caught Lazarus out of the corner of his eye sitting with the Tills. His eyes pierced Mrs. Tills, making it hard for her to breathe. She started shaking and pulled both kids in tighter.

"I—I just miss Willy," she answered Lazarus.

"Hey, what's your name?" he asked the boy.

"William, Dad hated Willy so I go by William," the boy's voice had an innocence to it.

Lazarus couldn't imagine what it must be like to watch your father die. Sure he loved to battle politics with his father, but he still loved him. He remembered back to when he was about William's age, ten or so. Mom wanted to start going to church and his father agreed. It seemed as if they went for a couple of years before something happened and his father stopped going. Lazarus stopped attending when he turned fifteen. He knew his mom still went every Sunday, but he often wondered what made his father stop. Because of that church, Lazarus had been able to worship a few times with him. That was an experience he'd never forget.

Lazarus looked up at Vance, nodded and smiled. The Congressman powered on an ending with the usual 'God bless you and God bless America!' He walked off the temporary stage and left the room out a side door with Phillip.

"God help us, sir," Mrs. Tills said and grabbed the arm of Lazarus. "You don't know that—that—that man. He's evil, he killed my husband," she finished.

Lazarus could see she believed it. "But, I watched him, on TV, he—"

"No, no, you don't understand. Those papers, those damn papers, they…they changed. They weren't blank, they had pictures…of the kids. They…they told him to—or else." She let go of Lazarus' arm and sat up straight. She wiped more tears from her eyes and cleared her throat.

"Ah, two of my favorite people," Vance said as he extended his hand out. He seemed to come out of nowhere. Lazarus was still trying to comprehend what Mrs. Tills had just said. "Now, Lazarus, I need you to go with Philip, he has some exciting news for you." Vance looked at Mrs. Tills with eyes that turned red—at least that's what she saw.

"But—"

Forrest Vance put his arm around Lazarus and said warmly, "I'll take care of it, son, you just go on now. You have proven yourself. I have big plans for you going forward."

"Yes, sir," Lazarus said. For one long moment he just stood there. The words had made absolutely no sense that came out of Mrs. Tills' mouth. That wasn't what bothered him, though. How could she think this about a man that had helped her so much? He figured she must be crazy; that was the only explanation that made any sense. He followed Phillip out of the room.

***

Vance asked the little boy to move and sat next to Mrs. Tills. He put his hand on her leg and softly rubbed. She couldn't look at him. She started to cry.

"Now, now, Mary, hush," he said. Vance put his arm around her and looked around. The room was filled with music and laughter and the sound of ice melting over an expensive cocktail. No one paid any attention to the widow and her children. The only light in the room came from the DJ's equipment. Whistles blew and signs were raised high in the air as people chanted 'Vance' over and over again. The 12-foot long tables had been pushed and pulled in every direction and not one person in the room drew a sober breathe—including Forrest Vance himself.

He took in the stage where he had delivered his winning speech. The banner stretched from one side of the room to the other hung high. It read: *I Can Fix That!* with Vote for Forrest Vance in bold black letters under it. He thought it was such a hooky slogan, but Phillip continued to remind him it really didn't matter.

Vance turned back to the widow. He seized a handful of her hair and forced a face to face meeting.

The smell of scotch filled her nose. She turned white and began to sweat. She tried to shake her head as if she knew what was coming. Behind his eyes she could see no life in him. She tried to catch her breath, but couldn't.

With force, he turned her head and whispered into her ear, "Mary, oh Mary, I know what you told the nigger. Now, you must pay." He breathed heavily into her ear.

She pleaded.

"Go home and wait for me, there's a car waiting outside that will drive you."

She shook uncontrollably as she clutched the hand of each of her children. Both of them asked if everything was alright. She couldn't answer. In her head she could hear a voice that spoke only to her, *You can't protect them.* She quickly looked over at Vance.

He grinned.

It was *his* voice.

***

It was Friday night. The election three days prior had lost some of its zeal for the Congressman. Phillip had already started to turn the storefront into the headquarters. Lazarus had helped out as well. Vance would be leaving on Monday for Washington since his seat was now an open one after the death of Willy Tills. He wanted to get started on all the furnishings of his new office. Tills had a couple of card tables and an old desk from his years as a prosecutor for the city of Irvine.

The newly decorated office here in California for Congressman Forrest Vance had a beautiful oak desk with a black, leather chair. Two chairs made of the finest mahogany with red leather cushions faced the desk. There sat the Chairman for the Democratic Party, Tom Sears, and Phillip. Vance leaned back in his chair and stretched his arms.

"Bottom line, Tom, you guys left me for dead," Vance said.

"Congressman, you know politics, what do you want? You're an all-star now, and I'm here to make peace."

"I want to be Speaker."

"Well, now, I'm not sure I can make—"

"Make it happen!" Vance said angrily and stood up. "Get out of my office," his eyes turned red—or at least that's what Tom Sears saw.

"I'll… I'll see what I can do," Tom said as he got up and walked briskly out of the office.

Phillip stood up, straightened his thousand-dollar black suit with pinstripes, and closed the door.

"Those bastards think they can play me. Not this time, not ever again. Is everything in place?" Vance asked Phillip.

He nodded.

"And the kid? Is he set?"

"He will be trained. Are you sure he is the one? I mean, I have plenty of kids to choose from that would follow you to their death. Why Lazarus?"

"A true believer is much more powerful than some fool on the juice," he answered.

"True, but it can be more dangerous as well."

Vance shrugged, "Perhaps, but there's something about him."

Phillip changed the subject. "Come on, it's closing time. And I have a surprise for you."

Vance gave Phillip a look.

"I know how upset you were that you didn't get to, well, take care of Tills yourself, so I set up a situation for you that I think you'll enjoy. It will complete your training as well," he finished and walked out of the office. Vance followed him outside.

The black Mercedes from the past came driving up. Vance glanced over at Phillip, excitement written all over his face. The driver stopped and walked over to let Vance in. The driver closed the door. Phillip got in on the other side and poured both of them a scotch.

"To the future Speaker of the House," he raised his glass up.

Vance, overcome with emotion, nodded and put his drink in the air.

The Mercedes pulled out of the parking lot and headed down Alicia Boulevard. Vance rubbed his hands together hoping to dry the sweat the moment had created. In a flash, the car stopped in front of the house with earth tone colors and a porch he remembered well. It was the Tills' home.

He looked at his watch, midnight. Hours had passed, but not for Vance. He shook his head and looked over at Phillip, who smiled. The driver handed him a butcher knife.

"Now, listen Forrest, not the wife," said Phillip in a condescending tone, and pointed his finger in his face.

The delivery didn't bother Vance at all. He was as giddy as a schoolboy. He could already taste the fear. He could see the terror develop in their eyes. He couldn't wait to touch the cold, lifeless body of the dead. The sound of the first scream filled Vance with a nervous excitement. He closed his eyes and could already smell the blood in the air.

The door opened. He stepped out with two hands on the butcher knife. The moment had come—

Forrest Vance was going to kill tonight.

***

Barry Parker couldn't believe the words coming from his own flesh and blood. He knew his son had a younger man's tendency to get swept away by the ideal world of socialism and its empty promises. In his own youth he remembered believing the perfect utopia could be created by man. But it didn't take Barry long to learn it was his hard work and money *they* wanted to exploit and take only to benefit those who were completely capable. Barry was more than willing to give to those who were helpless; he just objected to giving it to people who were clueless.

And yet here stood his son.

Not only was he buying into the notion that government was the answer to all their problems, but willing to spend the next two years letting *that* government train and brainwash him.

"What was the name of this organization?" Barry asked in a disapproving tone.

"The Domestic Peace League, Dad, the DPL," Lazarus answered. He wanted his approval. But Barry just sat in his black leather chair shaking his head.

"Never heard of it."

"It's a new program Congressman Vance set up, for guys like me, so I can be part of something." Lazarus looked over to his mom who sat on the couch.

She was crying. He wasn't sure if they were tears of joy or not. Mom cried at everything; Lazarus graduated high school with a 3.8 GPA, she cried. He got caught stealing a candy bar—he was nine—from Safeway, she cried.

"Great," his father said, "another government program we need to pay for. Has this Vance guy told you how we're going to pay for it?"

"Dad! This program is important, the rich need to pay their fair share."

"That 'fair share' you talk about comes from small businessmen like me. You know I almost had to close shop with all the costs Obama cost me. And I voted for the son-ova-bitch—at least the first time. Remember, son, the problem with socialism is eventually you run out of other people's money." Barry got up and went into the kitchen. He opened the fridge and pulled out a Coke.

"I'm no socialist, I just want things to be fair," Lazarus said.

"And what does that mean? Fair? Do you have any idea what that Vance guy wants—"

"Okay, enough you two," Mom started. She always had a way of ending the ideological warfare between her husband and son. "Our son has made a decision, Barry," she paused to catch her breath, and shed a few tears, "we must honor that." She walked over to Lazarus and embraced him. Both of his arms dangled helplessly and he couldn't breathe.

"Oh Lucille, I guess you're right." Barry walked over to his son and extended his hand, "Is this what you want?"

Lazarus nodded, and shook his father's hand.

"Well, son, you have my blessing. Are they going to pay for college?" Barry asked.

"Yeah, it's just like the military, only the training is more intense. The program is designed to get domestic terrorists. I'll be like a Special Forces guy, Dad, only instead of fighting in other countries my job will be to protect the home front."

Lazarus could see the disappointment fade in his father's eyes. "Maybe," he cleared his throat, "maybe you'll thank me for my service like you do to all those soldiers. Maybe."

Barry pulled in his son and gave him a bigger hug than his mom had. "I love you, son, you know that?"

Lazarus nodded. "I know, Dad."

"Hey, how the hell did this Vance guy pull off developing a program before even taking office?"

Lazarus shrugged.

6

Four months later…

Lazarus took in a whiff of the collard greens and homemade mac-and-cheese his father was making for lunch that day. Pots and pans clanged and crashed and made sounds that were music to his ears. Many of his fondest memories revolved around him and his father making mac-and-cheese. The process took hours and usually made a gigantic mess. It would drive his mom crazy since the cleanup—which she always got stuck with—was quite a task.

But she wasn't going to be upset about it today. Her son was scheduled to leave with Phillip at 2 p.m. from Vance's office. She and Lazarus sat at the dining room table laughing and smiling and watching Barry make a complete mess of the kitchen and himself. Bread crumbs could be found as far away as the front porch. No one knew how it got there. Melting cheese turned much of the white apron Barry wore yellow. Several spoons lay in the sink that had been used by all three of them. Each of them had claimed to be the 'official' taste tester.

It had been a long time since there had been a moment like this one. The conversation was about the past. Barry and Lucille reflected back on moments of their son's life that made them cry, made them laugh, and made them proud. Lazarus knew his life was headed in the right direction. The opportunity Vance had given him was bigger than even he realized.

Barry put a plate in front of Lazarus and Lucille: ham steak, mac-and-cheese, collard greens and hush puppies.

They didn't have soul food often but when they did, the three of them devoured every bite.

They dug in. The first five minutes were devoted to the ooh's and ah's of the tasty meal before them. Still, the day was bittersweet.

"They voted your boy in as Speaker," Barry said. "Impressive." The whole district was proud to be the home of the Speaker of the House, even if he was a Democrat.

"Yeah, I guess it's a pretty big deal." Lazarus scratched under his afro. He often thought about shaving his head but didn't have the courage to do so. Maybe this trip would present that opportunity.

"You're darn right it is, son, he's third in line for the presidency."

Lazarus puffed out his rippled chest and grinned, "That's right, I'm hangin' with the *man*."

"Just remember, son, don't compromise what you believe in your heart. Hang on to your principles."

His whole life his father talked about hanging on to his principles. Lazarus was never quite sure what he meant. Certainly he had no desire to ask with a plate full of mac-and-cheese. But it did bother him that he didn't have a clear definition of what his father was talking about. Perhaps he didn't have any principles. He wondered if he'd get those later, or if a person was born with them.

And what exactly is doing what you believe in your 'heart'? Is *bad* a choice? Is there such a thing as *evil*? His mom sure believed in it. But he didn't know if he did, or if his father did. The biggest question he wished he had the nerve to ask is: how do you know? What *does* evil look like? What does breaking your own principles look like? What if he had a *bad* heart?

When your back is against the wall, how do you find the courage or strength to do what is right? Lazarus figured it would just be easier to turn the other way. Someone else could pick up the slack and be the 'principle' police. He wasn't even twenty yet. Right then and there he decided not to worry about principle and the heart and what may or may not be the right thing to do. *What could possibly happen?*

"Are you packed?" Lucille's voice was shaky.

"Yes, Mom," he rolled his eyes knowing the crying was about to begin. He got up from the table and gave her a hug. There was a slight tug on his heart begging him to shed a tear. But it was only a slight one.

"We're going to drive you over," his father told him. Lucille had already broken down. Barry grabbed the box of Kleenex on the counter, put it in front of his wife, pulled one out and handed it to her.

The smile he gave her filled her heart with a love she never felt growing up. Lucille closed her eyes and whispered a small prayer to herself; first for her son, and then a thank you for putting such a loving husband in her life.

Lazarus just sat there not knowing what to say. Usually he had some sarcastic comment or told his mom to stop crying. But he knew today of all days that both of those responses were wrong. The problem was, he had been a teenager so long, he had forgotten what a sane person did in these circumstances. So, instead of making an ass of himself he decided to just sit there.

After the three of them cleaned up the kitchen—Lucille was very grateful—they loaded up the car and drove over to the newly refurbished headquarters of the newly elected Speaker of the House, Forrest Vance.

Phillip came out of the office to greet them, "Ah, Mr. and Mrs. Parker, a pleasure to meet you." They shook hands. "I'm Phillip Shaw."

"Nice to meet you, Mr. Shaw," Lucille said shakily.

"Call me Phillip. Look, Ma'am, we'll take care of your boy. I promise."

I told you not to call me 'boy,' Lazarus thought. There was something he didn't like about Phillip. It was probably that he was a pompous ass and carried himself like his shit didn't stink. But he knew the Congressman needed him and Lazarus trusted the Congressman. Still, he knew the eight or nine hour drive up north with this guy was going to be a long one.

Lazarus transferred all his belongings from his parents Ford Explorer to the shiny black Mercedes. There was something magical about the vehicle. The two separate feelings of rage and serenity seemed to come together in harmony when he was near the Mercedes. Lazarus didn't feel very comfortable, but figured it must be his own nerves—no way it could be the car.

The Mercedes began to drive away. Lazarus looked back. His mom and dad had their arms around each other. Both were crying. He wished he could bottle the last few hours with his parents and take it with him. But he couldn't. He took off his brown leather jacket and shrugged. It would only be a few months before he would see them again. That thought was comforting. He glared over at Phillip knowing the next few hours wouldn't be.

***

The drive was like a prison term for Lazarus. Phillip wasn't exactly a great conversationalist. And he listened to old country tunes. Lazarus wasn't exactly a fan of the stuff, but the old George Jones and Hank Williams country could lead to suicide for a nineteen-year-old black kid from Orange County. The twang mixed with the lack of any real beat was more than he could stand. He tried to read the books he brought, but the useless noise crowded out any chance of concentrating on the words.

"What are you reading?" Philip asked. It was nine hours into the trip.

"*Les Mis*, you know, by Victor Hugo," answered Lazarus smugly.

"We're almost there—yes, just a right—here." The car turned.

Lazarus had been busy either reading or hating the music when he realized they were in the middle of nowhere. He scanned the area. Nothing. The only light was the stars and headlights. The only thing he knew for sure was they were in the desert somewhere. He figured Death Valley.

"I read that book. It's long. Why are you reading it?" the condescending voice let him know Philip was asking only because he was young and black. This guy had waited nine hours to talk to Lazarus and then can't even avoid being a jerk.

"I read it in my honors English class my senior year," Lazarus said. "It's a great story. It's my mom's fault I love it so much. When I was twelve or thirteen she took me to the movie, you know, the musical one that everyone said Russell Crowe couldn't sing in, and that was when I was first introduced to Jean Val Jean."

"So, what did you think?"

"Oh, I loved the movie and—"

"No, about Russell Crowe."

"Oh, you mean his singing? I don't know, I thought he did a great job, but what do I know." Lazarus started to warm up to Phillip. Anyone who wanted to talk about literature, especially *Les Miserables*, was okay in his book. His father always wished for a baseball or basketball player, but Lazarus turned out to be a kid who loved story. He tried the sports scene and he had some talent there; plus the right build, but the passion was missing. His father came to the plays and listened to him go on and on about this book and that book or this play or how to play this role, but Lazarus always knew deep down there was a disappointment that lingered.

All that would change now. Everything was going to be different. He just knew it. Finally he was doing something that would make his father proud of him even if it was fueled by the other side of the political aisle. He wasn't becoming the starting shortstop for the Angels or starting tailback for the Raiders (both teams his father loved) but he was going to be a badass, that's for sure. In his father's eyes, this might even be better than being on some sports team. Barry did a ton of volunteer work for disabled veterans in the community and gave money to the Wounded Warrior Project, an organization that was close to his heart.

Lazarus hadn't said it to his dad, but the reason he decided to join the Domestic Peace League was for him. After all the years of being a mild disappointment he figured this might bring them closer together.

"We're here," Phillip said pulling up to a large gate that

looked like it opened up to nothing more than a vast desert. A man stood outside in a black kimono. The Mercedes stopped in front of him. He kept his arms crossed and did not move.

"Welcome," the man bowed his head.

Lazarus and Philip stepped out of the vehicle and approached him.

"Hi John," Phillip said. "Here he is, may I present Lazarus Parker."

John bowed and Lazarus did the same. "Welcome, it is an honor to meet you." John turned and faced Phillip, "Thank you, you may go now."

Philip got back into his car and drove away.

"Wait, my stuff," Lazarus cried, running after the car.

"Don't worry, my son, you will not need it. That is the first lesson in your training." John put his hand on Lazarus' shoulder and guided him towards the large door.

Lazarus was fuming. He wanted his books and clothes and other personal items that would remind him of home. But this guy wasn't interested in getting any of that back. He just kept prompting him to enter this place that looked about as entertaining as a car ride with a country western fan. Only *this* time there didn't seem to be an end in sight.

"Great, I have to say my first lesson kind of sucked."

"Listen to me," John said sternly, "there is something you must know."

Lazarus stopped and faced the man. He wasn't frightened or upset, but felt deep down that he needed to listen to what this man said. All thoughts of his bags and books and stuff floated away. Instantly he trusted this man and wanted to earn his respect. "Yes, sir, sorry sir," he said.

"Here you will learn how to inflict pain. Here you will learn all the ways to kill a man. But first, first you will learn how to heal. And then you will learn all the ways so you don't have to inflict pain, so you don't have to kill a man. You will know how to seek peace so that you and those around you can experience peace. No matter what happens, my son, don't ever forget that."

Lazarus listened and thought, *This must be one of those principle things my father talked about.*

7

Four years later…

The world's in chaos. Financial systems have collapsed. The last hope, the United States of America, is barely hanging on due to the weight of working desperately to help those at home as well as abroad. President Jefferson Smith had done the impossible; he kept enough political power to avoid the lame duck scenario in his second term, a term that usually plagues every president that holds the highest office. Many say it's a sign of the times; a need for leadership. Others call him a great man. Those who oppose him lay quietly waiting for the right time to strike.

Less than twenty percent of the American public voted in the last two elections. Since money was scarce, both parties missed opportunities to flip seats in their favor. Many states were in such financial distress they couldn't afford to have an adequate number of polling places. People had become so disgusted with the political system they didn't care, or, in some cases, didn't participate.

Speaker of the House Forrest Vance stopped concerning himself years ago with what the people thought. Deep down he knew the people couldn't be trusted with the vote, freedom, or thinking for themselves. There was a time when he had hope and faith in all these ideals. A time when *for the people and by the people* had meaning. But now he was going to have to enact Plan B. In fact, he *wanted* to enact it.

It's for their own good, he reasoned. He realized his rise to the presidency would not come the old-fashioned way.

His office in Washington was in the capital building. For the past two years he had tried to get permission to move to a Hotel Suite or a place more 'suitable' for the Speaker, but in these tough economic times he was told it would look unbecoming of the Speaker. He chuckled. *Now, after years of running deficits and basically stealing from the American public they're worried about appearances?*

He sat behind an oak desk created back in a time when furniture making was an art. Vance ordered his staff to clean and polish the desk every day—even on weekends. He ran a tight ship, but those who worked for him were loyal and dedicated. There was a faint redness with a slight glow behind their eyeballs. Not all of those who followed 'the Great Forrest Vance' as they often called him had it, but the vast majority did. The slight glow of redness had reached all levels of government as well as society.

Vance smiled knowing the time for Plan B had arrived.

Leaning down he opened the bottom drawer of his shinny desk. "Victoria," he whispered to himself. A black framed picture of his dead wife looked back at him, but he stared admiring his V shaped eyebrows in the faint reflection of the glass. He often wondered why he kept the photograph. He had burned everything else. But there needed to be some evidence that he loved her—even if it was only for the newspapers—what was left of them anyway—and the TV cameras. The truth was, every time he saw her he thought about the good times they had together. Funny how his career only took off *after* her death.

It had to be done, he thought. Even in his darkest moments he still loved that lying whore. The conflicted feelings that once dominated every other second of his life had moved on to minutes, on to hours, and eventually were months apart.

He punched the picture and the glass broke, shattering across his desk. The skin on his hand cut open, blood oozed its way out of his knuckles. A warm sensation filled Vance from head to toe. He brought his hand up and watched the blood work its way off of it. Bringing the cut up to his nose he took in the aroma of the thick, red metallic-smelling liquid. In his fondest memories a man begged like a baby, a cheating wife condemned no more, children screamed, and a mother lived in absolute terror.

"Sally," he yelled.

In walked the twenty-year-old intern with the better than average-sized breasts. She was short with beautiful, long auburn hair. She kept her hands plastered to her tan blouse and had a small hunch in her back. There was nothing physically wrong with her—other than the slight redness that hid behind her hazel eyes. Vance licked his lips trying desperately to recollect what she tasted like from the night before.

But he couldn't remember. *I'll just have her again tonight.*

When it came to sex he could never get enough or remember what it was like. All his twisted pleasures were the same. The need would be overwhelming. The desire would overflow only to leave a painful emptiness inside of him. Except killing, for some reason the killings always hit the spot and left a lingering satisfaction.

"Yes, Speaker," her voice was soft and distant.

Vance raised his hand in the air and showed it to Sally. "Bandage this up, then hold all my calls."

Sally had no response to the blood or the orders; she went to work bandaging his hand with the first aid kit under the wet bar on the other side of the office.

Forrest used his other hand to caress Sally's face. "Come over tonight," he said softly.

She finishes taping up his hand and stayed on her knees for over a minute, waiting. "Yes, sir," she finally said. Sally didn't look up at him, but instead put her hand on his leg and rubbed gently back and forth. "I can't wait." But her tone lacked conviction.

The Speaker watched her get up and scuttle gradually towards the door. As she closed it, suddenly he wished for the touch of a woman who could *feel*. The strong desire for a lover who wanted him and needed him brought tears to his eyes. He wanted these thoughts of the impossible, his longing for true love, to cease.

Look what love got you in the past.

"Yes," he answered the voices in his head. "Yes, so what do you offer me?"

Allow me to show you.

47

Vance nodded.

All the beauty of Plan B flashed before Vance like previews in an expensive movie theater. The vivid moments in a future where people felt the loneliness and despair Vance had once experienced brought an ease to his mind he had never known. The voices showed him the death and destruction his leadership would bring. He chortled. *The American people will bow down to me.*

AND YOU WILL BOW TO US.

"Yes," Vance dropped to one knee and offered himself to the voices.

"As for you, God of the cross, who did nothing but bring me heartache and embarrassment," —and *his* memories of church and pastors and hypocrites pleading with a God to enter heaven seemed so pathetic— "I ask nothing from you. Nothing." His voice deepened with each word. "But I tell you now what I will give you for what you have given me."

He motioned in the air with both his arms driving his hand through his dyed, jet-black hair.

"The same, nothing more, nothing less. I will terrorize and control your children here on earth as you terrorized me. I will take this once God fearing country and send it *back* to the dark ages, to a time when my Master ruled this world. Just as you darkened my world—I will darken theirs. I will enjoy watching your children suffer in more ways than even *you* can fathom. I curse you, and I hope you curse me." He stood up and inhaled a breath with his final transformation. Forrest Vance stood in his dimly lit office and embraced the moment. The devil's work was done.

He rushed out of his office past Sally and the other interns. Only one looked up and wondered for a split second where the Congressman was off to. But he was the one who lacked the dull redness that could vaguely be seen in the eyes of the other interns. Once he saw the others continue to work diligently on whatever it was they were doing, he went back to his own job logging in the names of those citizens, who for some reason felt it necessary to evoke their Second Amendment rights. The intern had just started yesterday on the final state, or perhaps territory, controlled by the United

States government, Washington D.C. By the end of the day the four year secret project would come to a close. The first stages of Plan B were in effect.

***

Jefferson Smith walked up to the podium and looked over at the rose garden. The scent of green grass perfectly trimmed floated in the air. He was reminded of better days in his first term when he and his wife and his son would tend to the stunning red, white and yellow roses that smelled like paradise. It was almost the third anniversary of his son's death in China. 'A peacekeeping mission to feed the hungry,' he told them. Even the president and first lady knew the dangers and had tried to talk him out of it. But his son's final argument of wanting to do something to change the world made it all but impossible to rebut. The speakers on the stage let out a squeak as the battered president tested it for the upcoming speech.

Jack Payne looked on from the first row of ivory-colored folding chairs. His thoughts went to his daughter, Abigail, as they often did. Someday he would see her again. The time in Dana Point Harbor when he had tried to tell her about her brother was the last time they saw each other. The painful years of growing up without a mother weighed heavy on Abigail he knew. Introducing her to his girlfriend on the anniversary of her mother's death was only one on a long list of mistakes Jack had made trying to raise a daughter on his own. Because of that boneheaded move, he had only a handful of phone calls to cling on to for the last seven years.

But Jack wasn't here now because he lost a loved one in the attacks of 9/11; nobody paid much attention to *that* day anymore. The president did appreciate the support Payne gave him during his reelection campaign. They did have a sort of kinship since they both chewed up some of the same dirt in Afghanistan and Iraq during the war on terror.

And maybe their friendship had something to do with his invitation to a small press conference in the rose garden about some obscure law he wanted passed to help some third world country in Africa. Maybe the president just wanted to duke it out with Jack afterwards, about why giving aid to countries that hated us was such a good idea.

For years Jack Payne had done his best to convince those in power that the real threat would come from within. But at some point the American people got sick of listening to some fringe thinking old war hero whom had an agenda. Or was just crazy.

The early February afternoon was unseasonably warm today. A thin man with black hair and slight beer gut sat next to Payne. He wore a black suit, white shirt and a silver tie. His hair was slicked back with some kind of oil that smelled like cheap perfume. He took off his overcoat and let the back of the chair catch it. He looked familiar to Payne, but he couldn't place where he had seen him before.

"Ah, Jack Payne, I remember you from my days when my political career looked bleak," the man said.

"Is that you, Speaker Vance?"

"The one and only."

"You shaved off your mustache, that's what's different. What are you doing here?" Jack knew Vance was not one to play nice with the other side of the aisle. Or his own side for that matter. The reports within the Beltway had Vance on the rise due to his uncanny ability to read the political climate better than Pontius Pilate. Most knew he hoped to be put in a much brighter light than Pilate, but planned on being just as famous. The Speaker would always say he wanted to be more like Abraham Lincoln—the Benevolent Dictator.

"Yes, just this morning—" Vance said to Jack. He looked at him askew, "—the mustache." Vance pointed to his upper lip and smiled.

The two news stations had brought their cameramen. This was rare nowadays since they would share footage and use what best played to their audience. The cable news wars had crippled every station except Tailored News Channel (TNC) and the Simply News Network (SNN). These two stations were holding on by barely a thread and a ton of government money. Familiar faces like Bill O'Reilly and Chris Mathews were long gone. New faces lasted a year at the most and usually ended up being caught in a scandal if they dared to report the actual news. Reports gave way to all day commentaries about race, sexual orientation, conservatives, liberals, reactionaries, and socialists. If it wasn't an extreme position, it didn't get on television, period.

"We're ready, Mr. President," the White House correspondent from SNN said. President Smith straightened his jacket and patted down his golden blonde hair. Jack noticed the stunned look on the president's face when he saw Speaker Vance. On the teleprompter he read the following sentence: "A crime has been committed on the American people by Speaker—" and then the words rolled back to the beginning of the speech.

Jack's stomach jumped up into his throat when President Smith approached the podium to deliver his opening statement. Jack made eye contact with Speaker Forrest Vance. The very essence of evil could be seen in Vance's eyes making Jack literally shiver. "Oh God, no…" His eyes grew wide as he saw the murderous look in the face of Vance. Plan B was revealed in a slideshow of horrible visions that made Jack's head ache.

Payne stood up and yelled, "The president is in danger!"

Vance stayed in his seat with his legs crossed. He turned to Jack and grimaced. The laugh that only *he* could hear drove Jack to the ground. He covered his ears in a vain effort to stop the laughter inside his head.

"God, please help—"

And then the cackling stopped.

Jack stammered to his feet only to see four Secret Service Agents racing towards him. Before he was tackled to the ground he swore he saw a dull redness escaping their eye sockets. The smell of freshly cut grass mixed with the putrid body odor of the four men made Jack gag.

Jack did nothing to resist the agents although he could've killed all four of them inside three minutes. He had been militarily trained by the very government that had him in a headlock on how to get out of these types of situations. But he knew it would only mean less protection for President Smith, and so he stayed down.

The rat-tat-tat of machine gun fire filled the Rose Garden. The stench of death filled the air. Two of the agents that were holding Jack made a bee-line for the president. This gave Jack a clearing to see what was going on. Vance still sat, calm as a butterfly, watching as if it was a Broadway play. Blood splattered the walls and four windows of the White House that looked out on this usually beautiful scene.

The air went out of Jack and he held back the tears he would need to cry for a fallen president. He wasn't quite sure how to make his next move. The situation told him that if they wanted him dead it would've already happened by now. The cameramen, the newsmen, some of the agents, a few politicians, and the president were all casualties of the day.

"Get him up," Vance said.

The two agents lifted Payne to his feet, and pulled him behind Vance, who was surrounded by scattered folding chairs, a now empty rose garden, and the stench of blood and gun powder.

The Speaker rose to his feet and put on his jacket. He bent down and picked up one of the machine guns on the ground, an old AK-47.

"What did you do? You're, you're—" Jack cried.

"I know, crazy, right?" he stuck the gun in Jack's gut. "My guys are pretty good, huh? Don't you go worrying yourself about it, Payne, that faggot Vice President Torres should be dead—right about—" he peeked at his watch and shook his head, "now."

The steel of the machine gun was still hot against Jack's stomach. He found his way to the trigger. He pulled it. Empty, just as he thought.

Just about the time Jack was calculating what it would take to kill this son-ova-bitch before the rest of these guys killed him a man grabbed Jack from behind. He dropped the gun.

"He's a tricky one, I've read his file."

"Thanks Phillip, I had it under control," Vance said.

"You're going to kill him, right?" Phillip asked.

"Oh no, not yet, first," he stepped right up into Jack's

face, his breath wreaking of stale coffee and 12 year old scotch, "I'm going to kill that snotty girlfriend of yours."

Jack tried to get out of the hold, but couldn't. It was a strange feeling being manhandled by a man that appeared to be more suited for a desk job than combat.

"That bitch daughter of yours will be next," Vance said. "Only, I won't kill her right away. No no, first I'll comfort her. Yes, I can see on your face that *that* will be the one that will finally break you."

Jack was trained to remain calm in times like these, but he was anything but calm on the inside.

"And then once I've seen you've lost all hope, Payne, and there's nothing but nightmares and horrible memories to fill the days of your pathetic life, then I'll kill *you*."

"There's a son as well, sir," said one of the agents. It was an old pal of Jack's from his mission in Kabul. But the tone in the agent's voice was hollow and a redness formed a circle in the white of his eyes.

"Good. The longer the suffering, the better." Vance started to walk away but turned back around. He pulled out a silver-plated Glock and aimed it at Jack's head. He took two large steps toward him. With each step, Vance's smile broadened. He fired one shot into Payne's left arm.

"Son-ova-bitch!" screamed Jack.

Vance nodded to Phillip, "Piss off," he said smugly.

The two agents dragged Jack to the side gate and tossed him on the ground, leaving him to die.

The sound of sirens grew louder. Jack knew his past would be used to label him the psycho with a machine gun. The years of telling everyone that the real danger would be domestic would create a storyline of how Payne himself had made his own vision come true.

He stumbled to his feet and found his way to the door across the street that led to the underground tunnels. His intimate knowledge of the Capital would make it easy for him to escape, if he didn't bleed to death first. He knew all the ins and outs, and was well versed in the how-to-get-a-president-out-of-the-city undetected scenario. Of course he never planned it would be him making the journey.

He tore a piece of cloth from the midsection of his favorite black button-down, covered in palm trees shirt and wrapped it around his gunshot wound. It would be a couple of hours before he could fix it properly.

In the tunnels, he pulled out his keys and used the small flashlight to help him navigate. His first thought was of his son and daughter, Miles and Abigail. How would he get a message to them? What would he tell Karen after years of not seeing her or even calling the boy? He had kept tabs on them and knew they lived somewhere near St. Louis.

The chaos that followed any assassination would be his greatest asset. Even Oswald was able to catch a movie before he was caught. Hell, John Wilkes Booth ran out the front door of the theater! The police and the Secret Service and the FBI and every other agency would be getting tips and calls and would be following leads no matter how farfetched they appeared to be. Plus, he figured Vance wanted him to get out. For some reason this guy needed a scapegoat that was living *and* at-large. He wasn't sure if this was for his own amusement, or if Jack was part of a bigger plan.

He didn't care.

Payne knew a bunch of old soldiers willing to put it all on the line for their country. This Vance character didn't know who he was messing with. "He should've killed me when he had the chance," said Jack angrily.

The time had come to get back into the swing of things. He failed once to kill that bastard—he wouldn't make *that* mistake again. By the end of the week he'd have a small band of badass motherfuckers highly trained in the art of kicking the shit out of bad guys.

And before Speaker of the House Forrest Vance could complete his rise to power…

***

The postcard with a picture of the Botanical Gardens in Berkeley was faded. The constant folding had created creases and wrinkles. Although it was old and worn, the photograph still captured the beauty of the redwood forest.

The half-circle seating of the amphitheater surrounded by the majestic redwoods was the perfect place for a wedding. For Abigail, the location was a deal breaker if he was going to propose. She folded the postcard back up and put it in the back pocket of her washed-out blue jeans.

Abigail Payne had been dating Barker Wilson for just over a year. They sat in her small, 700 square feet Laguna Niguel apartment watching an old 80s movie on the television. Barker was searching the internet on his iPhone 6000 (with the all new locator.gov app, secretly installed) when he started to laugh.

"What is it, honey?" she asked him.

"This movie is like, forty years old," he answered with a hint of snobbery.

Abigail's mind wasn't on the movie; it was on the ring she had found in his back pocket last night. She grabbed his hand with a firm grip.

Barker gazed into her eyes and smiled.

"I love you," she said.

"Me too," he responded.

"Hey," he turned to her; she bounced up and down to face him, praying this was the moment she longed for. She didn't say a word, but didn't need to since her actions showed him he had her undivided attention. Her body trembled all over. Since the day she bought the postcard on that Northern California trip her and her dad took twenty years ago, she'd been waiting for this very moment ever since. Barker was the perfect guy. She just knew it.

Barker cleared his throat and was visibly working up the courage to say something.

Suddenly, thoughts of Abigail's dad crowded out the excitement of the moment. He *had* to walk her down the aisle. There was no other way. She knew how unfair she had been to him the last few years. She didn't have the foggiest idea why she did it to her father.

I love you Abs, he would say, *and there's nothing you can do about it.* A grin formed on her face and she knew, just knew, no matter what he would be there.

Barker turned towards the TV still trying to muster up the

nerve to pop the question. "What the—hey, isn't that your dad?"

A picture of her father was on the screen. Under it the caption read: *Wanted in connection with the assassination of President Smith and Vice President Torres.*

"Turn it up, turn it up!" she said frantically.

He scrambled for the remote.

"Goddammit, Barker, turn it up!"

He breathed a sigh of relief when he found it and pushed desperately on the volume plus button.

"We take you live, courtesy of the Simply News Network, to the White House," the female anchor appeared shaken and way out of her league, although the terror on her face must've matched a good portion of the American people. It had been sixty years since a president had been assassinated. And never did the country have to deal with the decimation of the Executive Branch. The country was filled with millions of people who had no idea who their leader would be, or even if they would have one.

While Abigail and Barker sat quietly contemplating marriage, large sections of the United States had begun rioting in the streets. The violence was unprecedented.

"Good evening, my fellow Americans." Abigail recognized the man as Speaker Vance, and she knew, because of her father's relentless bantering that she learn about her own government, that he was the new president.

"I come into your living rooms tonight with a heavy heart. Both President Jefferson Smith and Vice President Sal Torres were assassinated earlier this afternoon. Right now as I speak, many of your neighbors are out on the streets looting, hurting other people, and causing unnecessary damage to both public and private property. Please only open the door for a policeman.

"Just a few minutes ago I was sworn in as the 47th President of the United States. I promised to protect and defend all of you from enemies both foreign and domestic. So, just moments ago I enacted Executive Order 59604, the collection and destruction of all firearms. Please, don't fight. We have detailed records and will not stop until we have accounted for every gun in the United States. The chaos in our streets needs to be stopped and that is the job of your government. And I assure you, your government is working hard for each and every one of you.

"Before that order I issued Executive Order 59603, the temporary suspension of the Constitution of the United States. This is absolutely necessary for the safety and well-being of all our citizens. If they can get to the president, none of us are safe. And that is my first duty, your safety. Your government is asking you to stay in your homes and keep your radio and TVs on for further instruction. A strict curfew has been set for 9 p.m., and being caught outside after curfew would not be advised.

"The maniac we believe is responsible for this heinous crime is Jack Payne." A picture that looked more like a mug shot appeared in the corner of the television. "Do not approach. Call the authorities if you see him. He is armed and extremely dangerous. We will be rounding up those we suspect are either aiding him, or helped him to pull off this unthinkable act. And yes, they will be punished to the fullest extent of the law.

"Your government has your back, America. You can count on it." The screen went black.

"Holy shit, we got to get out of here," Abigail said. She got up and searched for a suitcase or bag, or anything else she could stuff her crap into.

"Surely they don't think you were aiding him," Barker commented.

"What? Are you stupid? My dad didn't kill the president—that son-ova-bitch Vance set him up. They're coming for me, guaranteed."

"Now, darling, I know it's hard to believe—"

"Not another word out of you. I don't like you right now. Get off your ass and help," she said sternly continuing to run from her bedroom to the bathroom to the living room to the kitchen. Still, she had nothing in her hand or anything packed.

***

Barker stood in the middle of the living room watching his—maybe ex?—girlfriend mumble obscenities and incoherent phrases to herself in a frantic voice. Her breathing was heavy. Bending down, he blew out the banana nut bread candle on the coffee table. The smell of smoke entered his nose. He stood back up and thrust his hands into the front pockets of his beige slacks. "Look, Abs—"

"Don't you call me that. My dad calls me that," she went back to talking to herself. "Oh, why was I such a bitch, damn you Abigail," and the running and the talking and the cursing continued. "A-ha! Here it is," she exclaimed trudging out of the bedroom with a large red duffle bag.

There was a knock at the door. "Ms. Payne, it's the police, we need to talk to you."

With a stunned look on her face, she turned to Barker. "Shit, they already found me."

Barker shook his head and opened the front door. "How can I help you—?" But before he could finish, four cops busted their way in with guns drawn.

"Freeze!" the first one in the apartment yelled.

***

Abigail held her breath hoping the man didn't have an itchy trigger finger.

A tall, young African American male wearing a black leather jacket and a 1930s style hat entered her apartment. He scanned the room, pulled out a cigarette and lit it with a Zippo. Abigail thought about telling him it was a non-smoking complex, but figured she should probably keep her mouth shut.

So much for the deposit, she thought.

The smoking man peered down at the red duffle bag. "Going somewhere?" he asked.

"Not now," she answered. If her dad taught her anything it was that if someone wanted to kill you there's a good chance they won't spend the time to make small talk like in all those 007 flicks.

"Read them their rights, boys," he said.

"Do we still do that in this country?" she asked sarcastically. Her boyfriend gave her 'the look' that Abigail interpreted as 'Okay honey, time to shut up.' She wasn't that concerned. It had been almost a year since the last time her dad called her and she knew absolutely nothing about his whereabouts. A stranger would be more helpful in finding the fugitive Jack Payne than she would be.

"Make sure they're tight," the black man said to the officers, "especially on the girl with the smart mouth." He smiled at her.

"I just have an uncanny way of dealing with—ouch!" The handcuffs dug into her wrists. She glared at the man and stuck her tongue out.

They were taken down the front stairs and stuffed into a new Ford police car. The Laguna Niguel city had created a police department a few years earlier, and the new facilities were located at the remodeled City Hall.

The two of them remained silent staring out the side windows as the officer drove. The streets were well lit drowning out much of the stars above them. Most of the scenery was housing tracks with the occasional strip mall. The roads were unusually quiet.

Abigail could smell the mixture of stale beer and old sweat in the backseat upholstery. The vehicle cruised up Niguel road and passed China Moon on the right. Abigail had fond memories of the Shanghai Dumplings and the Ma La Chicken. Her stomach growled for the taste of the Mandarin food.

Without warning, Abigail got a big whiff of urine. She glanced over at Barker to see a man obviously frightened. He didn't notice her looking at him, or might have been too embarrassed to make eye contact.

The car passed Town Center Drive and put the blinker on. Abigail leaned up, using her restrained hands to lift, and peeked over the shoulder of the officer driving. He had signaled to make a left on to Crown Valley Parkway. Precipitately, her heart skipped a beat and she felt the fear Barker was experiencing. She muttered a silent prayer under her breath for their very lives.

The black and white veered into the left lane and stopped at the red light. The tick tock of the blinker screamed in her mind. The car turned left. Abigail gulped; she knew the way to the Laguna Niguel Police Station was right. *Where the hell were they going?*

***

The red had deepened in the eyes of the two cops that stood at attention by the door of the large room. The gray on the concrete walls had streaks of a faded black. The dismal white lines looked like tears streaming down a cheek filled with sorrow. A dull-looking steel table sat in the middle with two metal folding chairs on each side. In the corner sat Abigail. She shook with her head between her legs. The temperature and dampness added to the intended uncomfortableness of the place.

When she first entered the room she sat on one of the metal chairs. One of the policeman turned thug and had used his fists and legs to violently remove her from the chair. His blows were painful, but she had only cowered in the fetal position in a vain attempt to find heat. The thought of going completely nuclear on the person in charge brought some comfort.

The events of the day gave Abigail the impression that she had a six figure lawsuit on her hands. After all, this was still the United States of America, wasn't it?

She peeked at the two guards. The humid conditions of what amounted to a jail cell caused all kinds of trouble for her long, auburn hair. The curl caused by the moisture in the air was literally driving her crazier than the idea of being a prisoner of the state. She smirked at the one who would be fired by the end of the day. That would be the first thing on her agenda once she was free from this hellhole.

"Did you want some more, young lady?" the thug asked.

"You're so fired," she huffed and turned her head, arms folded. She didn't notice the red glow stronger in his eyes when she had turned away.

The man puffed up like something had pumped him full

of steam. He moved towards her with long strides.

Quickly she peered over at them. The other officer had a stronger glow. She stood up literally with her back against the wall. Abigail took the stance as she vaguely remembered learning from some speaker that came to her high school when she was a sophomore. The delusion that she could flip these two guys based on one lesson she had never practiced was all she had to hang on to.

A weakness began to develop in her legs. It was hard to breathe.

"As God as my witness," she muttered to herself, "if I get out of this alive I'll never be this unprepared again." Abigail finished her prayer. The bargain with Him was a glimmer of hope that He would get her out of this situation unscathed, or at least alive.

Her arms felt like two slabs of concrete.

Before she could make her first offensive move, one of the officers was already on top of her. She struck blindly, using whatever limb was available. Occasionally she hit her target. The two men used tactics that kept her wildness at bay. But with every bit of her strength and zero method to her madness, she tried to get free or inflict pain. The attempts were futile at best. Each calculated blow by the policemen lessened any effectiveness she could muster with her erratic moves. The first tear of her clothing sounded like a pin dropping in a silent room.

The action stopped for the briefest moment.

In the now bright redness of his eyeballs Abigail read the word *rape*. Her pulse raced. She squeezed her eyes shut and let out a primal scream. Each touch of the two men caused a quick jerk. She used her hands to defend against the constant grabbing of her jeans.

"Hold the bitch down," one thug said to the other.

***

"Let me talk to the president," Lazarus said with pride. It was the first time he used the word to describe his friend and idol, Forrest Vance. Vance was there when his parents were

61

ill, and Lazarus was still in training. He made it back just in time to hold his father's hand when he took his final breath. A huge debt was owed to Vance in the mind of Lazarus. He would do anything for the new president.

"Lazarus, my friend, how are you?"

"Good, I have the daughter and her boyfriend," he wanted to say once again how thankful he was for what Vance had done for his mom and dad, but he knew how busy the man must be. It wasn't appropriate now.

"I have some ideas on how we can best handle this situation," Lazarus paced the empty living room of the abandoned house. It was one of the many safe houses used by the Domestic Peace League. The DPL needed these places to be able to 'talk' to certain Americans about their activities. Lazarus felt in his gut there was something inherently wrong with spying on Americans, but he also realized the real danger of homegrown terrorism. The heinous acts by this woman's father were all the proof he needed.

"What do you have for me?" Vance asked.

"Well, sir, I've talked to the boyfriend. It looks as if we walked in right when he was going to propose to Ms. Payne." Lazarus searched the first floor of the house for somewhere comfortable to sit down. "Anyway, I was thinking," his eyes still wondered as he circled each room, "if these two are to be married, there's no way this Payne guy would miss *that*. So, this boyfriend will keep us posted on the when and where. I realize this bastard has no heart, and maybe he won't show, but according to the boyfriend there's some special bond between the father and daughter."

"What does the daughter know about Jack Payne's day to day life? Is there a chance of getting him before then?" Vance asked.

"He's too smart for that. Certainly we will have 24 hour surveillance on Ms. Payne and her fiancée. But, Jack Payne's work for the government is unknown and above my pay grade, which leads me to believe he's the type of guy that is prepared to disappear. Is there anything *you* can share with me about him?"

"I can't even find out what he did for us and I'm the fucking president!" Vance's voice raised with every word. It struck Lazarus like a bolt of lightning hearing the president use the F word. Certainly he knew that Forrest Vance had a foul mouth. It wasn't the first time he had heard him use such language. And he was by no means a prude. But there seemed to be something wrong about using that kind of language in the Oval Office, of all places. Lazarus knew he was being naïve—and at the same time hypocritical— but he still held the belief certain places were sacred. He probably got it from his father, who spoke many times about Ronald Reagan and how he 'never took off his coat' in the Oval Office. Or his mom's constant nagging about showing respect for our government—she wasn't fond of Reagan and let Barry know it—and the church, and other places that had a higher purpose.

"So, what? Are you planning on letting them go?"

"What choice do we have, sir? I mean, this is still the United States. Plus, she doesn't know anything." Lazarus finally decided to sit in the hallway with his back to the wall. "There's been a bit of tension for the last couple of years. That's why I think Payne will show at the wedding. There's no better place to mend family feuds than at a wedding or funeral. At least, that's what my mom use to tell me," he finished with a smile.

"Sounds like you have it all figured out, good. Keep me posted," said Vance.

"Yes, sir, and, I just—well, again, Mr. President, I have to say how grateful I—"

"I know, I know, son, you don't have to keep telling me. You're welcome," Vance said impatiently.

The air escaped his lungs like he'd been punched in the stomach. And when Lazarus finally caught his breath and was ready to speak, he realized the president was no longer on the phone. He cleared his throat and pushed 'end' on his cell phone.

Time to go talk to the daughter, he thought, shutting out the sting he knew was just plain silly to feel. He strolled back up the hallway to the living room and into the kitchen where the entrance to the basement was. He started to lift the portal up exposing the staircase; he recalled the doctor and the kids in that downstairs room years ago drinking that red stuff. The image came to mind anytime he saw a basement door. It was so rare to see a basement in California that no matter how often he traveled down one, it still felt awkward. He knew all of them were specifically designed to keep down on the noise and house possible terrorists. But deep down, it didn't feel right. He could never answer the question, 'if this isn't a good solution, than what is a good solution?'

Often he wondered if Vance really *did* know what was going on under his California headquarters all those years ago.

Lazarus started down the stairs purposely going slow to give him time to formulate his questions. A long rope was attached to the middle of the door; Lazarus pulled with force closing the portal once his head was clear.

He heard a woman scream. "Dammit. I told them to wait," he whispered to himself. Picking up the pace, the pain of Vance's words and the possible questions to Abigail Payne dissipated.

The door flew open and Lazarus saw the backside of both agents. In the corner, Abigail cowered, trying her best to cover her breasts and still find the energy to defend against the constant grabbing. Her pants were down to her knees; she still had her panties on. Bruises and razor thin cuts of blood were on her face and midsection.

Although the two agents seemed to be getting the best of her, the damage they had done had come at a price. The two men were covered in sweat and were defending as much as they were attacking.

"WHAT THE HELL ARE YOU DOING?"

The two agents stopped and turned around in unison.

Lazarus was stunned by the deep red in their eyes. Their faces were as primitive as a pack of hungry wolves. If the woman wasn't sitting in the corner fighting a losing battle, he would've ran. Even though he was well trained there were times when retreat was the smarter move. Certainly his mentor, John, didn't train him to be stupid.

The two men in black moved towards him.

Lazarus entered the room, closed the door, and quickly scanned the area. Abigail crawled around collecting her clothes. She used them to cover herself as she curled up in a ball. Exhaustion settled on her face. He could hear her crying.

He bent his knees and got into a fighting stance. His head moved from side to side, waiting to see which one would make the first move.

The two agents trudged forward, remaining in a very vulnerable position. They took Lazarus out of his game. He wondered what trick they might have up their sleeve.

This was the first true test of his martial arts abilities. He was confident he could defuse the situation, yet, still, doubt crept in.

The two men stopped and looked at each other. Then one of them made their move. The agent pressed forward wildly, with no real purpose. Lazarus ducked down and landed a punch to the man's gut, sending the agent back a couple of steps. The second agent flew in, fists blazing. A round house kick to the face knocked him back, but he remained on his feet. The two agents regrouped for round two.

Lazarus ran around them and jumped on the steel table, taking once again his crouching stance. He trembled, and could only hope his heart wouldn't beat out of his chest. The two agents turned around and moved forward and away from each other.

Taking a running start, Lazarus flew through the air. He landed a kick to the face of the man on his right, knocking him to the ground. Quickly he turned around, remaining in a fighting approach. He moved his feet towards the man still standing with a power-filled harmony.

The other man was now behind him and starting to get to his feet. With a yell that a Southerner in the Civil War would have been proud of, Lazarus applied the crushing blow with his legs leaving the agent on the ground for good.

He turned back to the agent still standing, "Your turn," he said with a grin. The man headed towards him in an absolute frenzy. Patiently, Lazarus hunted for an opening. He found it. He struck. The agent bounced back a few steps and stood frozen for just a moment.

And then he attacked again.

Lazarus parlayed to his right, dropped to one knee, and with the force of a runaway train punched the man in the kidney. The agent screamed. Holding his side, he stared at Lazarus with a coldness that made him shiver. Before the man could regain his composure Lazarus jumped in the air and kicked him with his right leg, knocking him unconscious.

The other agent began to come to. Causally Lazarus walked over to him, "Are we done here?" he asked.

The agent nodded. His eyes had but a dull flicker of red left in them.

Lazarus walked over to Abigail and offered her his hand. She sat up and took it. "I'm sorry," he told her. Tears streamed down her face.

Helping her to her feet he said, "I promise these two will get what they deserve."

"If that's the case, you should keep doing that kung fu shit till they stop breathing." She trembled in his arms.

He wanted to laugh. In the face of rape and possible death, this woman still kept her smart ass attitude.

He walked her out of the room, locked the two agents in, and stopped to retrieve a blanket from one of the hall closets. Wrapping it around her, he hoped to never come face to face with her father. Given her tenacity Lazarus couldn't imagine what the old man was like, especially knowing what he had done this day.

But now that Lazarus had the power to kill with just his bare hands he wasn't sure he could do it. It was one thing to stop a couple of thugs like the two agents trying to rape someone. It was much different to end their lives.

'Respect life,' his mentor, John, had told him. It was those words repeated over and over again that kept Lazarus from doing what Abigail had wanted him to do. What he wished he could.

She grabbed the blanket and pulled it over her shoulders.

He still had his arm around her, gently leading the way. She gazed up at him, when he looked down at her.

"Thank you," her voice cracked. Her watery eyes pierced his heart. Suddenly he remembered what it felt like to be cast aside for his own gratitude.

He squeezed her tightly and said, "You're welcome."

8

One year later…

The voices of reason calling for President Vance to lift the suspension of the Constitution had been silenced. His reach extended to every agency and organization at all levels of government. The soldiers that patrolled the streets—the "red-eyes"—were beyond strict. Many Americans seemed oblivious to the complete takeover by Vance while others had died in the streets, begging for anyone to listen. Resistance groups all across the nation had been dismantled by the Domestic Peace League; sometimes legally, sometimes—not so much. Fear gripped the nation. Many people had put all their hope in one man, Jack Payne.

Payne was the leader of the one resistance group that had escaped the DPL at every turn. Small pockets of men and women gathered in houses and abandoned buildings to pray for him and his band of freedom fighters. The lie manufactured by the government that Payne had killed the president and vice president was never taken seriously. The news that followed mixed with solid investigative reporting painted a picture of Payne and the events that day that was even more questionable than the circumstances surrounding the Kennedy assassination.

But none of that mattered to Jack Payne today, as he sat with his back against a large redwood. His daughter was getting married and he wasn't going to miss it. He knew the trip was dangerous. There was no doubt in his mind Vance and his minions would have a close eye on Abigail. Still, he had to ask himself what he was fighting for. And what he was fighting for was a future for his daughter and—

grandchildren? Perhaps there was a future he could look forward to.

"Payne?" a man whispered.

Jack got up on his feet and dusted off the black tuxedo with the matching grey vest and bowtie. He had wanted to wear all white, but keeping the suit clean while traveling through the dense sections of the California Redwood forest had been a bigger challenge than battling the evil forces of Vance.

"What did you find out?" he asked. The resistance back in the Smokey Mountains of Tennessee insisted a large group go with Jack to the wedding. He had wanted to go alone. The compromise was to let his good friend and former U.S. Navy Seal Frank Trippy go with him.

Frank had once took out twelve Iraqi soldiers with his bare hands, back during the Afghan civil war. Since the force to capture or kill Jack would be small to avoid being discovered, Frank was the perfect man for the job of getting him to his daughter's wedding unscathed. Plus he embodied the term 'one man army.'

"There's a small, white cottage the girls are in not too far up that path," he pointed to the ground. Jack could see the yellow stain Frank used to mark the way for him. The M-16 looked like a small toy in the arms of the six-foot-five giant.

Jack nodded. He inhaled the moist morning air and took in the fresh pine smell. Closing his eyes, he silently prayed for his daughter and her fiancée. Goosebumps raced up his arms, making the hair on the back of his neck stand straight up. Jack smiled, "My daughter's getting married today." Emotions got the best of him as his eyes began to water.

Walking by Frank, he patted him on the back and moved briskly towards the small cottage. There was a skip in his step followed by a fist pump. The day he dreamed about when he had first held Abigail in his arms had finally arrived.

"Hey," Frank started.

Jack turned around.

"She looks beautiful."

Jack continued through the forest to get a glimpse of what he already knew was true.

The white cottage had ceramic tan shingles that covered the rising rooftop. It had only one room used for the final preparations of a woman on her wedding day. In the distance Jack could see the half circle where the guests would watch the ceremony. The platform where he would deliver Abigail was decorated with red cloth draped at the top and purple roses strategically placed all over the stage. The awe of the surrounding redwoods and the perfect color of Spring green completed the masterpiece.

He made his way to the front door and knocked with one knuckle.

The door opened.

Jack could see in the full length mirror her wavy auburn hair. The traditional wedding dress extenuated her light, olive skin and baby brown eyes.

Abigail stood up. "Holy shit, Dad?" She covered her mouth with her hand and was unable to catch her breath.

Jack walked into the cottage and wrapped his arms around his daughter. The other three ladies stopped in their tracks, waiting, uncomfortably, to continue the work at hand.

"Damn you," Abigail was crying, "now I have to redo all my makeup." She waved her hands at her face hoping to save the work already done. "What are you doing here?"

"I'm here to walk my little girl down the aisle," Jack said.

"I'm so sorry, Daddy, if I could take it—"

He put his hand up to her lips and shook his head, then pulled her in for another hug. "I know, Abs. It's okay."

The women went back to work fixing the mess Jack had made of Abigail's makeup while the two of them talked about her fiancée, Barker, and her new job at UCLA. She told him she was working in the Admissions department and taking self-defense classes four nights a week. Barker had finally got on in a big law firm in Los Angeles and was working on some top secret stuff he wasn't allowed to share with her.

Jack never had seen her happier than at that moment. He couldn't help but think of her mother; Abigail looked just like her. His heart broke all over again remembering the phone call on that dreadful day in September of 2001.

Trying to explain to a six-year-old that her mother had just died was the hardest thing he'd ever done. God, how he wished her mother was here to see this.

Two hours had passed before Abigail was finally ready. It was quarter to eleven in the morning; the ceremony was only fifteen minutes away. She stood up and grabbed the arm of her father. The grin on his face was bigger than life.

***

Lazarus sat in the passenger's side of the Cadillac Escalade, staring out the window lost in thought. Not even the awesome sight of towering redwoods could bring him back to the present moment. Usually he spent a moment every day in a meditative prayer. He had learned the technique during his two years of training.

When the call had come in that Jack Payne had been spotted in the forest just north of the small cottage that held the man's daughter, Abigail, Lazarus knew today he would have to fight. Anytime it was necessary to use force his stomach turned. Lazarus chalked it up to nerves.

But now Lazarus' thoughts were on his mom and dad. Although he was grateful to President Vance, he often wondered why he wasn't given a pass to go see them both before they died. And then there was the one question that weighed heavy on his heart: *why didn't you just go anyway?* He whittled away many hours avoiding answering *that* one. The timing wasn't right. It didn't seem to be that serious. He arrived just in time to watch his father die; Lazarus didn't know if his father even knew he was there. The next morning he returned to John and his training.

Then why haven't you visited their graves?

Lazarus shook his head and exhaled. The voice in his head had grown louder. He called the voice his evil twin. That guy or thing or person or whatever it was that always played devil's advocate. It would tell him he wasn't good enough, or she doesn't really love you, or this world is better off without them. Without who?

Without them.

The world is on fire, he thought. His father had spent the last six months of his life fighting President Vance. Everything changed so drastically after Lazarus left home and joined the DPL. Russia and China joined forces and appeared to be too overwhelming a force for the United States. But President Vance changed all that. He beat down the Russians by singlehandedly destroying their currency. People in the U.S. paid pennies for a framed picture of the worthless Ruble. It almost became a sick obsession for Americans. Lazarus recalled a friend from high school who had put it up between a picture of President Lincoln and President Vance. It was as if the country began to believe Vance was a liberator of the Russian people, yet at home he was ripping away freedoms of the American civilians he said he fought for.

China was another story. The fight still went on to this day. In the beginning it looked bleak for the United States, but quickly the tables turned. After the Chinese leader was assassinated in September of 2023, China was like a boat with a small leak. The world held their breath as the two countries so intimately once connected began to flex their muscles. As China expanded out to the Japanese Islands and became more aggressive, America grew stronger. No one could explain it. Even the political pundits were speechless.

The only problem the president had were the resistance groups here at home. These pockets of rebellion were violent. Many of the guns were either surrendered or taken by force, but there were those who still considered the 2nd Amendment sacred. *Even after the assassinations*, Lazarus thought, *they still hang on to that silly belief.*

One bullet can end all that today.

The voice again. This time giving advice. He wanted to ignore its plea to kill Payne and end all this craziness. He remembered his father telling him violence only gets violence.

All the other resistance groups had been put down quickly and quietly, but not Payne's group. They had been a thorn in the side of the administration. Most Americans didn't even believe he was the one who pulled the trigger that killed President Smith two years ago. But Lazarus saw the recording. There was no question that the man was guilty. He often wondered why Vance didn't go public with it. He also wanted to ask President Vance why *he* hadn't done something to stop Vance since he was sitting right next to him. But he was afraid the answer might make Vance look like any other politician in Lazarus' eyes, and that would be more heartbreaking than missing his parents' funerals.

The glossy black Cadillac Escalade pulled up to the side of the road. Lazarus and the other three men in the car had practiced training techniques from this very spot for months. The tourist-created turnout was covered with light green grass. The smell of fresh pine invaded the car when the first door was opened. The redwoods stretched farther than any eye could see. The base of each tree thick enough to hide a full grown man, as the trees reached up past heaven. Not a word was spoken. Lazarus used hand signals to direct each agent. They moved with grace and without hesitation. The four men seemed to be swallowed up by the forest as they worked their way towards the final destination.

The only sounds of the forest were a chirp here and chirp there. The men progressed forward slowly, moving one foot over the other to keep the sound of rustling grass to a minimum. Lazarus raised his fist in the air and stopped moving. The other three followed suit.

He could hear voices. He pointed at Agent Kipling, pointed back at his eyes, and then towards the direction of the conversation. Kipling nodded and briskly made his way in that direction. Lazarus went up, stopped and kneeled down. He wanted to make sure he kept Kipling in his sights.

A man grabbed Kipling's arm and started to yell. Kipling reached up and wrapped his arm around the burly man's neck and covered his mouth creating no more than a muffling sound. The giant bit down.

"Son-ova—" Kipling pulled his hand back and tried to shake off the pain.

The giant thrust his elbow into Kipling's gut. He bowled over and took another punch to the nose. Blood painted the surrounding trees and moss like a Pollock canvas. Kipling fell to the ground and hit his head as it hit a tree stump. Still conscious, the man stood up, head swirling. The giant turned towards the path his friend traveled on.

Lazarus raced up and tackled him. The two quickly jumped to their feet. The giant, with no concern for himself, appeared to be preparing to once again warn the other. Lazarus trudged up and karate chopped the man in the throat. He coughed and tried to clear his throat.

Lazarus, for a brief moment, was taken by the simple gesture of the giant's need to put his friend before his own welfare.

In a drowned out voice Kipling said, "Ah, that son-ova-bitch, he broke my nose!"

The other two agents helped Lazarus surround the man. He figured this was probably Frank Trippy, the former Navy Seal who had joined the Payne resistance after the attack on Detroit. Vance had sent in a number of Seal teams to take out a terrorist group. It ended up being a slaughter. Many of the supposed terrorists weren't even armed. It wasn't so much the unfortunate events of that day, but what happened afterwards. Nobody knew what was said between Trippy and President Vance at the White House a few days later, but ever since then the two of them had made it their mission to destroy the other.

"You're Parker, right?" Trippy asked.

Lazarus nodded and asked him if he was Frank Trippy. Trippy confirmed.

"I heard about you. Rumor has it you're a good guy. So why are you still working for that evil cocksucker?"

The other two agents inched towards the giant. "I would keep your distance, boys," Frank warned.

Lazarus pulled out his Glock and pointed it at him. "Why don't we just go in, Frank, I promise—"

"My ass! You know Vance wants us dead," Trippy said and rushed towards one of the agents. He ducked and dipped. Then punched and kicked. Paul Sands, the other agent, headed over to assist. Lazarus cursed, holstered his pistol and hurried over. Trippy had already disabled the first agent. Kipling limped over with his gun drawn. Kipling wanted to kill him, but couldn't find an opening. Trippy got the upper hand on Sands and leveled him with a kick to the groin.

Lazarus escaped a punch and blocked a kick. A shot was fired. Trippy dived to the ground and Lazarus disarmed Kipling with a quick move followed by a punch to the nose.

"Son-ova-bitch!" Kipling yelled putting both hands up to his face to stop the bleeding. "WHY-Y-Y?"

Before Trippy could get up, Lazarus was already on top of him. He took a couple punches to the face and delivered a few of his own. He took hold of an arm and flipped Frank on to his stomach. Bending his arm up he whispered, "I promise they won't kill you. You served this country faithfully for too many years, you have my word."

All fight drained out of Frank. He put his arms behind him. Lazarus put on the handcuffs and helped him to his feet. The two men glared at each other. Frank looked away first. But Lazarus had seen the sincerity in his eyes.

"God help you if you're wrong," he told Lazarus.

"You could score big points by killing the bastard right now," Kipling said.

"Yeah, Parker, think about it, maybe you'll get your own country or something," Sands piped in. Sands' black suit was covered in dirt. He winced each time he tried to take a step.

Lazarus dusted off his leather jacket. He strolled over to where his hat was lying on the ground and picked it up, using his pants to dust it off. Straightening the rim of the hat out and putting it back on he said, "Nobody is going to die today. Sands, bring the prisoner, it's time to crash a wedding."

They traveled down the path towards the white cottage. The group walked single file down the narrow dirt path. Lazarus led the way. It took half an hour to get to the edge of where Abigail was going to get married.

Lazarus stopped and had the other agents huddle up, "So, any thoughts on how we should handle this?" he asked.

"Is the body count already *factored* in?" Trippy said sarcastically.

Lazarus stood up. "We've got some time, think about it," he told the other agents. "Kipling, do something about your nose." He grabbed the prisoner and led him away from the others.

"Look," he started, "I plan on bringing both you and Payne in alive, so long as neither of you give me a reason to do otherwise."

"Listen man," Frank said, "I trust that you believe that, but you don't know Vance like I do."

"That's President Vance, and I do know him; he's a good man."

Frank just shook his head.

"What really happened in Detroit?" Lazarus asked, hoping to change the subject.

"Are you sure you want to know?" Frank replied. "You won't believe me."

"Try me," Lazarus said, folding his arms.

"Okay. It was a night mission. We went in with specific orders to kill all enemy combatants. Only, they weren't where intelligence said they were. Instead, it was just a bunch of people hiding in the basement of a church. None of them armed, they were starving, it wasn't pretty." Frank put his head down mustering up the courage to go on.

Lazarus pulled out a cigarette and lit it. He offered to light one up for Frank.

"No, thank you," he responded. "I haven't thought about that day in a while. Christ has healed the wounds, but the scars are deep."

How does Christ heal wounds? Lazarus thought.

The comment brought him back to the church his mom and dad took him to when he was a child. Lazarus had wanted to understand what the preacher was talking about, but never had. There was a yearning deep inside him for something, a feeling, anything. The idea that He heals or saves never computed. And yet, Lazarus was still curious about religion and spirituality and God. When he gave it some thought, he believed, but didn't know what or who to believe in.

"They killed them all," Frank's voice cracked. "My team

took out every person in the room. I sat—just—watching—" Frank turned away and shook his head. "The guys—their eyes—they were robots— I—"

"Red-eyes? What did the president say?"

"The eyes of my whole team turned redder and redder. It was as if they didn't know what they were doing," Frank wiped his eyes on his shoulder. "The son-ova-bitch knew— he *knew.*"

Lazarus stood straight up and popped his head back. "Liar," he said then walked away.

"He's evil," Trippy called after him. "Vance is evil," he repeated.

Lazarus trotted over to the other agents and started to discuss their plans for Payne. Frank's words repeated over and over again.

Lazarus balled his hands into a fist. "Sands, shut him up!"

Sands walked over with duct tape. Using his teeth, he ripped off a piece. Before the man could react, Frank bull-rushed him using his head as a battering ram.

Sands lost his balance and landed in a mud puddle. Frank turned around and kicked him in the abdomen. A grunt. Sands grabbed the foot meant for his head and flipped him onto his back. The other three agents ran over to the skirmish.

Sands leaped to his feet and climbed on top of Frank.

"You bastard!" Sands exclaimed. Taking his right hand, he punched down on the man, reset, and laid another one on him. Instantly Frank's face turned purple and blood poured from his nose. The next fist struck him. A black eye formed.

Lazarus lifted Sands' body up and away. "Enough." Lazarus said, face to face with Sands. "Kipling, get the prisoner up and clean him up as best you can. Trippy, I'm putting duct tape on you. You can fight and get hurt, or you can let my men do their job."

"What are you afraid of?" Frank asked Lazarus.

Lazarus ignored the question and started directing his men to their places. *I'm not afraid of anything*, he thought to himself, *except, maybe everything*.

Lazarus stood in the front, not too far from the quaint, little porch that led to the front door of the white cottage.

With catlike skill, Paul made his way on to the deck and hid like a stealth fighter in the night. Kipling forced Frank on his knees and drew his pistol, the other agent, Ken Hewitt, stepped out of sight on the side of the house. Another man stepped out from behind the house and strutted over to Lazarus. It was Barker Wilson.

"Hey, your man's inside," Barker said.

"You better get lost until this thing is over. It might get ugly," he told Barker.

With a nod, Barker made his way over to the spot where they planned to deliver vows. He sat down on the decorated concrete circle and rubbed his hands together. Lazarus had promised him a cushy job in Washington for betraying his fiancée. The president had told Barker not to worry about losing this piece of pussy; he would be up to his eyeballs in pussy once he got to Washington.

Vance had been too crude for Lazarus' tastes. He laughed. But what else could you do but laugh when the president makes a joke?

Flipping open the pack of Marlboros with his thumb, Lazarus used his lips to grab a smoke. With his other hand he flicked his Zippo lighter open. The first draw was always the sweetest.

Blowing out the smoke, Lazarus scanned the area once more to make sure all his men were in place.

The door opened. Abigail stepped out. Lazarus couldn't help but think how beautiful she looked in her stunning white dress.

Out came Jack Payne.

Lazarus smiled.

***

Jack opened the door and the two of them stepped out onto the porch.

Lazarus Parker stood there wearing a black leather jacket and a fedora, smoking a cigarette. Next to him was a bloody Frank with his hands tied behind his back, duct tape over his mouth.

Jack could see fire in Frank's eyes. Another man wearing a band aid on his nose held a gun to his head. Payne smiled knowing the hell Frank must've raised before being captured.

"Jack Payne, you're under arrest for crimes against the state," said Lazarus.

Jack raised his hands in the air. "Fine, just leave my daughter out of this."

Lazarus nodded and another man in a soiled black suit, who seemed to come out of thin air, appeared behind them on the porch. He handcuffed Jack.

Abigail remained silent. She watched as Barker walked over to Lazarus and spoke to him. Her heart broke.

***

A caravan of brand new jet black Crown Victoria's made their way up the dirt road to the rendezvous spot Lazarus had chosen. The government had taken over all the car factories in Detroit after the supposed uprising. President Forrest Vance loved the name Crown Victoria; he said it reminded him of his deceased wife. The comment started a change that all government-issued vehicles used for transporting the president received that name.

Lazarus had sent away the wedding party and all the guests who had arrived early. All of them except Jack Payne and his old friend, Frank Trippy. Agent Paul Sands stood guard over the two prisoners.

The large open space was covered in tall grass. The five cars pulled up and created a perimeter in the shape of a crescent moon. A large man stepped out of the passenger's side of the stretch limo Crown Victoria and opened the back door. President Vance stepped out and slicked back his hair. The greasy-looking jet black hair with the matching V-shaped eyebrows gave the appearance of having just been dyed. Vance wore a black trench coat and used a cane. He waddled over to Lazarus.

"Something happen to your leg, Mr. President?" Lazarus asked.

"No. Where's the daughter?" he asked.

"We have her back at the cottage."

"Get her out here."

"Yes sir, Mr. President," Lazarus answered and pulled out his cell phone.

Agent Kipling answered and he told him to bring Abigail. "She's on her way."

Vance grinned.

There's something—different about Vance, thought Lazarus. He couldn't quite pinpoint what it was. Sure the dyed hair was something much darker than he did before, but who was he to question the vanity of an aging man? Lazarus wasn't even twenty-five yet. And there was the cane. What's up with that? Maybe he was hurt. But the cane, the dyed hair, the distant feeling he felt—that wasn't it. It was as if Lazarus could see something more—something deeper.

Perhaps it's just the enormity of the moment, he told himself.

Lazarus thought about what Frank Trippy had told him earlier that morning, about President Vance being evil. And laughed. That was just silly. Evil doesn't really exist. There's no way Vance would've planned the execution of innocent life. Lazarus could see now why the president had reacted when he was back in Washington two years ago for Operation: Sitting Bull. It was obvious how deeply disturbed the man was when the drone accidently dropped the missile on the Israeli Embassy in Germany after Putin's predecessor had invaded that country. He could barely hold back the tears during the phone call with their prime minister.

And then something Lazarus' dad once told him hit him like a bolt of lightning.

The greatest trick the devil had played was convincing everyone he didn't exist.

It sent a chill down Lazarus' spine and he shivered. President Vance made eye contact with him and grimaced. *Did he just read my mind?* Lazarus wondered.

Kipling led Abigail towards the group.

"Why isn't she in handcuffs?" asked the president.

"Well, sir, she's not under arrest," Kipling said.

"What?" he turned to two of his Secret Service agents. "Arrest her, and arrest him," Vance pointed at Kipling.

"Wait," Lazarus tried to catch his breath. "Mr. President, it was my decision, not Kipling's."

The other two agents put both Kipling and Abigail in handcuffs and on their knees before Lazarus could finish his protest. They were put next to Trippy and Payne.

Vance walked away from Lazarus and over to Barker Wilson. "Put her in the car," he ordered.

Barker couldn't get words out of his mouth. Finally, he just nodded a few times and stumbled over to Abigail. He bent down and gazed into her eyes.

She spit in his face.

"You bitch!" he screamed grabbing her arm and forcing her up.

She kneed him in the balls and began kicking violently.

Barker dropped like a bag of potatoes and took a number of stomps to the face. One of the Secret Service agents ran towards them.

Putting his arm on the man's chest Vance said, "Wait," and began to chuckle. "Nothing worse than a woman scorned, wouldn't you say, Mr. Wilson?"

Abigail glared at Vance. The president released the agent who took hold of Abigail and led her to the end car. With a handful of hair, he shoved her into the back slamming the door behind her.

Barker Wilson staggered to his feet.

"Look," the president pointed at Barker, "he's actually crying."

The agents laughed.

Lazarus stood, silent. He was stunned, speechless. The only noise he could hear was a thunderous crack. Vance strolled over to Barker. "You're pathetic, get on your knees."

"Wh-Wh—"

"GET ON YOUR KNEES," Vance crowed. The words came from him, but it wasn't *his* voice. The words were an echo, as if from somewhere deep and dark.

Every head turned towards Vance.

Fear gripped Lazarus like he never had experienced it before. He wanted to put an end to all this. He wanted to tell his hero, his friend, his idol, to stop. But he couldn't. He was too weak. His hands trembled. Then he heard a sound. He wasn't quite sure what it was, but he could *feel* it.

Barker cowered to his knees and lay at the president's feet. Begging for his very life, he openly cried without a shred of shame. The president kicked and told him to get off.

Lazarus finally moved. It was just a step. The moment felt like some kind of nightmare. "Mr. President, what are you going to do with the prisoners?"

"Whatever I damn well please," Vance answered.

It was then that Lazarus knew Vance's promise was empty just like Frank had told him.

"Come, Lazarus, come join me, and Jack and Frank."

Lazarus walked over and stood next to Vance.

Still on their knees, Jack and Frank looked up. Lazarus could read in their faces the reality of the situation. Unless he did something right now there was a good chance both of them would be dead by nightfall.

Vance pulled out a .38 he had tucked in his pants and handed it to Lazarus. "Kill him," he said, pointing at Trippy.

"But...but I promised. I told him if he came quietly that—"

"Do it!" Vance yelled.

Lazarus stared at the gun in his hand. The thought of killing himself came to mind. Then the idea of shooting Vance raced like a wildfire in his vision. Finally, what if he murdered Frank? What if? *Murdered?* Could he live with himself? Could he live with himself if he shot the president?

"I know what you're thinking, Lazarus. Kill him? Or kill me?" Vance whispered in his ear.

Lazarus tried to swallow, but his mouth had gone completely dry.

"I killed your parents, Lazarus," Vance paused, "and I liked it."

A fire raged within. "You bastard," Lazarus said. He

could hear *that* sound once more. What was it? He couldn't explain it. He shook himself and the inside of his stomach swirled like a tornado. "Why do you tell me this now?"

"I want you to kill, learn what it feels like. If you can't kill him, maybe you can kill me," said the soft sinister voice of Vance. He put his arm around Lazarus.

"Get your hands off of me!" Lazarus said. He stood straight up and backed away from Vance. Slowly he lifted the gun up. Vance stepped right into it.

"Fire, please," Vance spread his arms out. Lazarus was struck by how sincere the man sounded. It was as if in that moment Vance really *wanted* to die.

The gun began to shake violently in Lazarus' hand. He held his breath. Putting pressure on the trigger he saw a vision of his parents. It was the picture they took on their last trip to Chicago, at Navy Pier, next to a gigantic red and white boat they had told Lazarus was actually a restaurant.

Don't do it.

It was the voice. But it wasn't. It sounded different, calmer, comforting, from somewhere deep inside of him.

Don't do it, my son.

Could it be, he hoped, *could it be the voice of his father?* His arm dropped to his side. "I can't."

"If you kill him, I will give you your own empire. If you kill me, you could have an even bigger empire."

"I can't. I guess I'd rather be a good nobody…" Lazarus stopped, and for a second wondered if he was making the right call, "…then kill this man and be an evil somebody."

He thrust the gun into the president's chest and walked away.

BANG!

A gun shot. Lazarus briefly turned around. It was for Frank Trippy. The man's body made a rustling sound as it fell lifeless to the ground. Lazarus closed his eyes hoping not to hear the gun fire again.

Would he be next?

No, he knew for some reason Vance wouldn't kill him. Not yet. The idea of seeing him suffer would be much more gratifying. What his father had said about Vance being a charlatan and a dangerous man came rushing back.

"How could I be so blind," he whispered to himself. "I thought I knew the man."

He heard a crack in the air and realized what the sound had been all along. It was truth, and he didn't like it.

***

The flat patch of land between Highway 101 and Davison Road had become a makeshift military base. Sixteen thousand troops had been stationed in the National Redwood Forest after the great fire last summer after a group of environmental terrorists committed suicide by lighting a section of the forest on fire and burning themselves alive. But instead of destroying the forest, the fire jumped inland and took out dozens and dozens of residential communities. It grew out of control and almost made it to Los Angeles.

Lazarus watched the troop movement from inside the base. Night had fallen on the forest and he waited to catch a glimpse of where they might be keeping Jack Payne. He had scoped out and even entered countless tents. For the past three hours he had moved in and out of the tents searching for a sign of Payne and his daughter. Vance and his agents had already headed back to Washington leaving Lazarus to move more freely. His credentials still carried some weight with the enlisted men.

It was 10:00 p.m. His shoulders sagged and the circles around his eyes grew darker. "I can't give up until I find him," he promised himself. He marched into the next tent.

There two men stood over the body of Jack Payne. Payne's face was bloody and warped by continuous hammering. He spit out blood.

"Has he said anything yet?" Lazarus asked.

"What?" the soldier on the left asked. "Who are you?"

"Has he given up the location of the resistance?" Lazarus peeked over at Payne who slowly moved his head from side to side. *Oh shit, they weren't looking for information.*

"Sir, we're going to have to—"

Lazarus punched the soldier in the gut and grabbed his

head, pulling it down as he lifted his knee. Knock out.

The other soldier reached for his gun.

With a roundhouse kick the gun went flying against the side of the tent. The other soldier lunged at Lazarus with his fists blazing.

Lazarus deflected a punch and then another. The soldier lifted his leg and kicked. Lazarus dropped down and landed a punch right to the groin. The man fell with a thump. A final kick to the head knocked the soldier unconscious.

Moving quickly, he ran over to Jack and untied his hands and legs. With a jolt, he ripped off the duct tape that was half-covering his mouth. Jack took a shallow breath.

"Where's my daughter?" he asked.

"Not here, they've taken her someplace else." Lazarus hadn't found Abigail, but he knew Payne would want to search for her here. Lazarus needed to get this man as far away as possible. He needed to save *this* life. The shot that killed Frank Trippy still echoed in his mind.

"These guys were working on killing me, I owe you my life."

"Don't thank me yet, we're still on base." Lazarus searched through the tent for anything he could use for their escape. He grabbed two ropes and the duct tape. One of the soldiers began to moan. Lazarus grabbed him by the shirt and punched. And then he came up with an idea.

"Help me get this guy's clothes off; we're going to walk right out the front gate."

Jack Payne put on the man's uniform. It was a bit snug. The green fatigues had a little blood on them, but nothing that would give them away. The two men tied up the soldiers and used almost half a roll of duct tape on them.

"The shoes don't fit," Jack whispered. He caught a glimpse of his face in a mirror on the lone table. "What about my face, Jesus Christ, I look like shit!"

"Here, take this," Lazarus put his hat on him. "When we walk by the guard keep your head down. Try these." He threw Payne the other soldier's boots.

"A bit big, but better. Beggars can't be choosers."

"Great, let's go." Lazarus led him out of the tent.

They strolled down the pathway between tents. He could feel his heartbeat hard in his throat. The darkness hid Jack Payne's wounds. Laughter could be heard from the mess hall. The few soldiers who walked by paid no attention to the two men. Many of them were visibly drunk.

Jack peeked over at Lazarus and whispered, "Not the same Army I was a part of." Lazarus gave him a guarded smile.

"Sergeant," Lazarus called out to the man at the gate. A skinny looking runt carrying an M-16 came running out.

"How can I help you, sir?" he inquired.

"This man is drunk, he tripped and fell in the chow hall and I need to get him to the doctor."

"Jesum, is he gonna be okay?"

"It's an emergency; the man's face went into the fryer." Lazarus lifted up the hat and began pointing out the 'burns' on Jack's face. As the runt moved in to get a better look Lazarus disarmed him and used the butt of the gun to knock him out. He caught him before he dropped to the ground.

Dragging the man to the guard gate Lazarus set him inside. Jack ran over to the Army Jeep, jumped in, and started it up.

He met Lazarus just past the gate and they drove off the base towards the Northern section of the Redwood forest. About five miles up the road Lazarus asked him to pull over.

"Here's where I get off," he told Jack.

"Why don't you join us? I could use a man like you."

"I'm done joining. Sorry about Frank, I know the two of you were friends."

Payne nodded. "He was a good man."

Lazarus was tempted to go with Jack, but knew it would be the same old same old. He remembered hearing that the truth would set you free. For him, it would be more like a surrender. Like a prisoner watching the cell door shut for the first time. Lazarus had been stripped of everything he once believed in. To join another cause would be pointless.

"Are you sure I can't change your mind?" Payne said.

Lazarus patted the hood of the Jeep. "Your fight isn't my fight. I hope you find what you're looking for. I hope you find your daughter."

"Thanks. Good luck to you."

The act of freeing Jack gave Lazarus a clean slate. It wasn't perfect. He certainly wished he had been able to save Frank and Abigail, but that hadn't been in the cards. He also hoped for the best for his friend, Agent Kipling. But Lazarus had done all he *could* do. All he *would* do.

The Jeep sped away, kicking dust up into the air. Lazarus followed the vehicle until he couldn't see it any longer.

The night air had a chill in it. He wondered what was left for him—what life had to offer him. He turned back and started walking. Tomorrow would be a new day. He refused to glance back, toward Payne's path.

Part Two

A Bitter Sweet Surrender

"I have always thought the actions of men the best interpreters of their thoughts."
—John Locke 1632–1704

9

Lazarus walked into the dimly lit bar. It was two in the afternoon. The money he made fixing the porch at Mrs. Goldberg's house was just enough for dinner and to get good and drunk.

A bartender stood behind the bar with his arms folded. The mirror behind him had that foggy water-stained look to it that came with age and a lack of cleaning. Twenty barstools covered in black terry cloth probably installed during the Carter Administration lined the entire south wall of the building. The distance from the door to the bar wasn't forty feet.

Lazarus walked between two pool tables. He knew both were missing the eight ball from countless nights of playing.

"How ya' doin', Laz?" Joe, the bartender asked.

Lazarus sat down and rocked the spinning bar stools to the left, then to the right. He shrugged.

"TNT?"

Lazarus nodded and Joe went to work.

Joe, the local bartender, had the answers to everything. Legal advice? No problem. Politics? He had it all figured out. Women? Admittedly, he knew very little except who should possibly go home with whom on any given night. Joe had a nickname for everyone and once he got to know a customer knew exactly what they were going to order. Many of his customers would walk in and sit down in their usual stool to their drink waiting for them. Joe had an uncanny way of knowing when to talk your ear off or when to leave the customer alone.

Tonight he left Lazarus alone to his thoughts.

It had been over a year since that dreadful day in the forest. Lazarus thought about it often. Nightmares filled his nights; he would wake up soaked in sweat. Consuming large quantities of Tanqueray and tonics allowed him to sleep at night. On nights when he had a glimmer of hope he would think about what he *might* have done. What he *should* have done.

Using a little black straw he stirred his drink. He took the lime hanging off the edge of the glass, squeezed the tart juice into his drink, and dropped it in. In one move, he gulped down the entire drink and set the glass in front of Joe pointing for him to make another. For Lazarus, drinking was more of a job than a way to relax.

After the second drink, he finally had made up his mind. Today he wouldn't go to visit his parent's grave. He couldn't. Even loaded he didn't have the courage to meet his parents.

Why had God seen fit to leave an idiot like him alive and take his father, a man who would have made a difference, he asked himself each and every day between the gin and tonics.

"I might have another client for ya'," Joe said.

"Is that right? That would be great."

It was painfully obvious after spending six months searching for a job that Lazarus had been completely locked out. Prospective employers would be excited about getting a man like him, would make a few phone calls, and come back with some excuse on why he didn't get the position. He had become a pawn in some twisted game Vance was playing. Yet, Vance had never come after him.

Lazarus often wondered why Payne wasn't shot on the spot. Why *he* wasn't shot that dreadful day. It was as if in some sick way Vance enjoyed watching someone suffering.

After beating his head against the wall too many times, Lazarus found Joe. Joe owned the bar and gave him opportunities to make himself useful fixing this or that. It didn't take long for Joe to run out of projects for him, so he asked some of the patrons who visited the bar. As a result of spending way too much time on the wrong side of the bar, Lazarus was able to get to know many of the customers. It was the only way he could make any money—by doing odd jobs for them. Joe kept Lazarus' little business under the radar. It was an understanding between the two of them.

One thing Lazarus didn't like about Joe was his lack of morality. He let it slide since he wanted to eat and because he realized he didn't have a leg to stand on when it came to doing what was right. After all he realized too late he had gotten his parents killed. He was unable to fulfill a promise. He aided a man that might have killed a president escape from certain death. Now he watched on as Joe set up drug deals and found Johns for hookers. The man would probably sell his very soul to the devil so he could stay in business.

But it wasn't like Joe was a bad guy; he was doing what every other American was doing—what he needed to do to get by.

Lazarus chuckled to himself. *It's funny how a man will sell this and that, and not realize the slow slide into the abyss until there is nothing left.* Perhaps he'll wake up one day and ask himself who he really is—*really.*

For Lazarus it was different. Instead of selling his soul he would do nothing. He clung on to the idea that not participating in sick behavior and not making a moral judgment about it was in some way holier and just. But deep down inside, he knew it was really closer to defeat. He wasn't even thirty yet and already he was waiting to die.

"She's on her way in. Looks like she might keep you busy for a while."

"That would be great, thanks." Lazarus gulped down his third cocktail and pointed for another. He knew at the rate he was drinking it would take a big job to keep him numb each day.

A slight breeze caressed his face. The sunlight shone through then quickly dissipated just as fast with the sound of a closing door. Lazarus used the bar mirror to see the person who had entered. His heart stopped.

He trembled, but adjusted himself on the chair giving him perfect posture. No way did he dare turn around.

The click of each step on the dirty hardwood floor made music. His heart beat, faster and faster with each stride. The sweet smell of perfume lingered in the air. Lazarus closed his eyes; it was the perfect amount of fragrance.

"Hi Joe," her voice was soft but confident. "Is this him?"

Joe nodded, as he cleaned a glass with a bar rag.

The woman flashed a smile at Lazarus that wrapped around him like a warm baby's blanket. "Hi, my name's Angie." The sparkling gold in her blouse complemented her smooth, milk chocolate colored skin.

The moment he made eye contact with her he knew she was the one.

Lazarus remembered his father telling him once about how he felt when meeting his mom for the first time. How Barry was struck by a bolt of lightning. Lazarus had always doubted it growing up. No way can love happen so fast. It's impossible to know anything for sure—I mean, really *know*.

And yet here he sat knowing for the first time what his father had gone through years before Lazarus was born.

A life riddled with guilt and self-pity—his life—had been renewed. It was as if in an instant Lazarus was able to wear the world like a loose garment. The problems weren't gone, but the answer stood in front of him.

Lazarus spun out of his chair and offered his hand. "Pleasure to meet you, Angie. I'm Lazarus, Lazarus Parker. Please, have a seat."

He guided her to the stool next to his, then sat back down. The slight wave in her long hair glistened in the faintly lit barroom. The black skirt ended just above her knee exposing the beauty of her shapely bare legs. She was tall just like his mom. Almost six foot, he figured. She talked and he nodded. But all he could think about was what their life together would be like.

Focusing on the conversation, he listened as she told him about woodwork and plumbing and carpentry, but something much bigger was going on. It was as if the two of them had been aimlessly trudging through life until this very second. This was no chance meeting. Both of them knew it.

"So, when can you start?" she asked.

"How about tomorrow?"

"That will be fine." She paused as if waiting for Lazarus to say something. Finally she stood up and straightened her skirt. "Okay, then, tomorrow it is."

She headed for the door.

Maybe it's not meant to be, he thought.

Last chance, son.

"Wait," Lazarus shouted.

In the background he could hear the faint sounds of the news on the television. Angie stopped dead in her tracks, but didn't turn around. Joe made a secret fist pump and grinned.

An anchor man on the news said, "The terrorist known as Jack Payne is still wreaking havoc in all sections of the country. President Vance assures us that the resistance will be eliminated by the end of the year. He promises to restore the Constitution once he feels it is safe to do so. Here is what he said earlier today.

"'My fellow citizens, it has become apparent that although we have made the rest of the world safer, we are under attack here on our homeland. We will hold off on making any decision about having Congress reconvene until at least the end of this year.'"

"In other news—"

Lazarus ignored the reports. Day after day he listened to how dangerous Payne was and how because of him the U.S. was no longer a free nation. At least that was how Lazarus interpreted the message. There was always a slight tug within rooting for Payne to succeed. No chance he could be worse than Vance.

Power corrupts, and absolute power corrupts— absolutely, his father had said often.

Could there be a worse time to fall in love?

It's now or never—

"Wait," he repeated and flew out of his chair. "How about a drink?"

She smiled, "I'd like that."

He put his hand on the small of her back and gently led her back to the bar. They never broke eye contact.

Once they were both seated Joe spun a napkin in front of each of them. He folded both so they made a triangle. "What'll you have?" he said.

The lady ordered an iced tea with lemon. Lazarus glared

down at what was left of his gin and tonic. Sliding the glass towards Joe he said, "Just a Sprite. Thanks, Joe."

***

The cold concrete floor of the cell caused Abigail to shiver. The stubble on her legs had now become full grown hair. The all-white outfit of what was left of her wedding gown was covered in black stains. Once a week she was forced to strip down. The guards would use a fire hose to clean her. Yesterday one of the guards, the only one without red in his eyes, told her she hadn't left the 16' x 16' room in over nine months.

But today was moving day. At least that's what he told her. He promised she would be able to shave her legs, eat something that required a knife and fork, and shower without being slammed against the wall with a force that always left bruises. Abigail Payne wasn't dead, but she sure wished she was.

It was the isolation that was driving her crazy. No one would talk to her. It had been months before the rogue guard had finally whispered to her. Twice a day a guard would set a metal tray just inside the cell door. It would be some type of slop she would have to eat with her hands, and a metal cup filled halfway with tap water.

In the beginning of her imprisonment, she would scream at the top of her lungs for anyone to answer her. She wanted to know why she wasn't read her rights.

At some point she realized she no longer had any rights, at least not here.

"God help me," she whispered hopelessly. It was the same prayer she said each day.

At one point it became a much longer prayer. But she was tired, yet she still believed He was listening. Her faith had not given in, just her body. Physically she struggled just to pick herself up from the floor and crash on the cot with the ancient mattress. This suffering would lead to something— good? Was that the right word? Holy, maybe. She wasn't sure. Certainly God didn't want this suffering to happen to her, but regardless, she needed to remain strong.

Footsteps sounded outside her door. She could hear rustling and voices upstairs.

Abigail began to wonder if this time of suffering had to do with how she had backed off from the faith her father taught her growing up. Mistakes had been made. Certainly she didn't honor her dad as she should have. She dishonored her mom's memory by not living a life of love and grace. Sex out of marriage. *Guilty as charged*. And more than once. The only Commandment she hadn't broken was thou shall not murder.

But in Abigail's heart she had committed that act a thousand times. The hatred for Barker Wilson was strong. She was on her way to killing him before Vance told Barker she was a woman scorned. It wasn't the words so much as knowing that Vance *wanted* her to kill Barker.

She remembered her father telling her Jesus wipes the slate clean. Her father was always the forgiving one. Every time she thought about him, she prayed that he was still alive. But after watching what Vance did to Frank Abigail had accepted there was little chance of that being true. Hope was the one thing she held on to.

"I just have to remember to pray," she whispered to herself.

The noise upstairs began to make its way to the lower level. The creaks of the staircase echoed in her cell.

She continued to try and pray for Barker Wilson, President Vance, and the others that had ruined her life. The prayer was usually riddled with obscenities; she had not been able to use their God given names. Someday she felt she would be able to forgive them, but that wasn't going to be any time soon.

"On your feet, Payne." Two guards dressed in black uniforms with parallel red pinstripes down the sleeves and the pants appeared at her cell door. Both of them carried large, black sticks that looked like baseball bats. The sticks had a double circle opposite the handle. Their helmets had a visor and reminded Abigail of the bad guys in that 70s kid's movie her dad loved so much. Except they wore white.

Pain shot through her body, but she rose to her feet. She was hungry, dirty and suffering from a massive headache. Rubbing her temples, Abigail wobbled over to the bars that separated her from freedom. One of the guards used his key to open the door. He motioned for her to move in front of them. She obeyed. She had no other option. A chill ran down her spine; she feared she was going to die today.

She muttered a prayer. She didn't want to die, but she wasn't afraid of death. In the very essence of her soul, she knew she had more to do here on Earth. Not having an idea of what that might be led her to believe perhaps it was just wishful thinking rather than a message from God. It wasn't as if the Creator came down and whispered in her ear. Usually, it was a gut wrenching feeling of telling her what *not* to do. But other times it felt so pure, so right, so—from *Him*.

"Turn around," the guard told her. He put shackles on her hands keeping them in front of her. Bending down the guard connected them to the leg shackles he put around her ankles. "Move," he said pointing towards the staircase.

As she walked towards the stairs she noticed other cells with people cowering in the corner like she had. Plexiglas reached from the ceiling to the floor making the cells sound proof. But her cell didn't have it. A quick observation told her this was no ordinary prison; these people were left here to die. There was no way to get food and water into the cells. The people wore a look of defeat. They were literally starving to death.

How does God allow this to happen? Why am I being kept alive? Never did she feel more alone than she did at that moment walking by the living dead. One of the prisoners sat twirling a piece of hair around his finger. He pulled it out. No reaction.

Abigail bowed her head in horror refusing to watch the despair. She counted five cells on each side. Nine people dying of starvation. Her feet seemed to weigh a thousand pounds as she made her way up the staircase.

The door was opened at the top of the staircase and she was led inside a small room.

The guards sat her down at a long, wooden table. It had a dark stain on it and must've been twenty feet long. On her right was a brick fireplace. The style was old-fashioned throughout the upstairs with dull red bricks and a holder for the poker and other items. The hanging light above the middle of the table emitted a soft light that barely covered the table. The room was carpeted in light beige, but covered in plastic. Abigail had seen enough movies to know this was done to make cleaning up blood or a dead body a lot easier. Maybe she was being saved from the suffering of starving to death. Maybe she'd get a bullet in her head instead.

"How are you, Abigail?" President Vance asked, walking in through a door from the other side of the room.

She didn't respond.

"I get it, I'm not exactly your favorite person. After months without any real human contact I wasn't who you were hoping for." He strolled towards her, lightly tracing the table with his finger.

Vance twirled his cane with his right hand. "Ah, but is it the first contact you've had?" He pointed the cane at Abigail.

From another room two guards carried out a man with a white cloth in his mouth. Blood ran down his face. Abigail could hear the muffled screams as he violently shook his head and jerked his body hoping to break free.

"No, no, no, please… Oh, God no." Abigail recognized the man. It was the guard who had talked to her. Tears ran down her face. "Please, Mr. President, please, take it out on me, not him."

Vance raised his hand. Abigail stopped talking. "I will, Ms. Payne, but I have bigger plans for you. Gentleman, string him up!"

The two guards carried him over to the fireplace. A hook on the wall held a noose. The rope was attached to the ceiling. One of the guards wrapped it around the man's neck and pulled it tight. The man continued to fight a losing battle. An arm got loose and hit one of the guards. Using his elbow he caught him in the back. The man spit out the white cloth. Breathing heavily he blurted out, "Your father's still alive, he's still—"

Vance fired his gun, hitting the man in the head.

A large spatter of blood covered the red bricks. There was a tinge of sulfur in the air, and Abigail noticed a small puff of smoke. The man's body hung like a rag doll.

"What do you want from me!" Abigail cried.

"Oh, just to get you to swear your allegiance to me on national television," Vance answered; except Abigail was talking to God, not him. She scowled at Vance knowing he thought he actually *was* God.

"Never, Mr. Chairman," she said sarcastically.

"Chairman?" Vance looked up deep in thought. "Chairman Vance. I like it." He sauntered over to Abigail and caressed her hair.

Consumed by grief she did nothing.

"I guess the cat is out of the bag thanks to Gary." He seized a handful of her hair forcing her to look at him. "Not a problem."

He yelled in her face, "DO YOU HEAR ME!" and released his grip. Slowly he pulled a sword out of his cane and admired both sides of the blade.

Abigail exhaled and waited for death to come.

Vance flashed the blade in front of her.

She began to tremble.

"This," he started, "is not for you. Not yet." And with the power of a locomotive he turned and drove it into the guard who had elbowed Gary. "You screwed up my plans," he said, watching the life gradually drain out of the guard.

"That's okay," he turned back to Abigail.

She was crying, unable to hold back the tears any longer. "Just kill me, please, why don't you just kill me?" she pleaded.

"Can't do it, sorry," he said with sympathy, "but, here's what I can do. Rumor has it that Gary here—" Vance put his arm around the lifeless body, "—promised you a bath. How about it? I always feel much better after a bubble bath. So it shall be." He looked over at the two guards standing behind Abigail. "Bring her to the palace."

They nodded. Each one grabbed an arm and lifted her up. Carrying her, they made their way down the stairs and to the front door.

"Oh, and gentlemen, for your own sake, make sure she gets her bath."

***

The buzzing sound of a razor mixed in with rushing water from the garden tub echoed in her head, but Abigail was too tired to care. She watched as hair dropped in clumps on the bathroom floor. Her dirty auburn hair clashed with the Spanish style tile that covered the room.

She couldn't stand to look at herself in the mirror. She could only see a weak and skinny woman wasting away. It reminded her of those holocaust pictures her dad had once showed her when she young. That was the night she came home and asked if they could go to the movies because it was Jew night.

He didn't get angry. But he had educated her on the subject of racial slurs. He told her how, when he was young, he would tell jokes about black people or Jews or other races and everyone would laugh. Even he thought the jokes were funny. Until one day when he realized there must be a cost to spreading that kind of humor. That was the day, he told Abigail, that he remembered telling a black man a number of offensive jokes using the word nigger like it was any other word. Jack had told the man it was okay for him to use the word because *he* wasn't racist. But the man said nothing. Then it hit Jack, he explained to her, what had really happened and he was ashamed.

The buzzing stopped. Small strands of hair floated in the air. They seemed to remain suspended inflight and quietly whispered a long goodbye. Still, she couldn't cry.

The two ladies in the room with Abigail never said a word. She didn't feel much like talking anyway. They guided her over to the tub and helped her undress. The old wedding dress was filthy. One of the girls deposited the clothing directly into the trash can.

Hanging up on the back of the door was a lovely cream-colored dress covered in rose flower designs. The deep red in each rose caught Abigail's eye. She could almost see it begin to drip like the blood on that guard's face. Gary. Quickly, she turned away.

Each of the women held an arm and led her into the water. Steam made its way up as her feet made their way down. The water was hot, but Abigail didn't recoil. She sat down taking it all in. Goosebumps formed on her shoulders. She exhaled wondering how long it had been since she took a bath. The splash of water. The warm feeling of a sponge on her back. She sat with perfect posture as the two ladies wiped the dirt from her torso.

They were all business, not allowing her the luxury to soak. As the bubbles from the soap began to dissipate, the water turned dark like a muddy river.

They stood Abigail up.

She shivered. The suck of draining water gave way to the noise of shower water crashing down from above. She shook a number of times before once again feeling the heat of the water. The glass enclosed shower washed over her entire body removing the soap scum and allowing her to clean the stubble on her head.

She stepped out of the shower and shivered. The two ladies dried her off. Holding her arms close she wanted to feel warmth. She wanted to feel the heat of the water once more. She wanted to *feel* something.

And she wanted to cry.

The dress with the deep red roses fit perfectly and matched the flats they slipped on her feet.

But Abigail could barely keep her eyes open. She wanted to fall asleep on a nice comfortable bed with a thick comforter. But she knew that son-ova-bitch had more planned for her. At the moment she wanted to kill him. The moment just before that one she hoped he would kill her. She wanted to pray for strength, but was afraid He wouldn't deliver.

The door made an eerie sound when one of the women opened it. They pushed her into the next room. Whatever it was they had planned, she didn't want any part of it. Vance had cleaned and built her up only so he could tear her down once again. Abigail knew that. She wasn't stupid. This vicious cycle had no end in sight.

"God help me," she prayed.

"He can't help you, but I can," an older man said with a grin. He had dark brown hair and a clean-shaved face.

"Who the hell are you?"

"A friend," he answered.

"I haven't had much luck with friends lately. What makes you think you'll be any different?"

Somewhere between the door and the hallway Abigail had gotten a second wind and regained her strength. The only thing she knew for sure was Vance had no plans of killing her right now. This put her in a unique situation. She knew she could push. The real question was, *how far?*

"I can get you things." The man took her hand and led her down the narrow hall.

Abigail saw a very tall man before her, but he moved with a refined grace. So far nothing told her this man was here to hurt her. But—there was *something*—something underneath his proper manners and charm that was sinister, dark, frightening.

"Who says I need anything?" she asked.

The two of them turned the corner and the aroma of sweet-smelling foods filled her nose. Her stomach growled.

The long dining room table was covered in a white cloth. On top of it, a number of plates set filled with creamy chicken, potatoes and carrots. A bottle of red wine stood on the near end. It read *Opus One*, the same brand of wine Barker and her shared the night the two of them were arrested. The night her father became a fugitive. The night that changed her life forever.

"I'm not drinking that," she told the man, her voice stern.

He nodded and clapped his hands twice. A short, fat black lady wearing a white apron and dark navy uniform scampered out from the kitchen holding another bottle of wine. She exchanged the *Opus* for a nice looking *Beringer* Merlot.

"How's that? I'm usually partial to Cabernet, but since we will be having chicken, and white wine is so pretentious,

I thought the more prudent choice would be a Californian Merlot. After all, the French are such snobs." He motioned for Abigail to take a seat, then poured her a hint of the wine and waited.

She swirled it, tasted the fruity wine with a soft finish, shrugged and set the glass down. The man filled it half way.

She took the bottle of *Opus* as a sign she shouldn't get too comfortable in her new surroundings, but she figured she would play the game long enough to get a meal out of it. The hammer could drop any minute. She cut herself a big piece of boneless chicken covered in a parmesan crust and chewed it up so fast she didn't even taste it. One bite led to the shoveling of food as fast as she could into her mouth.

"Slow down, slow down, my dear Abigail, there's plenty," he told her.

She finished chewing the bite in her mouth. "I'm sorry, it looks like you know my name, but I didn't get yours."

"Ah, yes, introductions are always important. My name is Shaw, Phillip Shaw."

***

White. Everything was so white. Abigail didn't know what to make of it. The heavy cotton pants and shirts reminded her of the time she spent taking karate lessons. All that was missing was the stiff belt. Even the walls and floor were white. The queen-sized bed, a large sea of white.

She made her way down the spiral staircase into the ornately decorated living room, all the furniture in the perfect place. She could not find a stain or a blemish on the pearly white carpet. She entered the dining room. Windows from floor to ceiling on two walls. Sliding glass doors led out onto a patio that reached from one side of the house to the other. It was the type of house that dreams were made of. The layout was exactly the way Abigail had envisioned the home her and Barker would've lived in. A chill climbed up her spine.

"Good morning," Phillip said cheerfully. He was sitting at the other end of the long table, covered with a white tablecloth. A white plate with half a grapefruit sat in front of him. Removing the cloth napkin from the table, he gracefully placed it on his lap. He motioned Abigail to join him. She sat down at the other end where the other half of the grapefruit sat on her plate.

"I'm not really into grapefruit," she told him.

"I had a feeling," Phillip responded. He snapped his fingers and two ladies wearing white aprons, navy blue uniforms, and little hats that reminded Abigail of something a nurse would wear entered from the kitchen. One carried a plate with an oversized donut she just knew would be cream-filled. The other lady held a shot glass with some kind of red juice. The swap was made and Abigail picked up the donut and took a big bite. The vanilla cream flavor on the inside complemented the maple frost perfectly. She closed her eyes. The smell told her it was fresh baked.

"Can I get some OJ, or coffee, or something?" she asked.

"Once you finish the juice you can have anything you want."

A big red flag went up for Abigail. She noticed the shot glass was the only cup in front of her. She slowed down her chewing and finally gulped the donut down. *What is in the red juice?* she wondered. Growing up she hated tropical punch or Kool-Aid or any other red juices. There was an aftertaste that seemed to linger for the rest of the day. Not to mention on the lips. Her lips. The juice would turn her lips blood red. And *they* had called her bloody lips. It still bothered her to this day.

"Kool-Aid's really not my thing."

"Why? Still thinking about those kids in grade school?" Her heart skipped a beat. "Don't worry, Abigail, it's not Kool-Aid. It's just a little something to calm you down." He smiled.

"Do I need to be calmed down?" She paused. "What is it, really?"

"Oh, just a little something the Doctor cooked up."

"The Doctor? Who the hell is 'the Doctor?'" she peered over at him with suspecting eyes. "What do you and Vance want with me, anyway?"

"You're going to be the first guest on our new TV show," Philip started. "Our plan is to have you denounce your father and his *so-called* resistance. You see, Vance has big plans for the country, Abigail; he knows what's best for all Americans. To be honest with you, we don't trust you to do what we say, so, you need to drink the juice." He grinned.

"You're right," she stood up. "I won't denounce my dad. In fact, I hope he kills both of you." She grabbed the shot glass and chucked it at Phillip.

The glass bounced off the table and sprayed juice all over the front of him. He twitched, then slowly he stood up. Grabbing the glass of water in front of him, he dunked his napkin in it and dabbed his charcoal suit where the juice had landed. Finally, he used the napkin to wipe off his face.

"Well, it appears you are not ready to cooperate." He straightened his suit. "Nick!"

From behind Abigail came a man chiseled by the Greek Gods. Suddenly she found herself in a bear hug with little hope of escape. Slamming her foot down on his foot he loosened the grip just enough for her to bring her elbow up crashing into his chin.

He let go.

She caught her breath. The chiseled God seized a handful of her blouse and lifted her up in the air.

"Holy shit," she said.

"You really shouldn't fight with us, Abigail," Phillip strolled towards her as she remained suspended in the air, "especially with Nick. He has, well, special talents."

She prayed for a way out, for her father, for strength.

"Nick, she looks tired. Bring her upstairs to her room." Philip started to walk away but stopped. "And make sure she has a nightcap."

Nick pulled back his right hand, made a fist, and punched. Lights out.

***

Abigail woke up suffering from an aching head. The bruise forming around her eye felt like it was the size of a grapefruit.

She lay on the bed in the white room. Her focus was still a bit off when she noticed a shape on the nightstand. It was a shot glass filled with red juice.

***

Day one. Abigail wondered if she would ever get out of here. She prayed often. The first few hours dragged on like a bad movie. Calm. Depressing, with nothing to do. She wanted to remain composed hoping to outlast Vance and his sidekick. Lying on the bed she would try to rest, but the throbbing pain in her head wouldn't go away. Thoughts flew in and out at the speed of light. She found herself down on her knees begging God for the right answers.

Getting up she walked over to the door, tried the knob, and decided to knock.

"Hello? Is anybody there?" she said hoping to make human contact.

No answer.

Hours went by without sleep. Her mouth was dry and tasted like shit. She couldn't remember the last time she brushed her teeth. The growling of her stomach became her only company. There was no way they were going to let her go without water or food. No way.

Of course, she watched as they shot that friend of her dad's. Even the black guy just walked away.

The click of the lock echoed in the room and she jumped up, smiling. The door flew open and two ladies walked in.

"Hey," she waved. The two ladies stripped down the bed. They balled up the sheets, bedspread, grabbed the pillows and trudged back out. The chiseled Greek God peered in and closed the door. Abigail dropped to the floor when she heard the door lock again.

"Stay calm," she told herself. "Stay calm."

Twenty-four hours later Abigail finally broke down and cried. Hoping to stay strong, she did her best to hide the sobs. They needed her. Sooner or later she'd get at least a glass of water. Something other than that damn shot glass filled with the red stuff. She picked it up and threw it against the door. The lock clicked once again.

"Do you need to use the restroom," Nick asked in a voice that sounded more like a robot than a human.

"Yes, please." She didn't want to break. Not in front of him.

He escorted her down the hall to the bathroom. She closed the door quickly, locked it, and frantically turned on the water in the sink. Barely a drip. She huffed. The tub was her next stop. She turned and turned the two handles in every direction. Nothing. Lifting up the lid to the toilet willing to drink from it, she found a dry hole. On her knees she laid her head on the rim and cried. Light-headed and delirious, she couldn't get up. The smell of urine filled the room.

The door flew open with a kick and in stepped Nick. He picked her up with little concern of the pool of piss or the rancid odor. He ripped off her clothes.

Abigail looked up, hoping he would finish whatever he was going to do. For the first time she wished for death, welcomed it. Making eye contact she could see a distant red.

He must be on the juice, she thought.

"What's it like?" she inquired, her head circling around like a bobble head doll.

No response. *Typical man*. She attempted to laugh. She wanted to cry. She prayed in fragments and nonsensical babble. She struggled to keep her eyes open.

The air in the house was cold. When Nick dropped her back on her bed, stark naked, she realized the air conditioning was on.

"Just a sip, please. I'll do anything, I just want, I just…" She watched him walk out of the room. "Just a sip… goddamn it!"

Gazing over at the nightstand there sat another shot glass—filled. She reached over and slapped it against the wall.

Hours passed. She rolled up into a ball. Teeth chattering. Her mouth dry as sandpaper. She slept—or she thought she had. Occasionally she moaned. Visions appeared on the wall, in the bed, all around. It was hard to breath. She couldn't move.

"God, where are you?" she mumbled.

She begged Him for strength as she shook. She wanted to give in. Her stomach grumbled so much. The idea of death was so comforting, yet she knew it would not come quickly, or easy, or peaceful.

Another prayer. Her eyes closed.

Sixty-one hours. No water. No food. No heat. Abigail's eyes opened; she struggled to breath. Nighstand. Shot glass. Red stuff. Tears. Prayers. Hopelessness.

"God, oh God, I—" She reached to knock the drink down. Pulling back, she started to cry. A gripping twist of pain takes hold of her gut. She screamed.

"Abigail," the voice of Phillip Shaw filled the room, "all you have to do is reach out, and drink the juice. You've suffered enough; let us take care of you."

A brief moment of strength gives her the propensity to scan the room. *Was the voice in my head?* Delirious and suffering from every inch of her body being in constant pain, she rolled off the bed dropping like a rock onto the white tile floor. A one note thud fell flat in the room.

"Abigail, oh Abigail—"

"Shut up! Shut up! Oh God, please, help me," she yelled, lifting herself up from the ground. "I can't do it," she whispered. "I can't."

Reaching out she picked up the juice, her hands shook violently. She looked up, asked for forgiveness, and drank the liquid down.

10

Angie rubbed Lazarus' feet with continuous motions. A moment before, she had started with his legs softly caressing the top of his feet with the bottom of hers. Lazarus loved how she was the one who always initiated the action. A tingling sensation ran up his legs electrifying the sweet spot. Pulling her in, he kissed her neck. His hand wandered; hers explored.

Give in, he pleaded. Angie was already *there*. She could always get *there*. He couldn't. Ever. He didn't realize *it* was something impossible to *will* yourself into. When it comes to giving yourself to another human being the power of intellect is futile. Still, he tried. He loved Angie, but often wondered if, like with his parents, he would stand still when Vance ripped his guts out once more.

These thoughts, his fears, ran through his mind each and every time they made love.

She pulled him on top of her and ran her hands down his back.

Give in, he thought to himself once again. It was all physical. He couldn't escape his own head. *Give in.* The emotion became lost in a sea of guilt, shame and self-hatred.

Why can't I just give in?

The love making was good. Sex within marriage was so much more than he could have imagined. But, just as he would start to lose himself, to *give in*, the depths that existed simply couldn't be reached. There was a level beyond the physical he had hoped to attain. But he never did. He would pray for it if he really believed in it.

Lazarus rolled over. Angie cuddled up to him, wrapping her arms around his body. He picked up his cigarettes and lighter from the nightstand. "Want one?"

Angie nodded and turned away. Lighting two cigarettes in his mouth he handed one over to her. She sat up and took it from him. The distinct scent of burning tobacco filled the room.

He scanned her milky smooth body. "What's wrong?" he asked.

"It doesn't matter."

Lazarus knew this meant trouble. It was the typical female response to an age old question. He wasn't sure if she wanted him to probe further or leave it alone.

He asked again. Same answer. The silence was excruciating, and he wondered why he even *went there* as he took a long, deep drag off his cigarette. Everything within him screamed to reach out and touch her, hold her, love her. But he couldn't do it. A cloud of fear, confusion, and doubt filled his mind. Lazarus was caught up in it. The brewing storm was his creation; he was guilty. But the tools he needed to fully love her, to *give in*, were lost on him, or perhaps they had never existed.

Chairman Vance, that was what he was calling himself these days, would be back. Would Lazarus have the power to pull the trigger this time? Was that the right thing to do? Was that what held him back now from giving in to Angie?

A loud booming sound came from the living room. At first Lazarus thought it was an earthquake. The 'big one' had been predicted here in Los Angeles since his father was a kid. Suddenly he realized it was the front door. Four men appeared in the room wearing all black riot gear and helmets that hid their eyes.

Before Lazarus could react, one of the men punched him in the face with the force of a Mack truck. Angie screamed.

Filled with rage, Lazarus stood up, blood dripping from his nose. Lazarus tilted his head up, wiped the blood from his face, and growled.

Two of the black soldiers surrounded him. Kicking one of them, he noticed the man didn't budge. *No way rubber armor could be that strong*, he thought.

Each man seized one of his arms. It was as if the more he struggled, the stronger the hold. The shame of being completely naked settled in. Seeing Angie, Lazarus realized the two other soldiers had worked her over pretty good. She was a bloody mess.

"Cover her up, damn you!" He continued to fling his legs at the two men, in the air, towards those who held his wife. "What does he want?" he asked.

No answer.

"Why can't he just leave me alone? I don't care—" He wanted to cry, but couldn't. With each whimper from Angie the crack in Lazarus' heart grew. One of the soldiers pulled out a long needle and poked it in her arm.

"God damn it! Why? Why?" Lazarus yelled.

The lights drained out of her eyes and she fell limp.

Lazarus squirmed violently. The grip tightened beyond any possible human strength. Feeling a prick in his left arm a warm sensation traveled throughout his body.

They left him there on the floor. The other two soldiers dragged Angie, naked, out of the apartment.

His lights went out.

It was hours before Lazarus woke up.

Is she gone forever? he wondered.

There was no way to defend his wife from his past. She would continue to pay for his crimes. Vance held all the cards and could play them at his leisure.

And then a thought crowded out all other thoughts; Lazarus couldn't love Angie anymore. He couldn't, and no way would he ever be able to *give in*.

***

It had been three months since Angie first wandered back into the apartment. Lazarus still struggled to look her directly in the eyes. To this day they still hadn't discussed the events that transpired on that April day.

They sat in silence waiting for the other one to break it. Angie was fidgety, playing with her food, she hadn't taken a bite.

Lazarus didn't notice.

The bouquet of collard greens filled the air. He was trying

to admire the work he had done carving their new dining room table and the glossy dark wood finish he had applied early that afternoon. Even though everything in his gut told him to quit on life, he still took pride in his work. It was automatic. His mentor, John, had instilled in him that if something was worth doing than it needs to be done right. 'Give it your all. That's all I ask,' John had told him.

If only he could do that with his marriage.

"How was work, honey?" he asked Angie in the usual manner.

Their conversations lived only on the surface. When they made love there was no *giving in*—Angie felt dirty and told him so every time. Lazarus felt sick to his stomach not knowing what had happened the three days she was missing.

"Fine," she answered in her usual tone. "I have some news."

"Oh, yeah? What's that." He scraped his fork clean of mashed potatoes.

She waited.

He stared down at his plate.

"Will you look at me?" she asked in a stern tone.

Slowly Lazarus raised his head. Looking into her eyes was painful. In a way, he was grateful there was some emotion in her eyes even if it was anger. They lived in a world so numb that neither one of them ever noticed—anything. It was a fear so deep that to feel would be like committing a crime.

"I'm pregnant." He almost choked and dropped his fork.

"What? Really? Is it—"

"Yes, it's yours." She folded her arms and turned away.

"That's not what I—shit, I can't do anything right! I feel so...so trapped."

"I know." Angie closed her eyes, holding back the inevitable tears.

"I'm not sure that you do, damn it. Why on earth would you bring a child into this world?"

She stood up and threw the white bowl of mashed potatoes at Lazarus. "Don't you dare tell me I don't understand. Who do you think you're talking to? Huh?"

Lazarus put his head down and began to wipe the mushy potatoes off his shirt.

"Hit me, kick me, throw me out of this house, just—just do something that shows me you care about—something, anything, Lazarus." She shook her head and started to walk away.

He remained frozen.

***

She turned around and marched up to Lazarus. "Look at me." He lifted his head. "Do you see me? Do you?"

He made a half-hearted attempt at a nod.

She huffed. "What do you see?"

He shrugged.

"Say something."

The gaze was empty. She slapped him. He jumped out of his seat and pulled back his fist.

"Do it," she egged him on. "Do it, please, show some type of emotion."

"I can't," he replied. The tension drained out of him as he dropped his fist. "What happened, Angie? What happened to you—to us?" He flopped back into the wooden chair.

She began to cry. As if in slow motion, he rose and reached out for her. His arms retracted as if from a burning stove.

"Just—" she started and began to shake, "just, can you hold me?" Her voice trembled. "Oh god, please, Lazarus, just hold me like you use to?"

Silently he prayed to a God he didn't believe in. Maybe there were too many broken pieces to heal the wounds. Perhaps they couldn't get past that day in their bedroom. He often wondered if she felt he should have, or could have done more. Fear kept him from asking. Fear locked him in place, searching for the strength to reel her in.

She folded her arms and turned around. Then stopped—waiting—hoping—longing—for the embrace of her husband. Her shoulders drooped. Finally, she decided it was not meant to be and walked away.

"Wait," she stopped dead in her tracks, and a smile

appeared on her lips. "I… I love you, God if only you knew how much. I'm afraid, and I don't… I don't know what to do." She spun around and ran into his arms.

"Just hold me." She felt him quiver in her arms. Praying that God could put him back together, she accepted the man she loved for all that he once was and what he had become. She wished for the day he could get back what he had lost. The sacred vow of marriage meant sticking by his side— that she needed to be the rock in *his* life. She shook her head accepting from a power high above the duty she had, and the fight facing her.

"You're in danger," he whispered. "You must go, before it's too late." He pushed her away from him and turned his back.

"I'm not going anywhere."

"You must. He'll come, he will, and when he does he'll hurt you. Then, he'll kill you." Lazarus exhaled. "And he'll leave me alive to suffer." He turned around. "We are powerless, we are, and, I just—I can't stand losing you, too."

She rushed towards him, but he put up his hand, shaking his head.

She fell to her knees. "Pray with me, please, Lazarus. We are not powerless. God is on our side. He has to be."

"There is no God. We're bringing a child into this Godless world." He thought about how much of a coward he was for not taking his own life. It was better he not say *that* out loud. The day he learned Vance was responsible for his parents' death still haunted him. The nightmares every night were more intense after what happened to Angie.

First, he heard the twisted, evil whisper in his ear followed by a gunshot. He waited—and waited—but death never came to him. Vance let him walk away. Why?

Some of those nights were followed by a dream of all his teeth falling out. A sign he had no power and he's weak, that the evil son-ova-bitch holds all the cards, and the day would come when his losing hand ends with a bullet or a knife in his back. Probably by someone he loved. Lazarus welcomed death. He yearned for it. Hoped for it.

Some would say—Angie would say—he's already dead. So why doesn't she heed his warning? Why doesn't she just go away? He wished he didn't love her; that he never loved her.

"Angie," he said, "what happened when they took you?"

A pause.

Moving her head from side to side she answered, "You don't wanna know."

"Just go," he said sternly. His mind began to take him to places he avoided. When he closed his eyes he could see the worst kind of violations being done to his bride. The muscles in his arms contracted and the rest of his body stiffened. He knew Vance and Shaw took their turns. It made him sick. The visions took over like black storm clouds in the dead of winter. He was too helpless to scream.

"Stop it, just stop it!" she exclaimed. Picking herself up from the floor she stepped towards Lazarus.

He waved his hands in front of himself silently begging her to go away.

She persisted.

He mumbled a few words, including the occasional *no*.

Fighting her way in she held him tight, afraid letting go would mean falling to her death. She could smell the sweet aroma of his sweat. Not wanting to *give in,* he made no attempt to return the affection. "I'm here," she said softly, "for better or for worse—I'm here."

"This isn't going to end well," he predicted.

Filled with hesitation, he lifted his right arm up and around her waist. It was a mistake; he just knew it. But what else could he do? Throw her out? Where would she go? And would she still be in danger?

"What happened? Talk to me, honey."

She lovingly rubbed her face in the middle of his chest, tightened her grip, and closed her eyes. "I'll tell you, but you better make sure you really wanna know." She let go and held both of his hands in front of her, eyes still shut, and said, "How about we sleep on it? If you still want to know in the morning—then, we'll talk. Fair enough?"

He nodded.

She led him into the bedroom. Letting go, they escaped to either side of the bed. Angie turned down the sheets and started to get undressed. Lazarus sat on his side of the bed; head in his hands. There would be no sleeping tonight. There was no doubt in his mind that he now needed to know, no matter what the cost, what happened during those three days she went missing.

Slowly he pulled his solid black t-shirt off his body, balled it up, and tried to make it in the laundry basket. It missed. He huffed and trudged over to pick it up. There was a faint smell of rotting food coming from the dining room. He was too tired to clean it up tonight and figured Angie felt the same way. Turning back around, he noticed Angie kneeling down by the bed in her satin white nightgown. She was praying. She finished, and they slipped into bed together. They stared at each other. Just stared. Not a word was said. The small space between them felt a lifetime away.

She wanted to lean over and give him a kiss, but feared it might lead to more.

He wanted to reach out, touch her, hold her, love her like he did before that frightful day.

She inched her head closer.

He panicked and backed off. With a counterfeit smile, he turned on to his other side, fluffed his pillow, and pretended to fall asleep. In his thoughts he told her goodnight and that he loved her.

In her thoughts, she responded with a sweet kiss. She turned on her other side and soundlessly wept.

They laid awake, all night, hoping the next day would never come.

11

The White House lawn was pristine. Chairman Vance could smell the new rose bushes he planted earlier in the spring. After killing both the president and vice-president he remembered spending a late evening pulling out every last rose the Smiths had planted. There was nothing worse than people unaware of how to properly grow and care for roses. He reminisced about how bloody his hands got from carelessly pulling the plants out of the ground. The warm, salty taste of his blood when he licked it brought a sense of comfort.

Walking towards the nuisance known as the press, he grinned. Perhaps tonight he would get to kill again. And yet, he so loved keeping some of them alive. He reflected back on the day he sold his soul to the devil. Rarely did it feel like a mistake. How perfect life was with the power he wielded. The only problem was the desire for more.

Vance clutched the smooth, wooden podium and took in the moment. Only five members belonged to the White House press corp. Most had quit. Others were persuaded to leave their post. And still others disappeared or were found at the bottom of the Potomac. No one really asked the newly named Chairman any real questions. It had been two years since he had suspended the Constitution, and it didn't take him long to track down, and in one way or another, silence the opposition.

Of course there was the resistance led by Jack Payne, but having control of the media and television allowed him to shape the story to his liking. Plus, he had plans on how to kill two birds with one stone. A new television show was in the works. It would bring together the entertainment so many of his subjects—he liked to call them citizens—longed for with the continued punishment of those who opposed him. He didn't want to completely eliminate the resistance. It was fun having them around to treat like pawns on a chess board. Besides, his power was derived from their violence. Or at least that's what he had come to believe. It was as if hate generated more hate, violence was answered with violence, and suffering—his favorite—created even more suffering.

"Welcome to my citizens from around the world. I have only one announcement today, and I will *not* be taking any questions. Now—"

"Can you tell us Mr. Chairman when you plan on allowing congress to reconvene?" a female reporter to his left blurted out.

Vance hated to be interrupted. He glared at her. A force passed through taking the woman's breath away. Goosebumps formed throughout her entire body. She stepped back.

"Like I said, I will *not* be taking any questions. Is that clear?" Again he scowled at the reporter.

Eyes big, she nodded.

"Thank you. Now, to my glorious news. We will no longer be known as the United States of America. From this day forward, any citizen using that disgraceful name will face fines and possible jail time," he flashed a twisted grin and peered right into the camera, "from this day forward, we will be known as Jahannam." He turned and strutted back into the White House.

"Get me that bitch's name," he barked at one of his aids.

***

The five reporters dispersed back to their newsrooms to let the world know what had just happened. Since live TV was no longer legal, even the print media had a chance to be the first to report breaking news.

Grace Fillmore, the news reporter for Beltway Magazine, an online news rag dedicated to printing whatever smut they could get their hands on, rushed back to the coffee shop she used to write her articles. The days of newsrooms for any type of print, including online, were over. She yanked the silver ASUS laptop out of her bag and turned it on. She realized she only had about thirty minutes to post the news if she was going to be the first. Usually the first article posted became the source of the day. It meant more money in her pocket and a possible shot at getting hired at one of the bigger online newspapers. The New York Times was still around and the place to be, but she had hoped to get in at the Washington Post. So far she had been able to stay clear of the crap most of her colleagues wrote about, and this article would be a huge feather in her cap.

She banged away at her keyboard. The words flew from her fingers and danced onto the page. The smell of her stale coffee filled the café, but she didn't take any time to drink it. There would be plenty of time for that later. She needed to finish it. The money she was making would only allow her to steer clear of the filth for another week, two at the most. Boy, did she need this.

The final scan to make sure she didn't have any typos or nonsensical sentences happened after twenty-six minutes. Perfect. Most of the other reporters couldn't have possibly written a masterpiece like hers in less time. She wanted to shed a tear of joy knowing how she had sacrificed to get here. No more rice and beans for dinner. No more hitching rides from neighbors. No more *'who does she think she is'* comments from her peers. Her time had come. And on the twenty-seventh minute she pushed *Post*.

Almost immediately comments began to appear. That was good news. The phone call from one of the remaining big three would happen in a matter of hours. She had arrived.

After stopping by the local watering hole, The Breakroom, where all the great news writers hung out, it was time to head home. After spending almost five hours enjoying the drinks the other reporters bought for her she was now drunk. The Jukebox was playing old 80s music she vaguely remembered her mom talking about when she was little.

It was just after eight and getting dark. Grace wobbled down the street towards her second story apartment on Good

Hope Street. It was off the 295 close to the Metro she used to get into the middle of DC each morning. Stammering up the stairs to Suite 202, she thought she heard a noise behind her.

Quickly she turned.

Nothing.

She fumbled around in her purse and found her keys. They jingled in her hand as she shoved one into her door. The lock clicked. Turning the knob she realized the door was still locked. Finding that strange, she tried again. The door opened this time.

She flicked on the light and stumbled in, throwing her purse on the faded tan couch she joked was sold new in the 1800s.

"Good evening, Grace." The voice made her scream. "I'm sorry, I didn't mean to startle you."

"Mr. Chairman? Is that you?" her voice quivered. She regained her nerve and armed with liquid courage yapped, "What the fuck are you doing in my house?"

"Now, now, that kind of language will not be tolerated in my presence."

"What the—"

"Stop! Before you get yourself in more trouble than you're already in."

Her cell phone chirped. She knew it was one of the big three. She wanted desperately to answer it, but she was more than a little creeped out by having the Chairman in her house. Though, Grace didn't think she had anything to worry about. It was more of a shot across the bow rather than a real threat. Right?

Slowly he rose to his feet. "It's time I taught you some manners, Grace," he smiled.

It scared Grace. She wanted to run. Her heart beat faster. Sweat dripped down her spine.

"What is that supposed to mean?"

"You just don't know when to shut up!" he yelled at her, grabbing her by the arm. "Come here, you bitch." And he began to tear her clothes off.

She screamed.

***

He laughed. Vance looked forward to what he planned for her next. Regular sex didn't do it for him anymore. It was so straight forward. Even the twenty year old interns lacked the passion he now desired.

He salivated as he imagined what she tasted like. The recall of what Lazarus' wife was like came back to him. Her whimpers, her screams, the sound of her crying in the corner, actually praying to God. In Vance's world he was God.

Sweat dripped over his body. Smelling Grace's hair and cheap conditioner added a little something to the experience. It was the pain and suffering he was addicted to. The rape itself, his release, meant little to him. It was the power that he craved.

The cries, the screams, the absolute horror she was living through was everything to Vance. The twisted lust comforted him. It was all pleasure. The more she hated it, the more he enjoyed it.

She wept.

He smirked. The power was his, all his.

"Well, my dear Grace. I must be going." He put on his clothes.

Curling up in a ball, she prayed aloud that soon he would be gone, and he laughed. He made small talk. Telling her about his day and how this woman really upset him earlier in the afternoon.

Her body shook and she couldn't catch her breath.

"Oh, one last thing. Although I am partial to letting you live and watching you suffer over the years, that might be too dangerous. I can see in your eyes the need for retaliation."

"No, no, please. I won't do anything. I promise, oh, please God, no," she broke down into hysterics.

Pulling a blade from his jacket pocket he sighed, "I wish I could believe you, Grace. Not that it would matter if I did." He bent over her naked body and slashed her throat. As he watched her gasp for air, he said, "I have such an appetite for killing this evening."

The blood spilled out in waves. The life went out of her as she took in her final breath of air. Vance dipped his finger in the pool of blood and tasted it. "Not as good as mine," he said as he exited the apartment.

12

Lazarus rushed into the waiting room of Dr. Beck's office just off Cameron Lane in Downtown Los Angeles. He had been working up the street at the former Staples Center. More buildings were going down than going up nowadays, but at least he could make a few bucks as a laborer. The irony of it all was his love for basketball. He was tearing down a cathedral to the game all because Vance didn't think it had any real value. Baseball, soccer, and some of the other 'less aggressive' type sports suffered the same fate. Football was permitted to continue as long as they went back to the 1960s rules. No more being concerned over concussions or late hits, or any other part of the game that 'took away' from its violent nature. Hockey had become Jahannam's favorite past time. The self-appointed Chairman had control of all business, of all people, and even some individuals when it served his needs. If only the Parkers could stay under the radar until after the baby was born, then perhaps they could escape.

The doctor's office was an old sanctuary. The long, thin building begging for a paint job on the outside housed the only doctor in town taking on new clients. The inside had been recently updated with a light green color. A dozen or so metal folding chairs lined both sides of the small room. A makeshift wall with a half-moon cutout in it was used for checking in. The guy's commercials mentioned being on the 'corner of Hope Street' alluding to the idea their patient would get exactly that by being treated here. Lazarus had his doubts. If the look of the inside and outside was any indication, it would be more like getting medical care in Tijuana: quick, careless, and out to get your money.

"I'm a little late," he started to explain to the nurse behind the wall, "my wife is Angie, Angie Parker."

"Ah, yes sir, she is in seeing the doctor right now. Take a seat and I will see how much longer she will be."

"I would like to go in with her," he said apprehensively.

"Oh, I'm sorry sir, that's not possible. Husbands are not allowed in the offices or delivery rooms anymore. Chairman's orders," she finished with a finger in the air. He wanted to slap that smirk off the woman's face.

"Since when?"

"Ah, let me see, a couple of months ago, I think? It was in the Women's Protection Act the Chairman authored. It gives all rights to the fetus to the mother. Baby, too."

"Well that's crazy, it seems we are going backwards in this country. Let me talk to someone in charge."

She put her hand on the telephone next to her, "Now, Mr. Parker, I'm going to have to ask you to calm down. I don't want to call the police, but I will."

Thinking it would be best to be here rather than needing to be picked up at the police station, Lazarus stormed off and took a seat. "This is stupid," he said.

On the television SNN was playing an exposé on Jack Payne. The episode was titled, "Homegrown Terrorist: A Dangerous Man in Jahannam." More stupidity. Payne was a good man. He wondered what this world would look like if those in the resistance were in charge. Would it be just another version of Vance's tyranny? His dad had always talked about George Washington and how he *twice* gave up the power. 'I pray there's someone like him out there today,' Barry would tell him. But Lazarus reminded him that Washington would have owned their family as slaves, not given them freedom. Maybe the lesson his father was teaching had nothing to do with the few faults the first president had. Could Payne be that next Washington? He doubted it.

The idea of joining anything no longer had any appeal. In his mind, there was no such thing as a good cause. Even some of those black race hustlers he once admired had lost their charm. The majority of them became pawns in Vance's grand plan, or he had them killed. Those dead leaders were the ones to follow. But how stupid was that? To die for something that is lost. The United States and everything it had once stood for was no more. Gone. Slowly the country was slipping into some George Orwell version of existence. Big Brother was constantly watching. He just went by a different name.

Lazarus jumped out of his chair. Heart racing. Hands trembling. Something just wasn't right; he could *feel* it. That bastard Vance *is* watching now. His wife, his child, they were in danger. He marched through the office door and started entering exam rooms.

"Mr. Parker, stop," the nurse said. "I'm calling the police."

Lazarus headed right towards her with fire in his eyes. She froze. He grabbed the phone and pulled the line out of the wall. "No one's going to jail today," and he threw the phone against the back wall. He went back to his search.

"Angie?" he opened the next door. Empty. "Angie?" his voice a mixture of anger and fear. The door was locked. He kicked it in. The doctor had Angie in stirrups performing some sort of operation. Angie had her head turned and was crying.

"What the hell is going on here, doctor?" Lazarus asked.

"I'm sorry, sir, we couldn't save the baby."

"What—what the hell does that mean?"

The doctor shrugged. Lazarus landed a punch; the doctor fell to the ground.

The distinct smell of death and blood and sorrow was more than he could stomach. Lazarus threw up. His son was gone. A chill ran down his back as he remembered his mom telling him when a neighbor's baby died, 'It's not natural to bury your own child.' And now he knew exactly what she meant. This kind of pain never heals, never.

"Honey?" Angie reached for Lazarus.

"What did you—how could you—I have to get outta here!"

"No, wait!"

He ran out of the room. He ran out of the building. He ran down Hope Street.

Lazarus continued to run. And run. And run.

He ended up at the bar where he met Angie. Running didn't work. Maybe a drink would. It might even take more than one, but it was worth a shot.

He toiled down past the pool table to the bar, and sat down. A tall, balding man with a slim build spun a coaster down in front of him, "TNT, Mr. Parker?"

"What? Yes, but—where is Joe?"

Four officers busted in through the front door before he could answer. "Lazarus Parker? Hands above your head."

He put his hands straight up in the air. "Guess I won't be having that drink after all."

"Don't worry, Mr. Parker, it will be here for you when you get back." The balding man smiled and went to the other side of the bar.

The four officers circled Lazarus and one put handcuffs on him. He would have been able to take all them out, but the fight had left him. Plus, they weren't responsible for the murder of his child. Vance was.

Revenge zipped through his mind, but passed on like a summer breeze. It wasn't in him. In his gut he knew killing Vance would accomplish nothing. The satisfaction, if any, would be brief. But if the opportunity arrived once more he wasn't quite sure what choice he would make. This perverted dance Vance was leading had become even more personal. But Lazarus knew that was exactly what he wanted. There was no escape. There was no perfect answer. Maybe Vance was finally going to end it. He welcomed that idea; he longed for it.

***

The stink of jail was embedded in Lazarus' clothing. It didn't help that the cell was hot and all he did was sweat the past two nights. His own body odor was more than he could stand. He asked the cop at the desk who sprung him where Angie was. The guilt of blaming her, of leaving her in that retched place weighed heavy on his heart. The cop wasn't sure.

Lazarus walked down the steps of the police station and

headed to the apartment. There was no way he had the right words to say to his wife. Nothing would bring comfort. The same went for him. Their marriage had been filled with nothing but heartache. He would end it. She would be better off without him. Vance would never leave the two of them alone.

After a spell, Lazarus arrived at the front of his apartment complex. The shades were drawn in their second story unit. It was unfathomable what she must be going through. The guilt now covered Lazarus from head to toe for running away.

"Hey, Parker, tell your wife to stop making that nigger food. It smells like shit." It was the manager, Paul Hernandez. He would take offense to the man's words, but it would accomplish nothing. People's true colors (no pun intended) had surfaced since the takeover by Chairman Vance. The administration worked hard to create a divisiveness never before seen. Minorities were not only encouraged to hate white folks, but anyone who looked different than them. The Act that was used to keep him out of the doctor's office was just another ploy by Vance to separate people based on—well, whatever he could come up with. In this case it was gender; tomorrow it might be the state or county he lived in, if there still was such a thing; whatever worked to keep the people busy fighting each other instead of the government. It was as if Vance derived all his power from hate and violence.

Lazarus ignored the man and walked up the stairs to the second floor. The stench was awful. He took off his shirt and used it to cover his nose and mouth. The sweat rooted in his work shirt made him gag. The door knob was cold. He turned it. Unlocked. Strange for Angie—she usually had a lockdown routine at night.

Lazarus found it hard to breath. But not from the smell. An ache had developed in his stomach. In the very core of his being he knew something was wrong. A creaking sound pierced down the hall as the door swung open. He entered.

"Please, God, let it be a bad batch of chitlins." He tiptoed into the apartment. "Angie? You here?" he said, slowly making his way into the bedroom.

"Angie?"

The stench was stronger. Entering the bedroom he could hear the shower. He picked up his pace and stormed into the bathroom.

"Angie?" he said once more. Pulling back the curtain, her body laid covered in blood. It was her. It was his wife. He lost all control and fell like a box of rocks onto the linoleum floor. He dragged Angie's body out of the shower.

"Why, why baby? Oh, God, I should've been here." His tears fell as he rocked her back and forth. In the distance he could hear sirens. Good. He had no plans of leaving her. In death, he would finally be there for her even if it was for only a short amount of time.

Over and over again Lazarus apologized. He told her he loved her. His hold tightened. Softly he kissed her cheek. Again, he told her how it was all his fault. That he was the reason she was dead. Their child was gone because of him. She was gone because of him.

"I'm sorry," he repeated again and again. All hope drained out of him. The idea of God vanished.

After they stormed in and took her away, Lazarus remained on the bathroom floor. A numbing pain engulfed him. In a matter of fact way, he answered all the questions the police had. Suicide, they called it. But Lazarus knew better. *He* was guilty. No need for a judge and jury. It was no longer necessary for Vance to kill him—Lazarus was already dead.

Night came and went, and the next day arrived. He slept in the bathroom waking often. The pain was overwhelming. Child, wife, gone. He picked himself up from the ground and headed out the door. Slowly his stroll turned into a walk which turned into a stride and finally a full on sprint. He ran and ran. He moved as if there was something evil chasing him. And he believed it. Again, he found himself outside of the bar where he met Angie.

Compelled by an undeniable urge, he bellied up to the bar. The balding man walked over. He smiled. Lazarus grimaced. "TNT, Mr. Parker?"

"Please," he answered. The drink appeared and before the man could walk away he had finished it in one gulp. Lazarus snapped his fingers and pointed to the glass. The balding man refilled it.

"Another," he ordered after finishing the second.

"Don't worry, Mr. Parker, we won't run out. At least not for you," he said putting the third drink in front of him. The curiosity of where Joe had gone, why this man knew his name, what the hell was really going on in this strange world was lost. He no longer cared. It didn't matter. Nothing did. Only the next drink.

Funny how life had led him right back to where he was before he met *her*. A vicious cycle of hope. He would finally snuff *that* out. It was over. At that moment he decided never to hope again. It was too dangerous.

The balding man strolled over and put a bottle up on the bar next to Lazarus, "Here, this is for you."

He turned the bottle around and saw the face of Forrest Vance. It was Vance's brand of Gin. The evil grin with the slicked back hair and smooth, flesh colored skin actually brought comfort to Lazarus. His journey to hell was now complete.

"You win," he told the bottle.

From the other side of the bar Lazarus heard a chilling cackle. It was the balding man. He was talking with another patron.

Powering down the cocktail, he rose, grabbed the bottle, and headed for the apartment: a place he once called home.

***

Phillip Shaw entered the Oval Office just after noon. Chairman Vance was sitting at the giant, light-colored oak desk eating a sandwich. The curtains were a bright yellow and the room had been painted green. He also noticed the presidential seal had been removed.

"Do you like what I've done with the place?" asked Vance.

"You want my honest opinion?" Phillip asked.

Vance nodded.

"Not really."

"Excellent." They both chuckled. "What do you have for me?"

Shaw made his way to the front of the desk and sat down in an old, black hardback chair. It was not very comfortable.

"It was a chair used by the Supreme Court when they were in the capital building. I figured, why let it lay to waste in a room where no one can see it." Vance stood up and stretched. "Once it's used for a while, I'll throw it away."

"Hopefully that will be soon," Shaw commented. "As far as Payne is concerned, she's about as ready as she'll ever be." He stood up, turned the chair upside down, and broke off one of the chair's legs. "Does that make it ready for the trash bin?"

Ignoring the question Vance asked, "When does the first episode air?"

"October. We plan on calling it, *Welcome to Utopia.*"

"Very well. Have you leaked the information out so her father will make a cameo appearance?"

Shaw bowed and started to make his exit. The pictures of former presidents had been replaced by portraits and photographs of Vance.

The master would be pleased by our progress, he thought, *you have created a masterpiece in him.*

The admiration ran deep. Shaw knew the work that went into completely destroying a man to build him into the perfect specimen of ego. Vance had become everything the devil had hoped for and more. The lack of humanity was a testament to his new victory of *Him*.

And this beauty had spread to the people. They yearned to discard freedom and be led like ants to a food source. The last great hope on Earth would vanish from the world and finally from the memory of every man, woman and child. Complete victory would be his.

"Oh, Shaw, make sure you take this piece of shit chair with you. Tell—um, Marge to replace them both."

He smiled knowing Vance was so obsessed with self that no small detail left of this pathetic excuse for a country

130

would be left behind. Many of the people had already forgotten.

Strolling back, admiring still the newly designed Oval Office he grabbed the chair and leg, bowed once more, and walked out making sure to talk with 'Marge'—if that was actually her name—about finding a replacement.

The flight back to Chicago wasn't for a number of hours. Shaw thought about taking in some of the sights. Most of the Memorials had been closed and all of Washington D.C. area had become a military zone. The days of buses filled with school children and sweaty tourists snapping pictures every few steps were gone. The Tomb of the Unknown Soldier no longer was being guarded. All of the soldiers that had been guarding it when Vance delivered the order refused to leave. One by one he had them shot for treason. Their blood stains on the tomb itself. All evidence of their existence wiped out.

'If they so love the unknown soldier I will make them one,' Vance had said. He asked the Dark One to keep their very souls stuck in some sort of purgatory worse than hell itself. It brought him comfort when he was alone at night that he had personally sent scores of worthless men to his Master.

Phillip trotted down the landing strip to the small jet plane he would take back to Chicago. The show would be a big hit; he just knew it. The idea of having former resistance types swear their undying allegiance to Chairman Forest Vance was his. He had to admit the idea was stolen from his love of reading about Orwell's Oceania. So often he dreamed of turning that dream world into reality. But his show would be better. Like a game show. In just a few short months the first episode would air. Shaw was ecstatic. Some would have to be publicly executed on stage. People at home would root for the person to show their loyalty to Jahannam. Unless, of course, they didn't like them. Abigail Payne would become his first superstar.

***

The shot glass filled with the red juice sat on the nightstand.

It was there every morning. Abigail had stopped resisting months ago. Mr. Shaw had told her how wonderful it was to see her behave like a lady should. The only time she would fight was when he would take her. She felt so dirty afterwards. It appeared that the more she fought, the more he liked it. Vance had visited and done the same. He usually left his mark by slapping her. Once he slashed her face with a sharp dagger across her left cheek. The wound took over a month to heal and left a scar.

Lying on the white comforter completely naked she wanted to cry. She prayed for strength from a God she was starting to doubt. But still she prayed each morning. There had to be a silver lining in the future.

Her thighs throbbed in pain. Last night it had been Nick's turn. It was the first time she decided not to fight, hoping it was the answer to making it stop. No luck. His bad breath still lingered in the room. Her face was red from his rubbing it. After he was done, he licked the side of her face. It made her want to vomit. She trembled, reliving that final act. Tears fell from Abigail's face. *No one will ever want me again, no one*, she thought.

The red juice didn't seem to be working. She clung onto the idea that her praying was the reason for that. But deep down, she wasn't sure. She did her best to imitate the robot-like movements she had seen in others who were on the juice. Each day she prayed that God would give her the strength to make it just one more day. But lately her one-sided conversations with Him were simple: 'I can't take it,' she would say in a whimper.

She sobbed, hearing footsteps make their way up the staircase. *He* was home. He would need to feed his appetite.

Curling up in a ball, she wrapped herself up in the dirty comforter. The blood stains no longer bothered her.

The door flew open.

Abigail closed her eyes asking God to take her away, even if only in her mind. She could feel her soul slowly begin to leave her body. Would she be able to remain so detached from the physical world? God, she hoped so.

"Hey, get up, get dressed," Shaw barked.

With apprehension she rose. Slowly she put on panties and a bra he threw at her.

"Hurry it up!" he said abrasively.

She flinched and moved faster.

"Drink the juice, now!" he ordered.

Without hesitation she swallowed it.

Nick stormed into the room and put a burlap sack over her head. She didn't have time to scream, or moan, or object. For a brief moment she lost her breath and assumed she was on her way to the end. It was the only friend she had left, death.

He had a powerful grip on her arm to lift her up from the bed and began leading her out of the room and down the stairs. She grimaced. It will all be over soon.

He put handcuffs on her and tightened them to the point of agony. Again, she prayed. The pain became bearable.

Shoved into a car, they sped off.

The whole ride Abigail was thinking, *the end is near*. She was good with that. Mainly she wanted to know why she was made to suffer for so long without the opportunity to help another human being. Isn't that what He promised? That our suffering would at the very least benefit others? Now no one will ever know that she lived, that she died.

Anger swelled up within her and she wanted to tell God to go to Hell. Her father once told her when she was young it was okay to be angry with God. That it was okay to yell at Him, to curse at Him if need be. She remembered thinking her father was nuts. But then he explained that it meant you believed in God and knew He was there. The Creator forgave quicker than humans can ever forgive.

Abigail remembered her dad asking her if she wanted to play a game when she was just a child. Excited he had asked her, she said yes. 'Try and forgive, Abs, quicker than God can. Boy, I wish I could do that,' he smiled and kissed her oh so softly on the forehead. At the end, she wanted to hold on to that memory.

"Forgive," she whispered. "I forgive you." The words were more than a struggle to get out. Her eyes welled up with tears and the weight of the world seemed to dissipate.

It worked daddy, it worked. I played the game—

She knew she hadn't forgiven quicker than He did, but that wasn't the point of the game. She had forgiven. That was what mattered. Her father's teachings was to show her how to let go so God could come in and heal. The healing wasn't complete—it may never be complete, but it was a start in the right direction. Soon, perhaps she would be with her Creator. What a joyous moment that would be. The idea of seeing her mother again warmed Abigail's heart.

The black SUV stopped. The car door opened. Her palms began to perspire. The aroma of gas fumes found their way under the burlap and mixed with the sweat and tears running down her face. She could not escape the salty flavor that entered her mouth. Using her shoulder, she tried everything to itch her head, her ear, her cheek.

Nick forced her out of the car. The light brown sack was ripped off her head.

She exhaled. A cool breeze swept over her allowing her to breathe with ease. They were in a field covered in long grass and scattered brush. Scanning the area she saw a forest of trees off to the left and she noticed a building that looked like an airplane hangar. In the far off distance, she could make out a large city.

Phillip took over for Nick. His grip was not quite as strong.

"Listen up," Phillip whispered in her ear, squeezing her arm harder. "Your only job today is to swear your allegiance to Jahannam, to Chairman Vance. It needs to look convincing, or you will experience a whole new kind of hell." He lessened his grasp. "And *that* is a promise."

Abigail suddenly realized she was not going to her final resting spot. And *that* scared her more than death itself.

Once inside the building the handcuffs were removed. The hangar was divided into studios with dressing rooms for each one. Two ladies dressed in Victorian style dresses wearing white wigs and faces covered in white powder approached Phillip and Abigail and bowed in unison. They didn't appear to be surprised by her lack of clothing.

"Get her ready for the camera," he told them.

The women nodded and led her down a narrow hallway to a door that read, *Abigail Payne*. A star appeared on each side of her name. One of the women opened the door and the three of them stepped through. A high chair with Abigail's name on the back was the first thing she saw. Everything was decorated as if she was a movie star. The mirror was surrounded by large, round bulbs. A vase of a dozen roses were on the vanity with a card sticking out.

The two ladies guided her to her seat and immediately went to work. Her hair had grown out, but not enough to merit shampoo and conditioner. The ladies used brushes dipped in water and perfume to hide the stink of sweat and fear.

The ripping sound of removing her leg hair as one woman pulled strips down her legs was followed by a short shriek of discomfort from Abigail, as the other lady took the utmost care in applying her makeup. It was as if that woman was painting the Sistine Chapel.

A phone rang.

"Hello?" the doll-like lady answered in a high pitched voice. "Yes, sir, she will be ready on time." A pause. "That's the plan." And she disconnected and went back to her duties.

The final touch was the blonde wig. It made Abigail look like she had when she first arrived at the house. She hated it.

She read the card as she waited for their ministrations to be finished. It had three X's and three O's, and the signature of Forrest T. Vance.

Sick bastard.

Together the two ladies said, "All ready now." They clapped their hands and shook with excitement.

Behind the whites of their eyes Abigail could see the red. She wondered what sick tortures they had been through. Filled with sympathy, she forgot for a moment the absolute hell she had gone through over the past years. It had felt like a lifetime.

Out the door and down the hall they went ending up at the set for the show. A large neon sign hung down from the ceiling. Abigail could hear a buzzing sound followed by the deep red lighting of the words, *Welcome to Utopia!* The new stage had a long runway down the middle with seats for about 500 for an audience. Forrest Vance and Phillip Shaw stood on stage talking. A man dressed in a tuxedo appeared to be practicing his lines on the far end. Other people moved swiftly, bringing in more chairs or adjusting the lighting or checking camera angles.

Entertainment. That was what this was all about. Abigail knew it. It was like the Roman Empire towards the end. Keep the masses entertained and therefore, happy. She had more hope in the American people, yet knew how powerful of a ploy this was.

A light popped and a burning smell circled the studio. A man was pleading with Chairman Vance. She couldn't hear the words, but knew he was begging for his very life.

The whole set made her sick to her stomach. Death had a presence. Evil had engulfed the entire production. All she could hope for was strength. Silently she prayed.

The ladies led her up to a chair that was set mid-stage. They sat her down and praised each other on a job well done.

Shaw ambled over. "Ready?"

She didn't know what to say. The king-sized seat, without warning, sprouted metal guards that captured both her hands and legs. She was trapped.

"Remember, you don't want to disappoint me."

Lights flicked on from everywhere. Blinded by the light, she squinted in a vain attempt to see—something. Vague silhouettes and blurred shadows danced from every direction. As her eyes began to focus, she saw people rushing in to find a seat, the low roar of chatter hummed within the walls.

"Check—check—check 1 -2 -3—check—"

And then—the stage went silent. Cameras and lights moved in and out. The show was ready to begin.

"Hey, hey, hey folks and welcome to utopia!" a male voice said from one side of the stage.

The applause from the crowd erupted.

"Tonight is our very first episode, and boy, do we have a show for you!" The man dressed in the tuxedo was hosting.

His slicked jet black hair was made to imitate Vance. It was creepy. "I'm Willy Randolph, your host. Yes, as promised, we will get to the public executions, but first we start with Abigail, known by those who love her as Abs or Abby. She is a twenty-something little hottie, as you can see, who gets the chance to dishonor her father tonight." He stopped and waited for the crowd to applaud. "Yes, yes, a practice all of you should do often. But for poor, little Abby, it's a game she doesn't get to play often. Her father is busy terrorizing all of you. He's the terrorist, Jack Payne."

"BOOOOOOO!" came from the audience.

The cuffs on her arms and legs retracted. Had her prayers been answered? Or was this part of the show? She glanced to her left, then to her right, and back to her left again.

There stood a man—*could it be?* Was it just an illusion?

"Abs," it was *his* voice, her father's voice. "Run to me, now."

She darted off in his direction, a child running into her father's arms.

The host, the audience, the crew: all of them were stunned into silence. She took her father's hand and headed for the exit.

"How did *he* get in here?" Vance growled.

Instead of trying to explain, Shaw ran after them.

Pushing a few buttons on his watch Shaw yelled into it, "Code four! Code four!"

***

The first guard was met with Jack's right foot to the groin. He went down like a sack of potatoes. Two other men from the resistance joined Abigail and her father.

"I can fight, Dad, let me go," Abigail said, and he did. The four of them raced out the front double doors that led to the outside.

"No matter what happens, make sure you get to the edge of those trees," Jack told her, using his head to point. One of the resistance men was shot in the head and died instantly. The other three stopped. Four men dressed in suits wearing sunglasses appeared.

"Nice job, gentlemen." It was Vance. "I have to give it to you, Jack, I never thought you would come after her."

He walked over to them. "On your knees and put your hands behind your head," he ordered.

The three of them did so.

Shaw caught up. Vance ordered the four agents to go back inside and 'work' on crowd control. "You," he pointed at Shaw. "I will deal with you later. For now I want you to make sure those idiots do what needs to be done."

Filled with shame Shaw walked away.

"What to do with you three. Hmmm…" Chairman Vance pulled out a .45 and shot Jack's soldier in the head. His body fell forward. Blood splattered all over the wild grass.

Next, he sauntered over to Jack and shot him in the arm. He screamed.

Abby cried.

"Take care of your brother. Run," he whispered to his daughter. "Run now!"

Abigail ran as fast as she could.

With all the force he could muster, Jack drove a dagger into Vance's foot. "Now you have a reason to use that cane."

A piercing, evil hiss blew through like a tempest. Abigail found herself at the edge of the small forest. She turned, hoping her father was right behind her. Instead he remained with Vance, towering over him. In what seemed like slow motion, she watched as the pistol raised to the back of her father's head. He brought his hands together in a final prayer before the gun went off.

"NO!" Abigail cried.

Vance turned. Bending down, he removed the knife from his foot. Blood dripped from it. He chortled.

"Come with me," a man whispered behind her. Startled, Abigail turned around and readied herself to attack. "I'm one of your dad's men. Follow me." She could hear the crack in his voice.

A brother? she pondered. *I have a brother?*

The two of them traveled briskly through the dense forest. It was all but impossible for her to shake the image of watching her father die. Blindly she followed the man she didn't even know, hoping the future had something better in mind. The entire journey she prayed for salvation from the evils of Shaw and Vance. She asked for any forgiveness she could receive.

But more than anything, realizing that she had been spared, she asked for guidance. For direction. For the strength to go on. She owed that much. Not only to God, but to her father. His sacrifice would not be in vain. And she ended her prayer by breaking the silence, "Your will, not mine, be done."

***

Vance hobbled back into the studio to see the work he asked for was complete. Dead bodies were everywhere. He hated wasting bullets and was more than pleased with how the entire mission was accomplished by the four agents using their bare hands. He decided not to chase Abigail at this time. The leader of the resistance was dead, and he needed someone to take his place. The fight must go on. It must. Maybe she would be the answer to that call. At least her story might inspire some fool to take up arms against him.

Walking among the dead, he thought what great opposition Payne had supplied. He liked using guns and violence and dynamite and fire. Sure, he worked hard to keep the so-called innocent from becoming casualties, but that didn't matter; the need for perpetual destruction was there. Vance could only hope Abigail would be as eager to use weapons with the same love and care that her father did.

A person in the crowd of dead bodies was moaning close to him. He peered over to one of the agents. "Left that one for you, sir."

Giddy as a school boy, Vance lifted the man up and cradled his head. Giving the man words of comfort, he placed his hand over the man's mouth. A tingling sensation moved through Vance as the man struggled for air. He grinned once life had left the man's body.

***

Several hours passed. Although all the bodies had been removed the rotten smell remained. Vance loved taking it all in. The final blood stain had been scrubbed away when Phillip appeared.

"Ah, my one and only friend."

"Yes, sir," Shaw said cautiously. The penalty would be severe, he knew it.

Vance rose, needing his cane like he had never needed it before.

Phillip dropped to one knee and bowed his head.

"You know it has to be done."

Phillip could almost hear the last bit of humanity in Vance.

"I know, sir, I welcome it." Shaw knew it was the end. The master's puppet couldn't have friends. It would not be prudent. He was excited to go back and be with the One. They had never come this far before. It was not the only time in history they had tried to take over the supposed 'last great hope' for mankind. Washington refused to keep his power, Lincoln ruined their chances during the Civil War, and Wilson actually gave in to the pressure of those pesky women who wanted the vote. He succeeded in making the country *more* free. The exact opposite of what they had asked those in his administration to do.

Finally, they had a man in Vance that could fulfill the dream of total darkness for the former United States.

Vance pulled his shiny blade from his cane and placed it on Phillip's neck. He lifted it up and placed his other hand on the handle. "Goodbye, my old friend," and with those words he sliced downward, decapitating Mr. Shaw.

Your evil is now complete.

Part Three

Hope Rises

"For how does it benefit a man, if he gains the whole world, yet truly suffers damage to his soul? Or what shall a man give in exchange for his soul?"
—Jesus Christ

13

Eight years later…

Chairman Forrest Vance had come a long way from those days in grade school when big Billy Thurman chased him around the playground. In sixth grade it was every day. Finally, when Billy was sent off to one of those 'special schools,' Forrest thought the terror would come to an end.

But it didn't.

His mother picked up right where Billy had left off, his *own* mother. Her drinking had reached its pinnacle during his thirteenth year. The name calling and physical abuse still had not healed. No amount of destruction, human or otherwise, could cure that wound; to this day it still festered.

And yet the time and care he took to kill Billy Thurman could still bring a smile to his face. The opportunity *to teach his mom a lesson* was not possible since she had passed years ago. So instead he dug up her body and threw it in a landfill. There was no rest for the wicked.

These memories entered his mind as Air Force One began its decent. The drop left him queasy. He took a sip of his Dewar's on the rocks and licked his lips. Constantly he drank alcohol, but never could he get drunk. At least not like he yearned.

"We will be landing in Kingman in twenty minutes, Mr. Chairman," the pilot announced.

The entire country had been renamed now. Kingman was once the city of Colorado Springs in what was formerly known as the great state of Colorado. Kingman was the last name of the governor Vance had put in charge. He decided, since he couldn't possibly be everywhere, to divide

Jahannam into three sections. Each section had a governor. Vance oversaw the entire country.

There had been rumors of a resistance taking hold in the Black Hills of what was once known as South Dakota. He wanted an update, personally.

Any type of resistance was futile. Sure, there was the occasional explosion killing governor's troops in all three sections, but they didn't stand a chance. Chairman Vance had sent the nation back to the stone ages. Food was scarce—unless civilians lived in one of the capitals, gas and oil was heavily regulated, making it all but impossible to get, and the internet was but a memory. The entire skies belonged to Vance's Air Force One—he liked the name, so he kept it, and his legions of drones.

The plane landed. The limousine was late picking up the Chairman. The streets of Kingman were deserted. Vehicles sat in auto cocoons waiting for fuel or were discarded wherever they stalled. Brush and weeds were slowly surrounding every structure. The people had become so dependent on government that none of them lifted a finger to fix anything. Showing initiative was frowned upon. Filing grievances with the governor usually led to a civilian's disappearance. Vance knew secretly people planted small gardens and hunted for food when times became desperate. The times the government came through the meat would be in the final stages of spoilage, except his food of course. He ate the best of everything, imported from other countries. The smell of garbage and rotting human flesh forced Vance to keep the window rolled up.

Governor Lawrence Kingman had built a castle on top of Pikes Peak. It was made of marble and came with a draw bridge and manmade moat. The back side of the castle had a large open area he used for entertaining guests.

It was early October and the mountain was already snow-capped. Despite the white on the ground the day was gorgeous with a slight chill in the air. The four wheel drive limo cruised over the bridge and parked in the roundabout that circled a fountain made of stone depicting Cupid with his bow.

A tall, handsome young man wearing slacks, a white button down shirt and a bow tie opened up the Chairman's door. He bowed and gestured for him to follow. Up the gold-plated stairs and in through a pair of doors that reached at least ten feet in the air. The doors opened automatically upon the young man's request. The white marble flooring with a hint of grey was dull and dirty. Passing by the kitchen, Vance could smell frying oil and something sweet baking. Many of the servers, boys no older than twelve, carried trays full of fried appetizers of all kinds. Others carried desert trays of chocolate truffles and tiramisu. The servers were nearly naked except for their perfect white bowties and loin clothes.

The glass sliding doors were open to the expansive back patio. The governor lay in a hammock wearing a speedo. Since he was over 300 pounds, Vance figured he might break it. Two boys provided human air conditioning with large feather fans. The governor was playing 'the touching game' with two servers that were in the hammock with him.

All around boys and girls ran around nearly naked, performing in one way or another for the governor's guests.

"Hey, mister, can I dance for you?" a little boy asked Vance.

He led the boy over to the far edge. The Chairman, using his cane, had an obvious limp. It was a thousand foot drop over the four foot wall. He picked up the child and threw him over.

"Damn faggot," he said wiping his hands.

The entire party, once a constant buzz of chatter, went silent. Kingman jumped out of his hammock, tripped, and fell on his ass.

Rising to his feet he said distressingly, "Sorry, sir, I mean, Mr. Chairman. I... I didn't know you were coming."

"I know. I made sure of it." Vance walked around the room, memorizing each and every face. "What the hell is going on here?" he asked the governor.

"Well, sir, it's just a party."

"A party? Really? Didn't I make being a faggot like you illegal?"

"Well, yes, you did, but, I didn't think that applied to me." The governor shrugged.

Seeing the distasteful look on Vance's face he quickly wiped the grin off his own face and dropped to one knee, pleading for mercy.

"Mercy? Get up, faggot. Look at you: fat, ugly, you make me sick."

The governor rose and Vance walked him over to the wall. "Throw yourself over," he insisted.

"What? But, sir. I'm the governor."

"Do it, or what I do to you will be much worse."

Governor Kingman cried and begged, as he promised to change. But it fell on deaf ears.

Everyone in Jahannam knew, once Vance was done with you, he was done with you. The crowd remained silent and still. No one dared move.

"Everyone, come, watch your governor fall to his death. I insist." And with those words everyone moved towards the edge. "Ah, yes, an audience, is that what you were waiting for?" Vance asked Kingman.

Kingman's words had become nothing more than blubbering nonsense. A warm liquid started to puddle under him. Vance could smell the piss.

"Jesus Christ, man," he said backing up away from the stench. "Did I really put this pussy in charge? And where do you get off wearing a speedo; are there no mirrors in this house?"

There were some who laughed. "Oh please, laugh at my jokes."

The palace erupted.

Vance bent down and whispered in his ear. "Don't you know you're nothing more than a fat fuck? It's time, before I get very angry."

Kingman got to his feet, legs unsure. He put one foot over the side and peered down. Turning to Vance he started to say something, but decided against it.

"Wait! Wait!" Vance cried.

The governor sighed in relief.

"Whew, thank the devil, I was afraid you didn't hear me,"

Vance said.

Governor Kingman puffed out his chest and smirked. Right then and there he made a promise to pay more attention to his duties. Vance wouldn't regret keeping him alive.

"I think what we all want to see is a dive."

Kingman's heart jumped into his throat.

"What do you all think?" Vance asked, turning to the crowd.

"Dive! Dive! Dive!" the chant continued.

Vance tilted his head and glared right into the governor's eyes. He could hear his voice, but his lips did not move. *Fatty, a head first dive, or else.*

Lawrence Kingman had no idea what *or else* meant. What he did know is the suffering would be horrendous. With a huff and a grunt, he stepped up onto the four-foot wall. He closed his eyes and dove off to his death.

The crowd transitioned from the chant to an out and out cheer. Some clapped, others rooted him on all the way to the bottom, and a few prayed they would escape the castle alive.

Everyone turned and saw four agents guarding the glass doors. They stood, arms folded, mirrored sunglasses, in black suits and a determined countenance.

"Before we begin the after party, do I have any volunteers for the governorship?" Vance scanned the area. "No? Okay then, boys, get to work."

14

"Mr. Parker. Mr. Lazarus Parker?"

Lazarus sat on the floor knowing what the men at the door wanted. His television. It was all he had left. It was all he was living for. Leaning up against his emerald-colored couch with a missing leg, he wondered if Vance was watching. Or listening. Or even knew what was happening to Lazarus.

Another knock at the door. They called out to him again. Sooner or later they would just break it down.

It had been at least two weeks since he last worked. The money had run out. In his hand he held the last swallow of gin. Now was as good a time as any to polish it off. And that's what he did.

Another knock. More like banging now.

The TV was on. He was watching a rerun of *Welcome to Utopia*. He hated it, but never missed an episode. Often he wondered why Vance never put him on the show. Maybe because there was no doubt he would swear allegiance to Jahannam. They were just words. Lazarus no longer had anything left to fight for. Chairman Vance must know if he had decided to fight against him Lazarus would have done it long ago.

Angie, the baby, his parents; they still entered his mind. The booze worked sometimes, but not very well.

He grabbed his filthy white shirt and put it on. He was still wearing the same Levi's he wore to work the last time he had labored. His usually shaved head had stubble and he had a scraggly beard still with last week's food in it. He didn't care anymore. It didn't matter.

The timer on the microwave dinged. He could smell the mac-and-cheese. It was all he ever ate. The meal reminded him of the last time he saw his mother and father alive. It wasn't nearly as good as his father's homemade recipe but it was food.

"Mr. Parker, open the door, now!"

"Coming!" he yelled. Lazarus got up and set the now empty bottle of Forrest Vance Gin next to the other ten empty ones on the counter. He made his way to the door and peered through the peep hole. Rapidly blinking, he tried to focus. Both of the officers wore the dull black uniform with the red badge on the right breast. They carried night sticks now that guns were illegal; except for Vance's personal guard. It was still possible to get a gun through illegal channels, but getting caught was a fate worse than death.

Behind Lazarus on the TV he heard, "So what will it be? Allegiance, or death?"

"Death, Willy, but you probably already knew that." Lazarus said in answer to the host's question as he opened the door.

"What did you say?" the officer asked, his voice stern, pushing Lazarus out of the way.

Lazarus grabbed the man by the throat, shaking him, and barked back, "I was talking to the television."

"Mr. Parker," the man's partner said, "put him down, now." The officer had his hand on his side ready to strike with his baton.

Lazarus let go and walked over to the couch.

"Sit down!" he was ordered. Lazarus remained standing, putting both of his hands into his pants pockets.

"What stinks in here? Smells like nigger." The two cops laughed.

Lazarus fumed.

"I'd tell him to take a shower, but it probably wouldn't help."

"Now, Mr. Parker, we're here for the television. I must ask if there are any drugs or weapons in the apartment."

He shook his head and sat down on the couch, folding his arms.

The two men began rifling through the kitchen drawers, the medicine cabinet in the bathroom and under his bed.

The studio apartment Lazarus moved to a couple of years after Angie's death didn't take the officers long to search. The only window was covered with an old Los Angeles Raiders blanket he had kept of his fathers. It was the only thing hanging on any of the walls. The five volume set of Victor Hugo's *Les Miserables* sat on his nightstand against the small, gold lamp with the tan-colored shade.

Last year when the Chairman banded pretty much every novel, he pursued permission to keep the set since it had belonged to his mother. He was told no; he kept them anyway.

Often he wondered if there was a Bishop in *his* future that would release him from *his* bondage like Jean Val Jean in the story. Since religion was outlawed a couple of years ago it didn't seem likely.

"Don't touch that!" he told one of the officers.

It was the only two pictures he had left. One was a picture of Angie on their wedding day. She was wearing a beautiful solid white dress that hung just below her knees. It was not a traditional wedding gown but made her the most beautiful woman in the world to him that day—and every day since. Her dark brown hair was braided with beads on the ends, almost golden in the sunlight. The photo was taken outside the Justice of the Peace where they were married in Los Angeles. It showed a smile on her face that told a story of love and joy and togetherness the two of them had shared before it all went to hell, literally.

The cop flicked the two pictures on to the bed, exposing the other photo underneath. It was from Angie's ultrasound. So many nights Lazarus had wanted to give the child a name. But he couldn't. He would call his child *little one* as he outlined the shape of the unborn's body with his index finger.

The first few years he did this every night as he wallowed in a drunken self-pity crying himself to sleep. Nowadays it was different. There were no more tears left. It was only on the nights that seemed the darkest he felt the need to outline the picture. Tonight would be one of those nights.

The partner unplugged the television and headed out of

the apartment. The other officer handed him a card. "The Chairman thanks you for your sacrifice to the collective whole." He walked out.

It was an E card. Either you traded in the black market or you were blessed with an E card. E cards gave the holder about three to four months of food and drink. And drink could be booze. Right then and there, Lazarus decided to drink himself to death. He was already two weeks into doing nothing, why not continue.

Dropping to the floor he laid down in defeat. A musky mixture in the carpet of smoke and gin and filth filled his nose. He was tired. Too tired to get up and trek over to the liquor store for more of that bastard's gin. He crawled over and sat down on the couch, lighting a cigarette. The end was near.

It was always darkest before the dawn. How true it was at this moment in his life.

He slid off the couch and onto his knees, overwhelmed by futility and despair. Then, he caught a glimpse of the digital alarm clock slash radio lying upside down in front of him. It had sat next to the television unused since his last day of work, but it was still plugged into the wall and the red number 12:00 blinked constantly. Death continued to call his name, the gin's calling screamed in his head, but a stronger force reached out for the radio. He turned the thing over, turned it on, and heard through the static a woman's voice.

Moving the dial, he worked to make the voice more clear.

"*You are not alone.*" Her message echoed through the studio apartment.

Lazarus sat up hoping this was an answer to a prayer he was too ashamed to make. The calling of the bottle of gin went silent.

"*You are not alone,*" she repeated, her voice filled with a fire that struck a chord deep inside of him. He stood up and placed his only chair in front of the door. He sat back down next to the radio, turned down the volume, and without so much as a squeak, listened to the voice.

"Welcome to our pirate broadcast. Thomas Paine once

wrote, 'These are the times that try men's souls: The summer soldier and the sunshine patriot will, in this crisis, shrink from the service of his country; but he that stands it now, deserves the love and thanks of man and woman. Tyranny, like hell, is not easily conquered; yet we have this consolation with us, that the harder the conflict, the more glorious the triumph. Heaven knows how to put a proper price upon its goods; and it would be strange indeed, if so celestial an article as freedom should not be highly rated.'"

Words like *freedom*, *patriot*, and *tyranny* raced through Lazarus' mind. What does this mean? Who is this woman who speaks so boldly? He wanted to hear more.

"We are calling out to those who are *not* sunshine patriots, who are *not* summer soldiers." She spoke about freedom and the American Revolution and how the people needed to rise up once more. She lashed out at Chairman Vance for turning Americans all into slaves.

Lazarus scanned his small apartment. His heart raced knowing the danger in listening to this broadcast. Yet the words ignited a new fire within, making it all but impossible for him to stop listening. Just a few minutes previously he was willing to die, his soul already dead. He had to ask if an intangible idea like freedom was worth living for.

"Again we find ourselves in a time that will try men's souls. Our cause is simple, liberty. We have been lied to." The voice called on Americans, on Lazarus, to revolt against this tyrannical government. He sat, his legs crossed one over the other on the floor, in awe of the words echoing through the apartment. He ignored the fear that shouted in his head.

"The people around us disappear in the middle of the night never to be seen again."

She was right. His parents, his wife, his son were all gone. He thought about those he knew that had railed against the Chairman and how they too had disappeared. Many of them were committed to the reeducation hospitals or 'terminated' at once for treason. He had stopped talking to anyone. Everyone stopped talking to him. Within a few years, the voice of opposition had completely vanished. But here it was once again rising up in his living room.

"The trials and TV shows and the fear we live in must end. If we hang together, we won't hang separately. It will not be easy. The times demand men and women willing to risk their very lives so future generations can once again live free. Chairman Vance is evil. Pure and simple, evil. He has taken from us the very will to live as our Creator wants us to live. Once again it is up to us to demand our God given right to life, liberty and the pursuit of happiness. Don't be afraid. You're not alone. We surround *them*. Look for us, search for us, join us. The time to fight for liberty is now."

The radio went silent.

He sat for hours wondering if *she* would return or if all this was just a dream. He had lain down next to his new friend, and her words continued to echo through his imagination. *Freedom, tyranny, we surround them.*

Finally, Lazarus closed his eyes and smiled. "I am not alone," he whispered in a tone filled with a hope he thought he had lost a decade before. He dreamed of this new world, this world he caught a glimpse of years before but thought was lost. He promised himself he would no longer be a slave. Life had meaning once more.

The words hit him hard. It was time to look for these freedom fighters; suddenly he wanted to join the fight. What was left to take away from him? Nothing. He felt a power surging inside. It was unexplainable. Maybe it was—freedom. Something had awakened.

"God," he said, not knowing or even wanting to believe, "let me find them. I need them." A warmth filled his heart, and he cried tears of joy for the first time. A force surrounded him as he lay next to the radio and he slept peacefully.

***

Fear crept in the next morning. Lazarus still thought about freedom—about the voice on the radio. All night he had left the radio on hoping she would return—then praying it was just a dream. He sat staring at the radio, begging it to tell him what to do next. The need to be inspired grew.

Looking down, he still held in his hand the E card. The gin called out.

Determined to resist, he tore off his clothes and jumped in the shower. He shaved his head and face clean. Putting on what he liked to call his 'dating' Levi's and a clean t-shirt with a faded logo of some motorcycle rally that happened eons ago, Lazarus decided the need for gin was stronger than one radio broadcast.

He left his apartment building where everything looked—different. People walked by in silence with their heads down. He studied the apartment building across the street—grey, dirty, and plain. Vance had torn down and rebuilt all apartment buildings in town so they would look exactly alike. It was frustrating when Lazarus would come home after a long day of work. More than once he entered the wrong building.

The buildings had five windows across going up twelve floors. They were replicated, in both directions, all the way down the endless street. A few strip malls where goods were sold interrupted the uniformed appearance every four or five blocks. He wondered if he had ever looked up before today.

What was different about today? Was it a feeling? Was it a thought? No, it was more like a mood. Gloom, despair, and misery appeared in the buildings, on the faces in the crowd, in the sky above. Would he ever be able to live here in ignorant bliss again? The radio broadcast had awakened him.

All these years he had been walking around like the living dead. On the faces of those who passed by he could see it. Sure, they breathed, their hearts beating, blood flowed through their veins. But, like Lazarus, they'd stopped *living* years ago.

A man in a long black coat walked by.

"Hi, how are you?" Lazarus asked.

The man peered at Lazarus with suspicious eyes, pointed his head back down, and picked up his pace.

Lazarus made his journey to the liquor store.

"Hi, how are you today?" he asked a woman who walked by him. She looked up in shock, gave a guarded smile, but remained silent.

Another man was heading toward him. Lazarus was on a mission just to hear another human being speak. The man was tall, balding, had his fists clenched, and walked briskly. A strong feeling that maybe he could make his day better overcame Lazarus.

"Hi, sir, how are you today?"

"Don't talk to me!" he snarled.

Lazarus shook his head and grinned—but at least he got to hear another voice.

He stopped walking when he heard a plea for help. Across the street a man was being beaten by two policemen. The scream went unanswered. The abused was curled up in a fetal position pleading with them to stop. The man stared right into Lazarus' eyes.

Through the tears on his face he could see how the man wished for death—begged for it.

The two officers stopped beating the man and looked over at Lazarus. "Nothing to see here, sir. Move along." The officer's tone was surprisingly friendly. He wiped the blood off the nightstick on his left leg and went back to beating the man.

Putting down his head Lazarus continued towards the liquor store. The gin would take away the guilt and shame of not helping the man.

He tried to remember what society was like before it had transformed into this so-called utopia. His teenage years were filled with social activity. Do they play sports in high school anymore? He remembered playing football—he was okay at it. And basketball. He had been a good student, maybe too good.

On his walk he passed many other people, but said nothing more. His little experiment might attract attention and bring trouble.

He looked up. 'Liquor Store,' was the name on the marque. He entered and said, "Can I get a bottle of Forrest gin, please. How is your day going?"

"You gotta card, mister?" the man behind the counter said. His blond hair was all over the place and it was obvious the man hadn't shaved in days. The bloodshot eyes gave away his hangover.

Lazarus handed him the card.

When he raised his arms to pull down the bottle of Forrest gin, Lazarus could see the sweat circles under his arms. He handed over the bottle and swiped the E card through the computer. After handing it back, the man pulled a white cloth out of his pocket and wiped the sweat from his forehead and exhaled.

"Thank you."

A nod.

Walking out of the liquor store, he headed back to his apartment. In the pit of his stomach he felt a strange sensation of delirious shame. He couldn't wait to crack open the bottle and taste that first drink. Yet he knew once he finished, all hope of finding this freedom *she* talked about was done for. His fate was inside the one liter jug of gin. He knew it.

He peaked down at the label—another picture of Chairman Vance with that sinister smile. The Chairman on the bottle nodded in an arrogant assurance that Lazarus remain his slave.

He picked up the pace in some twisted hurry to put on the chains and throw the key away forever. When the card runs out, he figured, he'd just take his life. Was it really *his* life, anyway?

The saliva building in his mouth made him queasy. His hands shook and he could feel the sweat forming on the back of his neck. He grabbed the bottle with both hands. In a weird way, he looked forward to ending this fight, to crushing this desire to be free, to silencing *her* voice that continued to call out.

Building 223. Finally.

He went up the stairs still holding the gin with two hands. *Her* voice again. The silent nod of the Chairman on the label of the bottle. Lazarus opened the door, stopped, and stared at the staircase leading to the second floor where the apartment waited.

Closing the front door of the apartment, he set the bottle down on the counter. He dropped to his knees once more.

155

He looked up at the gin—turned and could see the radio.

Closing his eyes, Lazarus said a little prayer, "God, help me." He stood, reached for the bottle and started to twist off the cap, then set the bottle back down on the counter and sighed.

He hoped this was all just a nightmare—prayed that *she* would return. And that the sinister smile on the jug would fade.

***

"Welcome to our pirate broadcast. You are not alone." *She* was back. It had been six days since her last message. Six bottles of Forrest gin sat un-opened on the counter.

"Our cities are filled with misery, disease, and death. The tyrant has taken what once was called the American dream and turned it into a nightmare." *She* talked endlessly of crimes against the people. Chairman Vance, *she* said, handcuffed us and certainly didn't pray to the God of love and forgiveness she had faith in.

Americans. She used the word Americans. Lazarus tried to remember the last time he heard the people referred to that way. Chairman Vance always called the people citizens. He claimed to be just like the rest, calling himself, 'the first citizen.'

His father would be disappointed to learn how afraid he was, how he had allowed Vance to turn him into a slave, and with the idea that he feared using a simple term like American to describe himself. He no longer felt like his father's son. He wasn't even sure who or what he had become. Can *she* change *that?*

Lazarus found comfort in *her* words. He sensed danger in the hope he was beginning to feel. He began daydreaming about what it would be like to meet *her*. He wondered if *she* looked like the angel he envisioned. Some nights he questioned if *she* really existed. Each day he left the apartment wanting to find these freedom fighters. He didn't know how to search for them. He wanted to join, but struggled with a fear that begged him to keep his head down and remain subservient.

'Nothing to see here, sir.' Those words from that policeman still haunted him. He had just walked away. He was use to walking away. It was all he knew.

In the distance he could hear *her* continue *her* diatribe on freedom. Right in front of him stood the bottles of Forrest Vance gin. The sinister smile reappeared. He removed the cap from one of the jugs.

"The tyrant entertains you with television, stale music, and drink." Her voice echoed throughout the apartment. That's right, he thought, and I'm going to finish *this* bottle tonight.

"Programs like *Welcome to Utopia* and liquor like Forrest Vance gin are tools the Chairman uses to control you."

Lazarus wanted to shut her words out. Each step he took closer to tasting the first sip was interrupted by *her* attempt to sell him on certain ideals. *She* claimed this freedom thing could outlast the booze. Could he trust *her?*

Bottle in hand, he walked over to the sink. "God, help me," he prayed.

He watched in horror as the liquid traveled down the drain. His hands shook. He hated what he was doing but felt a sense of power surging inside.

The voice on the radio used words like *self-reliance*, *individuality*, and *duty*. Then she spoke about the evils of the current society, of fighting wars without honor, and how to take off the shackles of slavery.

With each bottle, it became easier to pour the gin down the drain. Yet again, he dropped to his knees after the final jug swirled down the hole.

"I hope you're right."

The radio went silent. He sat down next to it, smiled, and wondered if *this* is what freedom felt like.

***

October, 2033.

The last couple of months had been a series of ups and downs. Lazarus still listened for his new friend each night hoping to hear *her* voice. Each day he ventured out in search for those who fought for freedom. The broadcasts were uplifting. The twisted trips to the liquor store tore him down.

Where are they? Where is *she*? Who is *she*? He craved the sound of *her* voice, not knowing what to do without it.

The four blank walls of the apartment were closing in. He got weaker every day when he arrived home with yet another bottle of Forrest Vance gin. He prayed to a God he didn't know, doesn't think is there, that he really doesn't believe in. His voice cracked each time he spoke to Him.

"Just drink the damn bottle."

But *she* tells him to remain strong—*she* claims this freedom thing is worth it. "I don't have the power." He refused to make eye contact in the mirror as he repeated the words. "I don't have the power."

All the empty bottles remained on the counter in some twisted monument to this small dose of freedom he was experiencing. Lazarus often wondered why he continued to bring home the bottles. *Her* voice, the bottles, they comforted him. That was the only answer he could come up with. Comfort.

He pulled on the faded jeans he wore yesterday, and a dull, plain t-shirt like all the others he owned. Owned? Mine? Do those words still mean anything anymore? He pulled out the dull razor and began shaving, starting with his head. Finishing by wiping his face clean with an old, ragged towel he's ready for the day.

"No bottle today, God." Lazarus stared down at the razor. "God, are you really there? Take these thoughts—"

The idea of suicide vanishes. Lazarus smiles for the first time since *her* last broadcast. The search for *them* will continue.

"God, how about a little help here!" he yelled.

Still, he doesn't think this God is powerful enough to help. To hear his pleas. To take the time and care for such a lousy excuse of a human being. His parents, his wife, his— he had strength, training, knowledge, the opportunity to blow Vance's head clean off.

Instead Lazarus had stood there, silent, and just walked away. *Just walked away.* This nightmare would be over. *There must be a special place in hell for a guy like me*, he thought.

A few hours later Lazarus entered the apartment, bottle in hand, defeated. The frightening thought that the radio was some sick joke by Vance caused his heart to skip a beat. He popped in the individual size mac-and-cheese and boiled some hot dogs. He liked to cut them up and mix them into the noodles. When he was a child he had asked for it pretty much every night for dinner.

His journey to childhood didn't last long.

'Nothing to see here, sir.' The haunting words of that officer.

From the hallway he heard a loud thud. He cracked open his front door to see what was going on. Most people stopped being curious about odd noises years ago. It only made things worse for them.

"No, no, I'm not guilty. I'm free." A skinny man in his late forties wrestled with two officers in the hallway.

"Sir, if you go quietly, Chairman Vance will not terminate you, I promise."

A promise. When was the last time Lazarus heard that word? It was from Vance himself. He promised him it would all be okay after his parents died. That he would take care of him and be a father figure; one that he could look up to, and ask for advice. An unsuspecting deal with the devil. How could Lazarus ever trust anyone again, even *her*.

The man stared right into Lazarus' eyes. "She can lead you to freedom," he said.

Without hesitation, Lazarus closed the door. Fear gripped him. *Does he know about her and I?* he thought. *Are they coming for me next?*

He tried to listen to what was going on across the hall. Resting his ear against the door he prayed to the God that betrayed him. "God, please not me."

What choice did he have? He was out of options. The first strike against the man's flesh with a nightstick made Lazarus flinch.

The man laughed. "Free! I'm free." The thumps continued.

A mountain of empty bottles sat on his counter. It was time to get another one—after they left. By the end of the night he would forget the voice of that cop, 'Nothing to see here, sir.' He would forget the laughter and words of the man next door, 'I'm free.' And the plan included the destruction of that damn radio. All his problems would be solved in a single night.

An envelope sat underneath one of the empty bottles of gin. The Chairman's smile on the label began to dissipate. He picked up the envelope. In the light he could see a handwritten letter inside. The smell of mac-and-cheese mixed with the aroma of anticipation.

Quickly he tore the top off and took out the paper inside.

> Keep buying the gin. We are watching and will contact you when the time is right. Hang in there, freedom is closer than you think.
>
> The Radio

He scanned the apartment. Where had this come from? Had the cops seen this letter? A mixed feeling of relief and fear swirled within Lazarus.

He grabbed the long, blue lighter he kept next to the stove. Lighting all four edges of the letter he dropped it in the stainless steel sink. The fire stopped. His hands shook. The words could still be read on the page. He relit it. The fire balled up in a black swirl only to turn grey and *poof*; the flame went out.

Sweat covered his bald head. The smell of ashes tickled his nose. The blaze wasn't going fast enough. "Hurry, hurry, hurry," he whispered.

He fanned and blew on the small rolling fire. Burn out. *Shit*. Re-light. *God, help me*. Not fast enough. *Help*. The burning caused a yellow streak on the bottom of the sink. *I'll never get rid of this smell*. He kept lighting the paper.

Just a small square of white was left of the letter. Gone. He turned on the water and rubbed like hell to get the yellow stain out. The remains easily found their way down the drain. The nightmare was over.

A knock at the door. *Oh shit, they're here for me. They know about the letter. There's no time; there's nowhere to run.*

"Mr. Parker, are you home?" The cop opened the door and walked in. The dull black uniform of the officer still had shades of the man's blood. "Is something burning in here?"

"Oh, I'm just trying to light the pilot. You know, old stove," Lazarus answered. The lingering smell of ashes still floated in the air.

"I have some questions for you, sir." The officer closed the door behind him. "How well did you know the man across the hall from you?"

"I don't know anyone who lives here," Lazarus tried to stop the trembling; he knew the officer could hear it in his voice.

The officer moved closer.

Silently, Lazarus prayed for the right words. "What did he do?" he asked pretending to clean his kitchen counter with a sponge.

"That's not important now," the officer perused the apartment. "Why haven't you bought any gin lately?"

It had only been three days, yet they *knew*. How did they know?

"To be honest with you, sir, I was just getting ready to head out to the liquor store. As you can see, I'm out." *Please God stop my hands from shaking.*

"I see. Look, if you hear anything strange going on you must let us know. There's been rumors of a radio station spreading lies about the Chairman."

The cop moved across the apartment and over to him. He put his hand on Lazarus' shoulder, "You haven't been listening, have you? If you tell me now I might be able to keep you safe. You will be able to keep your freedom."

He calls this freedom? No choice in work, no choice in what home to live in, *and* in what radio station he can listen to. The new laws don't allow travel. The law even stripped him of that shitty one-channel television set.

"I would have to take the radio," he finished.

Why not just take my sanity?

"No, sir, I listen to the radio but haven't heard anything like that. Just music, it's the only entertainment I have, except the gin, of course." His hands had stopped shaking. He prayed the officer wouldn't turn the radio on.

The officer stared at Lazarus for what felt like eternity. Slowly he walked over to the radio.

Lazarus' legs were wobbly.

"If I turn this on, Mr. Parker, what will I hear?" he asked skeptically.

"Music," he answered in the most convincing voice he could muster up.

"We'll see." The officer bent down and lifted up the radio.

Lazarus trembled from head to toe. He knew another prayer wouldn't work. God didn't exist. *She* had screwed him. These damn freedom fighters had killed him before he even had the chance to fight.

He flashed back to Angie in the tub and the policemen who questioned him that night. He wanted to die that night more than at any other point in his life. She was gone. Nothing was left. The same feeling came back when they took the TV. Why? He didn't know. It was as if the last bit of humanity had left in this God forsaken world was neatly boxed up in it. Even if the information the television gave was bullshit, it still connected him to the world. A false sense of contentedness had lived in that television set for Lazarus.

But now with *her*. With the radio. It was different. There was real hope. It scared the living daylights out of him. But it was there. Faint. Just a whisper. A small piece of what he had lost many years ago. Even before he met Angie. She was working on building that back up. He literally owed his life to a woman that saw something in him he couldn't see himself. A new woman had crept in. Not to take the place of Angie, but to finish what she started. Angie would tell him she was a gift from heaven. He would nod his head finding strength in her faith.

"Are you *sure* there's nothing you need to tell me, Mr. Parker?" the officer asked once more.

He shook his head. The knot in his throat made it hard to breath. Thousands of visions appearing like snapshots raced through his mind. His life had amounted to nothing. He stood for nothing. He fought for nothing. He believed in nothing. He had become nothing. And now, he would die for nothing. He wished the officer would shoot him now so he didn't have to spend his final days dreaming of what could have been. He didn't want to die, and that was what amazed him the most. He wanted that freedom *she* talked endlessly about on the radio.

He closed his eyes. *Perhaps another life.*

With his hand on the dial, the officer looked over at him once more and smiled, "Here we go."

Music! It was music. The sweet sound of a piano played in the background and the loud blasts of a thousand trumpets. Lazarus turned around and put the empty bottles into the trash can. He smirked and struggled to keep his composure. Wanting to laugh. Wanting to cry. Wanting the officer to leave.

"I love this song."

The red in the officer's eyes retracted, "Everything looks good here, Mr. Parker. Enjoy your evening. The Chairman thanks you for your continued support." He marched out of the apartment, closing the door behind him.

Lazarus fell to his knees and started to gag, his shirt covered in sweat. The smell of B.O. overpowered the lingering order of ashes. His hands began to shake once more.

He crawled over to the radio and embraced it. The need to cry was strong. *Freedom, is it worth living for?* The jury was still out about this freedom thing, but now he wanted to find out more than ever. He wanted to believe *her.*

Getting up from the floor he pranced over to the front door. He slipped on his tennis shoes and put on the dark blue jacket he bought at the thrift store years before, when those types of places still existed. He knew exactly what to do at that moment. It was time to buy another bottle of Forrest Vance gin. But the sinister smile on the bottle began to fade. The jug *knew* he wasn't going to drink it.

Closing the door behind him Lazarus headed for the liquor store.

***

Boom, Boom, Boom. The sound from the door echoed throughout the thin-walled apartment. The chair held.

"Mr. Parker, don't make me break this door down!" The cop continued to work his way in. It's over, so Lazarus remained seated by the radio. He could barely make out *her* voice due to the ruckus the officer was making in the hallway. He turned up the volume disregarding the certain consequences that would follow.

"The idea of freedom and liberty are lost. But we can get them back. That's what we are fighting for."

Lazarus felt a deep regret he wouldn't be able to join. This small token of rebellion would be his shining moment, *his* liberty, *his* freedom. Again he cranked the volume louder.

"Don't be afraid," the radio cried, "the choice is a simple one for me, liberty—or death. The evil empire Vance has created must fall. We need your help. Raise up, let your voices be heard, tell the devil to go back where he came from. We are Americans, and we do not cower to anyone."

"Mr. Parker. I demand you turn off that radio and open this door at once."

Turning it up to ten Lazarus whispered, "This is for you, Angie, my little one, Mom, Dad."

The room went silent as visions of his life flashed by like snapshots taken from one of those old Polaroid cameras.

He began to pray. "Angie, oh God Angie. I'm so sorry I couldn't be the man you needed me to be. Forgive me, please forgive me. Mom, Dad, forgive me, I knew not what I was doing. My little one, I—I don't have the words. My mentor, John, let your training guide my future actions. And God, believe in *me*, please, believe in *me* since I cannot believe in you. I will follow—just show me the way—"

And one word crowded out everything he was trying to say, the pounding and the yelling of the two officers outside his door, even *her* on the radio, it silenced the guilt and the pain and the suffering for a split second and it filled him, almost literally knocked him over. It sang to him.

Peace. And just as he heard it, it was gone.

"Mr. Parker! We're coming in." The officer's tone was not pleasant. The thump against the door shook the very foundation of the building. The chair held, but he knew it wouldn't be long before the door collapsed.

So Lazarus prayed. Not for what would happen to him, but instead for others, for their freedom, for the very soul of his country now in turmoil.

"Damn it Mr. Parker, open this door at once."

"The Chairman doesn't like foul language," Lazarus said, his voice filled with defiance. He was in some state of surrender. Certainly he didn't fancy himself a hero. For years he had been hiding in shame and fear. *Her* words had awoken in him what once was dead. He had been blind but now he could *see*. The gin still called out, the obedient one within wanted to answer the door, yet, still, he remained the rebel with no idea where this power was coming from.

Fear gripped him. *Walk through this fire Lazarus, walk through it.*

BOOM!

BOOM!

BOOM!

The door began to give.

Lazarus got up and put his back to the door, wanting to hear the final words of freedom blaring from his radio. A new, colder chill covered his body with each thunderous pounding at the door.

BOOM!

BOOM!

"The search is over. The time is now. We must rise up as one, we must! Caesar had his Brutus. Washington had King George. Hitler his Bonhoeffer."

BOOM!

"God, give me the strength." And Lazarus was reminded of his high school years. His love for poetry led Mr. Duma to share a poem he memorized. It was title *Who Am I,* written by Dietrich Bonhoeffer. The preacher fought against the injustice of the Nazis during World War II. Lazarus remembered his high school teacher telling him how Bonhoeffer attempted to assassinate Adolf Hitler. Was it possible to have *that* kind of strength?

The preacher wrote this from prison. Lazarus figured if they didn't kill him that he soon would experience the inside of a jail cell. But would he understand the freedom Bonhoeffer speaks of in this passage? Or, will Lazarus follow blindly their demand for his obedience? Will he act without question, or instead search for meaning?

Is God on my side? he pondered. *Perhaps He doesn't take sides. Maybe He doesn't care what has happened to me.*

Lazarus rocked back and forth, his arms around his legs.

"There's no saving you now, Mr. Parker," the officer laughed. "When I get in there you're going to beg for the Chairman's mercy. I'm not going to kill you quick."

Crash!

Large and small fragments of the door and chair that had been placed against the door flew in scattered chaos across the room. The two officers entered the apartment with weapons drawn. The officer used his nightstick and struck the radio, silencing it. The next blow landed squarely on Lazarus' temple.

A flash of pain and then—blackout.

***

Lazarus awoke with a groan. His head pounded in agony. The floor was covered in a pool of blood. His, he suspected. He could feel the warm liquid seeping from the right side of his face. The police officer pushed down onto his stomach, cutting his knee into Lazarus' back.

Lazarus cried out. Then he couldn't breathe as he swallowed his own blood.

"Mr. Parker," the officer leaned over and whispered in his ear, "you will die today. But like I promised, it will be slow. Unless, of course, you tell me where *they* are."

"Who?" Lazarus groaned.

"Don't lie to me," he said, his knee digging deeper into

Lazarus' back. The officer grabbed his head and turned it. Nausea set in with the taste and metallic smell of Lazarus' own blood. His mouth too dry to spit out the thick fluid. The officer pelted the nightstick like he was on a horse in the long-gone derby.

"Do you want more of *this*, Mr. Parker?" the smirk on the man's face led Lazarus to believe he just wanted to inflict pain. The man didn't want the truth. *Blind obedience, that's all Vance wanted*.

"Yes." Lazarus tells him. He prayed to remain strong.

The officer chuckled. "Hey Henry! He wants more."

"Give it to him." Henry's voice was flat, filled with malice.

The officer beat Lazarus a few more times, then paused. "We got to get this fool back to the department." The officer looked back at Lazarus. "Then, Mr. Parker, you will feel the wrath of our great Chairman Vance in ways *you* can't even imagine."

Bending close to Lazarus' ear, he whispered, "The best part? I get to do it." The officer lifted his knee off his back and stood up. "Let's go. Get up, Mr. Parker."

Lazarus knew it was vital to get up on his own. The time had come to make a stand. His head ached, legs wobbly. He stared at the officer who would be his murderer and grinned.

"Don't smile at me," the officer slapped Lazarus down to one knee.

God, give me strength. Lazarus picked himself up.

The officer struck again. In a futile attempt to believe all this was just a nightmare Lazarus closed his eyes. Nothing happened. Cautiously, he opened his eyes at the officer to see that Officer Henry had stopped him.

"We have to go. I am in no mood to carry this nigger out of here," Henry said. The other cop took Lazarus' arm and began to lead him out of the apartment.

That word, *nigger*. He remembered hearing it when he was a teenager. A memory lost in the cynical world he had been living in began to cascade. He was fifteen and sat on his bed listening to the latest flash-in-the-pan rap star following along with what could only be described as hateful lyrics.

His father had walked into Lazarus' room and turned off the CD player.

"Son," his father said, "what are you listening to?"

Lazarus told him.

"Let's listen to the song together," his father suggested.

Lazarus hoped for a defining moment between him and his father. They would unite in the music of his generation, thinking this time 'son' was a term of endearment, not foreshadowing impending doom.

They sat and listened to the entire song. He bounced his head back and forth to the beat, but his father just stood there, arms folded, concentrating on each and every stanza coming out of the stereo.

"Son, let's kneel down and pray together." Lazarus knelt down with his father and they both folded their hands. His father said a powerful prayer he wished now more than ever he could remember. It was the only time Lazarus had seen him pray.

When he was finished praying he looked over at his son and said, "If you want to listen to that stuff I can't stop you. I suggest you think hard about what this man is really doing by writing lyrics like that." Barry stood up and walked out of the room. That day was the last time Lazarus ever uttered the 'n' word.

Reality crept back in. The officer led him out of the apartment. He could feel the blood begin to dry on top of his head and plastered to the side of his face. The officer slapped handcuffs on him.

Lazarus looked down the hall. A man in a 1930s style hat stood there staring at them. The hat looked familiar.

The officer told him to put his hands behind his back. Lazarus obeyed.

"Phil, look," Henry said, pointing to the man at the end of the hallway. Officer Phil started down the hall towards him wearing a look the devil would have been proud of.

"Sir, there's *nothing to see here*, move along." Phil's voice was surprisingly gentle.

Anger boiled up inside of Lazarus. That voice was *his!* The words hit a chord. Decades of silence, indifference, of 'moving along' filled him with fury.

He looked up, staring with vengeance at the back of Officer Phil's head. Reaching out, he wrapped his hands around his neck throwing him to the ground. The cry from his lips released upon the man, all the pinned up vexation Lazarus had been carrying around for years. The man's body bounced off the floor like a ragdoll. Every bone in his body wanted to jump on top of Phil and beat the life out of him, but he knew there was another cop to deal with first. His wrath set its eyes on Hemry who stood there like a statue. Lazarus stepped closer. Henry started to babble.

"Please!" Henry knelt and folded his hands together. "Don't kill me, please, I beg you." Tears streamed down his cheeks and he began to blubber like an idiot.

Lazarus wanted to kill him. He walked over, grabbed his hair.

"Look at me," Lazarus said, and punched him with everything he had. Henry dropped to the ground; tranquility settled in. He turned and walked back over to Phil. He was still breathing. His turn to die had come.

"Mr. Parker," a man called out. "Mr. Parker."

The sinister smile was now on the face of Lazarus. A graphic image of tearing Phil's arms and legs off his body created a confused sense of peace. *You will die today*. He wanted to savor the moment. Thousands of voices chanted the word 'revenge' inside his head. The officer began to move. He grumbled. Murderous thoughts churned in Lazarus' mind.

Peace echoed from above.

"Lazarus!" the man with the funny hat stood behind him. "What?" he asked.

"Don't do it. Come with me."

"But it was *him*. *He* is the reason I walk around with shame. *He* is the reason I can't sleep at night. Killing him will give me my life back, I just know it."

"No, Lazarus, it won't. Killing him will only bring you a new nightmare. You might lose the shame, but I promise you will inherit guilt."

"Who the hell are you? How do you…know…anything?"

169

Lazarus inquired. Slowly he was regaining control. He knew the man was right. Still, he clenched his fists, the rage beginning to rebuild. He had never killed before. Was he prepared to do it now? No. The answer was no. But still—

"I have stood where you are. I know the power you are fighting. *Don't become them.*" The man put his hand on Lazarus' shoulder. His thinning blond hair mixed with the tiredness around his eyes convinced Lazarus the man was telling the truth. "Come with me, I know the way out."

His body began to tremble. '*Don't become them.*' He stood there wrestling with the man he thought he could be. Hoping not to become *them.* Praying to become something *more.*

"Freedom is closer than you think, Lazarus," he said, "but it starts with not killing these men." A warm smile reminded Lazarus of his parents, of Angie, of the little one that lived in his memory. It was absent of malice. He knew he was right.

Peace, the inner voice whispered once more.

"Can you hear that?" he asked the man.

"Hear what?"

"Nothing." Lazarus glanced at the officers lying in a heap in the hallway. "Why are these men free to do as they please?"

"Do these men have freedom? You must realize like you once did, these men live in fear." He gently took his arm and guided him away from the bodies. "Don't you understand they're already dead?"

Lazarus bowed his head. The man slowly lifted up his chin and peered deep into his eyes. There was a moment of silence.

"Don't look down. That God you have been praying to believes in forgiveness. He's a loving, caring God that wants you to be free. He wants you to be happy. At least that's the God I believe in."

A flurry of emotions brought tears to Lazarus' eyes. "How do I know He's real?" he asked, hoping to keep his composure.

"You know," he paused, "you know because your gut

tells you murdering these men is wrong. You know because there's a fire burning inside of you longing for freedom. You know because when you look at these men you see the hate in their eyes, you see they have lost their souls; you see no life in them. And you know that killing them will take your life away as well."

The man gave him that warm smile once more.

"I know." Wonderful images came roaring back, like falling in love for the first time. Angie, sweet Angie. He could see his parents dancing at their 10th wedding anniversary. The love in his wife's eyes. He remembered his father telling him, "Son, life's a journey, not a destination."

This moment was not an end, but a new beginning. He had a choice to make.

How do I start this new journey? Do I want life? Or do I want revenge?

Silently he prayed; then looked down at Officer Phil. He sobbed.

And then he knew *peace*.

15

One week earlier...

Most nights were filled with a reoccurring nightmare. She would turn, freeze, and watch her father being killed over and over. Each time Abigail was helpless to do anything.

But last night's dream was different.

Often she wondered how he had found her and why he had come to get her. Had he sacrificed his 'baby girl,' they might have won the fight years ago. Instead the past eight years since his death had been filled with heartache and set back. Abigail did everything she could to keep her father's dream of freeing America alive. She had learned so much, but was it enough? Doubt crept in on a regular basis.

But that had been true of her father as well. His letters had explained so much about leadership, tactics, and passionate but persuasive arguments to support why he did what he did. He could've been the next George Washington, his followers had told her. They had set up camp a few years ago in what was once known as the Black Hills of South Dakota.

Abigail ran through the camp. With a few minor tweaks and some ingenious designing, the new resistance had turned the National Park at Mt. Rushmore into a fort. Each day their numbers grew from people who had survived the Great Starvation from Governor Kingman. He wasn't cruel; he just didn't care, leaving most people north of Colorado and Nebraska to fend for themselves and not offering government support.

Abigail had taken charge from the moment her father was

killed. It didn't take her long to gain the confidence of the men and women who fought alongside Jack Payne. The real problem was rebuilding.

Vance had learned about the secret camp her father had created in the Smokey Mountains of Tennessee that currently resided in Section One. As she had watched her father being executed, an army of 'red-eyes' had torched the entire National Park. It would've broken her father's heart knowing all that history and hard work building the camp had went up in smoke, and how many of his freedom fighters had died that day. So many of them were children. Those who tried to escape were shot on sight. Only a handful made it out alive. The new base at Mt. Rushmore brought with it a new hope.

The Visitor's Center where tourists had once upon a time bought some Thomas Jefferson ice cream and a hamburger had become the chow hall. When the resistance could get the ingredients they still made Jefferson's tasty treat, but it was enough for Abigail and the cooks to make sure there was enough food to feed the growing community.

Abigail ran, searching every square inch of the large open area that included a library on the far end. Pockets of people were sitting at round tables with attached chairs. The cream-colored tables had black, round seats she figured were stolen. They just didn't fit right. For Abigail, it reminded her of being in high school all over again. The strong smell of bacon and scrambled eggs lingered. A false wall separated the dining area from the kitchen where she could hear the loud noises of cooks, dishwashers and servers bantering back and forth. Some things never changed.

"Hey, sis, what's up?" Miles asked walking up behind her.

She jumped. "Oh, shit, there you are. I need to talk to you," she said.

Miles could sense panic in her voice. He could always tell when something was bothering her; after all, they were family. Abigail had raised him since he was eleven. Karen Bey, his mother, was killed in the fires in Tennessee. Jonas Quinn, who had fought with her father, had saved Miles from the fire, but couldn't save Karen. Jonas' 1930s style head gear was legendary, and he loved leather: jackets, pants, and hats. Whatever he could find.

Abigail often prayed for Karen's forgiveness. She knew the woman had wanted to marry her father, but he hadn't done it without Abigail's blessing.

Abigail remembered that day long ago in Dana Point when she ran away like the brat that she was at the time. Since Karen was dead, there was no way for her to escape the guilt. But that's not why she had raised Miles—she loved him.

They never talked about the past. It was the big elephant in the room. Even so, they were close and there was nothing they wouldn't do for each other. Nothing.

"Let me grab some coffee and we can sit over there. What some?" Miles asked as he moved away. She nodded, but started to chew on her finger nails all the same.

"Boy, it must be serious." He stopped in his tracks. "Stop that, Abby."

She gave a nervous smile and put her hand down by her side. And laughed once he had trotted off for the coffee. What the hell was she going to tell him? That a dream told her to tell him to go off on some wild goose chase? She knew he would do whatever she asked of him. But this was different.

Miles put a cup of coffee in front of her, loaded with cream and sugar, just the way she liked it, and sat down next to her. "What is it, sis?"

"Once you finish that cup of coffee I need you to go to Centerville." Abigail sat up and took a sip of her drink.

"What? You mean Los Angeles, in old California?"

"Yes," she sat back and folded her arms.

"O—kay. And what should I do once I get there?" He wore a confused look.

"Well, we have about a week to get this guy out, and… and well, Jonas is already there but you need to help him find this guy."

"Wait, sis, what the hell are you talking about? What guy?"

"Lazarus Parker. That's all I know. Oh, and he's black." She took another sip of her coffee. "This is good, Miles, just the way I like it."

"Yeah, nice try. Where is this coming from?"

"Well, you see, I had a dream." His face tightened and those light brown brows drew closer. "I know it sounds crazy, but," she sighed, "look, you have to go. He is the *one*. I wish I could explain why I know besides saying I had a vision."

Suddenly she had regained complete control. "It was from God. Don't look at me like that. I'm serious and no, I'm not drunk or anything. This man will be dead if we don't find him. He is our last hope—our only hope to defeat Vance. I saw it clear as day."

Miles sat up, but remained deep in thought. "What is this Lazarus supposed to do? How could one man be the answer?"

"I don't know. All I can tell you is we need this guy on our side, and we don't have much time before it's too late. I realize that—"

"I'll do it." He finished off his coffee. "Tell me about your dream."

She started to go into it when he cut her off once more, "You know what? Forget it. I don't need to know, sis, I'll do it, no questions asked."

They sat back for a moment savoring the moment before they got up and hugged each other goodbye. She held on for dear life knowing he would be in harm's way.

Miles wasn't doing it because of a dream or because he thought it was some message from God. He was doing it for *her*. The dream was a bit alarming, but she had been known for ideas that were even crazier than this one. The move here to the Black Hills seemed impossible, but it was her drive and vision that had gotten the resistance this far.

As for God, well, He had taken away his mom and dad. How could Miles ever forgive that? And it was on the same day. Being raised by his big sister had its perks, but nothing could replace the love of his mother and father.

"Zack is stationed outside of Centerville. He'll get the

message to Jonas, who is our asset in that town."

Miles often wondered how his sister was able to go from huggy kissy to all business in a matter of seconds. "Both you and Zack will need to help them once they are in the tunnels."

"How do you know all this?"

"It was in my dream."

"Oh." Miles looked down.

"And one more thing," she sighed, "I have a past with this Lazarus guy, our father, too." And she told Miles what she knew.

Miles was even more confused than before. "Why would we save a man who had been Vance's right hand man? That's insane."

Abigail couldn't give him a satisfactory answer—only that the resistance needed him. Miles was only nineteen, but he took orders like a seasoned soldier. He slid his hand through his light brown hair and shook his head. He wasn't convinced. But it was Abigail asking, begging him to take this journey. He'd go, reluctantly, but he'd go.

***

The last time Forrest Vance made the woman wrap his foot the gangrene had traveled up his left leg, stopping just shy of his knee. Since she wasn't a nurse, she gagged at every step but the bandage covered it all. He didn't want to see any of it. And the constant throbbing kept him in a bad mood.

"It's time to change the dressing," he told her from the hammock. He had decided to stay in Kingman and rule from there for a spell. The view was incredible and now that only his staff remained it was nice and quiet. For the past two days he had hoped for a feeling, a sign, some news from Section Two that the resistance was alive and well once again.

Nothing.

Kathy, the latest intern, gently asked Vance to follow her to the large bathroom so she could get started on his bandages. He hopped out of the hammock onto his right leg and grabbed his cane.

"Well?" he barked. "Lead the way." The pain had become more manageable. The Chairman walked with ease through the house and up the spiral staircase. The constant white marble had drove him crazy, so he had ordered his decorator to fly out and take care of it.

Once in the bathroom Kathy helped him take off his pants. The bandage was soaked in reddish, green ooze. Kathy's stomach turned and she glanced away. A putrid stench of rotten eggs mixed with sewer water arose from the wound.

Vance lifted her head up by the chin. "Don't worry, honey, your debt is almost forgiven." He sat back in the metal chair.

She was renewed with energy hearing about the possibility of her release.

Her husband's gambling had been so innocent in the beginning. Just a bet here or there with friends on the big game. The emotional charge it gave her husband had been so exciting for her to watch. It was that kind of passion she fell in love with. Kathy never imaged her husband would mortgage the house for another shot at getting even. Or how far down it would take them.

When Chairman Vance came to her with a plan to help, she jumped at it. Then later she realized it was Vance all along that had booked the bets. It was as if he desired her and worked this all out just to get close to her. And yet, Vance had never made a pass at her or forced her to do anything. She would do it in a heartbeat if it meant saving her husband. But Vance had never asked.

Cautiously she removed the tape and started to un-wrap the bandage. Clean. Skin. Perfect. The next section was revealed. Again, no gangrene. She moved faster. Two more sectors showed the same thing. She continued. The ankle was miraculously flesh colored and dry as a bone. She removed the bandages from the wound, showing only the scar Jack Payne had created eight years prior.

The pain was gone.

Forrest Vance peeked down at his leg and quickly looked again. He erupted in a cackle that raised the hairs on Kathy's arms. Evil was about to rise up higher than ever before.

He flashed a grin at Kathy. "The resistance is back! Praise the devil, the resistance is back!" He twirled his cane, pulled on his pants, and ran downstairs to begin plotting his next step.

This time, he told himself, *their torture will last a lifetime.*

16

Lazarus looked up from his knees at the man in the funny hat. His hate for the two men on the ground had disappeared. Sirens echoed in the distance.

"Lazarus, we must go."

He followed the man down the stairs and headed for the front door. He yelled stop and directed him towards another staircase. They ended up at a brick wall. The yellowish stain and remains of graffiti suggested the wall was quite old. The man pushed on the wall. It opened and they stepped on through. Together they closed the hidden door behind them.

In a faded black on the brick wall was an arrow pointing them to the right. Lazarus could still make out the words, 'Hill Street.' *Streets are all numbers and letters today. Chairman Vance has taken the idea of secularism to a whole new level.* The street names, stores, towns, nothing was allowed to have a name that would be construed as personal. *The rumor was that he wanted to make everyone all a number to completely remove individuality.* Lazarus guessed it was easier to kill that way.

The man walked with purpose. Lazarus realized they were down in the old subway tunnels.

Los Angeles had a subway system?

Painted black markers directed them down a staircase that led to an old platform that must've been abandoned before either one of them were born. The walls and ceiling were covered with that brown, yellowish stain leaving no doubt that these tunnels had been forgotten. On what once was the railway laid pieces of broken track and a dirt road that led into the abyss.

Lazarus stopped. "Hey, what's your name?"

"Jonas." He walked over to the edge of the platform,

179

picked up a lantern, struck a match, and lit it. "Take this."

After handing off the lantern to Lazarus, Jonas reached back into the same hole and retrieved a rifle, large knife, and a map. "Stay alert, sometimes I think there is more to fear down here than Vance," he said.

Lazarus held his breath.

The light from the lantern lit up the abyss like the rising sun. It shimmered in the distance to the beat of his shaking hands. Graffiti filled the sides with signs and words from a forgotten time. Some of the artwork remained from the war between gangs, the final battles depicted on the walls. Nobody won. Except Vance. He used his own version of *social justice* to put an end to the gang violence.

"Beauty being destroyed by the hate of this world," Lazarus said, "at least down here beauty still exists."

"Don't give up hope. Where I'm taking you is filled with all kinds of beauty." Jonas stopped. "Hope is stronger than fear, that's why Vance works hard to take it away from you."

They continued on for about twenty minutes in complete silence. The graffiti on the wall told a story of good versus evil. Scenes of death crowded out the simple message of love that struggled to find a home on these ancient walls. He tried to remember back to Angie, to his parents. To loving another human being like there's nothing he wouldn't do for them. The voice on the radio had told a story of what he hoped to become. He had always thought he loved like that, but it wasn't the case.

"What's her name?" Lazarus asked Jonas.

"What? Who?"

"The voice on the radio. I need to know her name."

"Abigail Payne. She's our leader, you'll love her," he answered.

Lazarus stopped dead in his tracks. Abigail Payne? He couldn't believe it. The reports had her dead along with the victory over the resistance. He didn't want to give away the fact that he knew her during the time he worked for Vance. It was him that had ruined her wedding day. What would he say when he saw her? There was a good chance she'd still be pissed. And how could he blame her? There's a good chance no one knows he helped her father escape. All she knows is he walked away.

"We will stop here until the sun goes down."

Lazarus looked up at what appeared to be a dead end. He could barely make out the outline of another hidden door. He grabbed the lantern, found a backpack in a dark corner, and pulled out some cans of food. The rustle and bustle of life in Centerville seeped through the ceiling. And they could hear the sounds of sirens and helicopters circling in the air.

"They're looking for me?"

"Yes."

Lazarus felt safe with this man. Jonas appeared to be all business. His receding hair line told the story of many adventures. He handed Lazarus a can of beans and they began to eat. The beans were cold, but the hint of sweet barbeque made it tolerable. He already missed his mac-and-cheese. It's funny how he had found little comforts to make the pain of life go away.

They sat there for over three hours. Jonas told him to get some sleep but the days' events continued to play in Lazarus' head.

Then Jonas stood up and pushed on a door. It began to move outward, and Lazarus could see the full moon and street lights light up the town of Centerville. The smell of fresh air brought comfort to him.

"Let's go." The two of them squeezed through the opening.

"Run," Jonas said, and he took off.

Lazarus was in a full sprint behind him. He had no idea where they were going. Soon they stopped. He was out of breath. It had been months since he got any kind of exercise.

"Get down!" Jonas cried and slipped behind an old, faded brown house with a picket fence. Lazarus obeyed.

A familiar sound moved towards their location. It was an engine, but different than a car. The vehicle moved passed them in the street. It had the shape of a dump truck but was made out of steel. Shame filled Lazarus knowing how he helped Vance spread this evil. His parents. His wife. His son. Suddenly he felt so unworthy to be chosen to fight side by side with Jonas.

A puff of black smoke escaped the truck. A whiff of diesel. Lazarus was propelled back to his childhood and how he took the bus to the beach in the summer of 2015. His father had told him to get off on 32nd Street in Newport. He had, but never understood how a black man would think to get off there. It was a great stop if you were white. He often wondered if his father had said that because that is what he heard growing up. His father would always joke about how his entire high school had three token blacks out of two thousand students.

The smell of diesel would simmer throughout the bus. Lazarus had spent an entire summer catching that moving, sorry excuse for an air polluter bus to the coast. It was a blast. The next year he stopped going after reading the book about Malcolm X. He remembered feeling out of place on that beach and felt people were looking at him because of the color of his skin. His friends told him he was crazy, and screw them even if it was true. Lazarus stayed home the next summer and read books. That was the same year he first met Forrest Vance. Boy, was he impressed. How easily fooled he had been. He wondered if that was happening all over again now with Jonas. If he was playing the fool to join the resistance.

"Let's move; this way," Jonas said.

They walked briskly, half crouched, through a number of bushes between houses. Weeds grew wild and the mess that was once well manicured lawns showed the surrender of a society long forgotten. Every house had a cold emptiness that made him shiver. Remains of 20th century furniture sat in a wooden cocoon on many of the porches. A haunted silence replaced human interaction.

The brownish green on the ground became a dirt gravel mix. They traveled down a slope towards a wall that had graffiti covering every square inch. The large letters on top spelled 'CAR.' Underneath that was the letters, 'LSC.' Lazarus couldn't help but wonder what that meant. A gang sign? The initials of a man or woman the artist wanted to remember? He could still make out the half-moon shape that once was the entrance for a railcar. A thick layer of dirt and age made the rest of the artwork impossible to read.

Jonas stopped at the door and shrugged off his backpack. He pulled out the lantern and handed it to him. Out came the shotgun and he loaded it. Lazarus flinched when he heard the sound of a round entering the chamber.

"Be ready for anything," Jonas said.

Anything? What the hell does that mean?

Jonas pushed open the door. The grumbling sound sent a chill up Lazarus' spine.

Jonas held the door open and handed Lazarus the matches. He lit the lantern and stuck it inside the tunnel. The light reflected off the graffiti like the lights on Broadway. The hair on his arms stood straight up. The scenes on the wall appeared to be new. The colors radiated off the wall, but the art itself seemed a bit primitive. The graphic novel painted there showed an underground people, filled with happiness, laughter, joy, living a wonderful life under what was once the great city of Los Angeles. They snatched people from above at night. They slept in the day. Underneath the happiness Lazarus could sense some deep secret the underground people didn't even talk about.

"Take this," Jonas handed him the shotgun and pulled out a pistol from his backpack. He checked the magazine to make sure it was loaded.

"I haven't shot a gun in a… I don't know how long."

"It's a shotgun, just point and shoot. Hell, the sound of racking it will scare away most." He fluffed up the backpack and used it as a pillow. "You're on first watch. If it moves, shoot it."

"Great," Lazarus responded. He wasn't comfortable with the idea of killing someone. Had that been the case, those two cops back at his apartment would no longer be breathing.

Jonas had no trouble falling asleep. Lazarus kept the light on but couldn't see much. On his left he could hear a dragging sound, it was faint but thunderous. Straight ahead he swore he heard whispers. He couldn't sit still. His heart was exploding out of his chest. Constantly he moved his head from side to side, refusing to blink. He wanted to throw up.

"Lazarus?"

"What!" he jumped. The gun slipped out of his hands but didn't go off.

Jonas laughed.

"Oh, you think that's funny? Well—" Lazarus began to chuckle. "Well, I'm glad it was you." A sense of relief came over him.

"My turn. Try to get some sleep, you're going to need it," he told Lazarus.

He hated how Jonas never explained what was going on. What is it he should be 'on the lookout' for? Why does he need to get some sleep?

"Jonas."

"Yes."

"Nothing."

"Hey, get some sleep and don't worry. I won't let anything happen to you."

Lazarus somehow believed him. He slept.

***

"Hey, time to get up," Jonas whispered. Lazarus was dreaming that dream where he said what needed to be said, he did what needed to be done; that dream where life was truly like living in nirvana, a utopia. Of course, once he came to he couldn't remember a moment of it. He hated that.

The sunlight made its way in the tunnel through the cracks in the door they entered from. Jonas filled the lantern with oil and handed it to him.

"Give me the shotgun and take the pistol. I will lead the way. Don't drop that lantern. Its light is the difference between life and death."

Lazarus nodded.

They walked towards the darkness, and the lantern showed evidence of life as they went. On the ground he could see fresh footprints. Jonas kept them right in the middle of the half-circle shaped tunnel. On each side there was a platform that went on for as long as the lantern could see; it was about two feet wide. There appeared to be dark spaces up ahead in the wall. Upon further examination Lazarus realized they were holes.

Is that where the underground people sleep?

"Holy shit," Lazarus said.

"Shh," Jonas put his finger by his lips.

Lazarus mouthed sorry and scurried up next to him. He whispered to Jonas, "I saw someone in one of those holes."

"The last thing we want to do is wake them up." Again he put his finger to his lips.

In the distance Lazarus could hear snoring. This guy must drive his family crazy. The snore echoed through the tunnel and had a faint, whistling sound at the end of each harmony. There was a strange comfort in the clamor. As long as this man sang on and on Lazarus figured they were probably safe. The deeper into the tunnel they traveled the louder the carol became.

Jonas waved for him to come closer, "Up ahead on our right. I want you to watch closely," he gulped. "I will be watching the left. Draw your gun."

Lazarus slowed down. He kept a close eye on the right as they came to another platform once used for waiting passengers. *Pasadena,* it read. Last he heard the drones had destroyed that entire city. No one was killed in the attack according to the reports. Pasadena was used as a training ground after the nuclear scare last summer. The governor had evacuated the town after the nuclear plant was rumored to have sprung a leak.

Jonas slowed down his pace. He crouched down and crossed his legs from left to right, keeping an eye on the left side.

Lazarus did the same. His training came back in a flash. The light from the lantern swayed back and forth like a ship lost at sea. Both of them held their breath. The gun bounced in no particular rhythm. The hope was there would be no need to use the weapon. In the distance he could still hear the man's song. The trip across the platform lasted a lifetime. Once they had made it to the other side Lazarus heard a snap. He turned to Jonas. A thumbs up.

He exhaled as they continued on.

A cool breeze whisked past. His shirt was soaked with sweat, and he wiped his forehead. A strong whiff of body odor filled the enclosed area. He didn't know if it was him or Jonas. Death by the Chairman would have been a much easier way out. Waiting for some creepy underground thing that probably hasn't heard of a shower to attack was getting old.

Then, the comforting sound of snoring song came to an end.

The light caught a shape in the distance. It was human.

Please God, help.

They moved with caution closer to the shape. It was a girl. Her face was lightly covered with a dirty film, and her hair looked as if it had never seen a brush. She was short and wore a ragged, black dress. A white, cloth belt was wrapped around her waist tied in a perfect bow.

"Why is she shaking?" Lazarus asked.

He let out a breath and looked all around.

"Jonas?"

"Oh shit," Jonas finally said, "the red stuff. That's why she shakes. These people were the first. It didn't quite go right, and, well, they eat human flesh."

Great, I get to be dinner.

"Should we try and move past her?" Lazarus asked.

"Are you kidding? I vote we shoot the bitch!"

Each of them took baby steps keeping a close eye on her. She just stood there. Her head tilted to the left. She smiled. She was a child. No way Lazarus wanted to start by killing a child. Jonas' face filled with concern.

"Shit," he said again.

"What?" Lazarus asked.

He turned to see what Jonas was looking at and felt his heart drop into his stomach. "Great." There were at least twenty flesh-eaters standing about thirty feet away. He could literally see their mouths water like they were looking at a couple of two hundred pound rib eyes.

"Shoot to kill," Jonas ordered.

God was nowhere to be found.

And then he heard: *Peace, Lazarus, peace* but didn't know what it meant. Why was he the only one to hear it? And what did this voice want from him?

The group began to move in an effort to circle them. The dirt on the ground turned to dust swirls. The grimy smell of human waste grew stronger. He realized what Custer must have felt like at *his* last stand. He looked behind to get a final glimpse of the young girl; she was gone. How long had they been watching us? It doesn't matter. Lazarus suggested they go back to back to cover all angles.

"Some should run after the first shot," Jonas told Lazarus. *Should run?*

"You're just filled with good news." And Lazarus shot in the air; then put the pistol away.

Jonas elbowed him. "Hey, we don't have a lot of ammunition. If you're going to shoot, shoot to kill."

One of the red-eyes approached. Lazarus stepped up and kicked him, knocking him to the ground. Another holding a pistol slithered towards him like a zombie. Quickly Lazarus grabbed the barrel and pointed towards the ground. The subhuman began to struggle for control, for the gun, for the opportunity to kill. The gun fired. Some fled. Another shot. A burning odor. The heat from the barrel scorched him. He switched hands as the weapon discharged once more. The man cried out. Lazarus still held the gun. The red-eye dropped to the ground. He was dead. Lazarus threw the weapon at the wall.

Peace, Lazarus, peace.

Jonas began to shoot, plucking off the few that still remained. Both of them then saw a large group gathering to attack. The flesh-eaters crept forward and attacked. Lazarus used his martial arts skills to fend them off.

"Shoot the bastards!" Jonas told him.

"I can't, I—"

Again the words rang out—*Peace, Lazarus, peace*. He knew then what they meant. He knew he couldn't kill. They would only become more powerful.

But how does one have faith when faced with death?

"What do you mean 'I can't'? We're going to die!" Jonas fired the shotgun again taking another life.

"God, help us!" Lazarus yelled.

Suddenly light filled the entire tunnel. He ducked.

Gunfire. From where? Am I dead? What the hell is going on?

Bodies began to fall all around him. Jonas whispered in his ear to stay down. The tunnel became a haze of black smoke.

"Quinn, how ya' doing?"

"Zack! Boy, I'm I glad to see you." Jonas picked himself up from the ground. "Hey, Lazarus, meet my old friend, Zack Thorn."

They shook hands. The aroma in the tunnel was like burnt firewood mixed with firecrackers.

"You must be Parker," Zack grinned from ear to ear and continued to shake his hand long after proper etiquette requires.

"Who's with you?" asked Jonas.

"Bey! Get over here and be social for Christ's sake."

Zack was a huge man. He reminded Lazarus of a big guy that was really just a teddy bear. He had a brown mixed with grey mullet that begged to be cut off. His five o'clock shadow was well groomed. He set down the lantern and dusted himself off.

Out of the shadows came a brown-haired teenager. He wore a light blue shirt with a pair of black jeans. Fashion was not his thing. The boy walked right up to Lazarus and offered his hand.

"Miles Bey, pleased to meet you."

"Lazarus, Lazarus Parker. Thanks for getting us out of—"

"Yeah, hey, why don't we get outta here?" He walked away.

Lazarus was not impressed. Who did this kid think he was?

"We gotta' get a move on, boys. The crazies will be back," Zack said with a grin.

Jonas grabbed the lantern and handed it to Lazarus. Miles refused to make eye contact with him.

From the shadows appeared one of the red-eyes. Miles cocked his shotgun and took aim. Lazarus rushed up and pushed the man out of the way. "Stop!"

"What the—I almost shot you!"

"We can't kill him."

"What the hell." Miles said and looked over at Jonas, "who is this guy? As far as I'm concerned we can leave him here."

"Are you saying we shouldn't kill him? Or do you mean, not killing at all?" Jonas asked.

"I mean, yes." Lazarus paused, the voice echoed *Peace, Lazarus, peace*. "Yes, I mean not at all," he finished with confidence.

"Really? Jonas, Zack, this is a mistake. This guy doesn't know what we're up against," Miles said.

"I have a tendency to agree with Miles," Jonas piped in.

"Wait a minute, now, what do you *really* mean? Like, we just stand around and let this son-ova-bitch Vance cut us down in the streets?" Zack wanted to make peace hoping Lazarus would change his tune—even if he just tweaked it a little.

"Something like that."

"This is bullshit, Jonas. I mean—what the hell are we risking our lives for? This?"

"Alright, everyone just calm down," Jonas started. He could see Miles was ready to abandon the mission. Jonas knew that Miles was skeptical from the beginning. This bizarre twist wasn't helping matters any.

"Look," he faced Miles, "she wants us to bring him back. Plain and simple. She hasn't steered us wrong yet." He rubbed his chin, then turned to Lazarus. "I don't know if I buy into this whole not defending ourselves thing, but she tells us you're the chosen one. You better not get in the way of my gun. I guarantee you'll end up dead. I don't use deadly force unless I'm absolutely certain, and just so you know, I'll pull the trigger."

Lazarus nodded.

"Whatever, let's just get him back before he gets us killed." Miles started down the tunnel.

Peace, Lazarus, peace.

Lazarus caught up to Jonas and handed him the .38 he was carrying. "You might as well have this; I won't be using it."

***

"Kathy!" Vance yelled.

She ran from her room to his. Rushing through the door she could see the Chairman sitting on the edge of the bed in his black, silk PJs. He had just awoken but his hair looked perfect. He pointed down at his foot.

She sauntered over. The gangrene was back. It had started to circle the scar of his wound.

"Wrap it," he ordered.

She disappeared into the master bathroom to get the necessary supplies.

He sat with a pernicious appetite. The top of his lip quivered; all he could see was red. The idea of peace made him ill. He spent the last eight years searching, finding, and destroying so he could continue to feed his brand of evil. The collecting of souls for his Master was job number one. The past year of peace was painful and frightening. Once his leg had healed he knew he could find a way to keep the hate and violence going for years, decades, perhaps centuries. Why the sudden change? Had the Enemy broke the rules and sent a message to one of his minions?

He had swirled up hatred all over the world, but his army defeated it easily. The rest of the world was towing the line of One World Order like they were born for it. The opposition needed to come from his own country. It was his fault. He knew it.

Over the past couple of years he had become soft, too easy on his subjects. What he needed to do was turn up the heat. They had too many comforts here: *Welcome to Utopia* provided the greatest in entertainment, food was too easily attained, and some were actually starting to like him. The need to be hated was strong. The balancing act of being hated just enough to get the people to rebel was no easy task. Some would be too afraid if they considered him too brutal, and then there were those who welcomed another to control them.

A new law. But what? He already made it illegal to speak out against him. Getting married, having children, none of those things could happen without his permission. The gay community was back in hiding where it belonged. That was his personal favorite. *Those people* actually cheered when he became president. *Beware of those claiming to be your ally, especially when they are so willing to do anything to get their way. At some point your* 'special interest' *will be on the chopping block. Guaranteed.*

But the one that brought the greatest joy was his banning of religion. Vance wanted to go so far as making it illegal to believe in Public Enemy number one, but that would be difficult to monitor. The best part was using the people against themselves to accomplish it.

One of the greatest assets for the former United States was their stand on religious freedom. With the stroke of the pen Vance had eliminated it. His Master was pleased. The beauty of Christians hating Muslims, Jews concerned about every group, Muslims hating, well, everyone, and the nonbelievers continuing to tout they were offended made it quite easy to strip the Enemy from the very fabric of American life. All those nonbelievers, offended by a God that claimed he forgave and loved him. Nonsense.

"How does the devil take over?" he whispered. "By giving the people what they want."

"What's that, sir?" Kathy asked.

He patted her head and said nothing.

She wrapped his foot, noticing the green ooze getting bigger.

Lazarus Parker echoed between his ears.

"So *that* is the problem," he grimaced. "Oh goody, my old friend Lazarus is back. The prodigal son has returned. The dead has risen. HA!"

She stayed down, finishing quickly. She had seen Vance

in this state before. It usually was followed by death and destruction. His pulse beat faster.

The name was all he had needed. Vance knew exactly what to do. He peeked down. Kathy would be his first test. The need to drive out the agonizing pain of his growing foot fungus was the first step. The ball was still in his court. The idea of love, peace, tolerance and all the crap that went with it was still a spark. It would take that type of convincing Lazarus was not capable of providing. It was almost too easy. His Master had already put an idea in his head on where to begin the destruction of *he who has come back to life*.

How pathetic.

He yelled at the Enemy asking if this was the best He's got. Kathy got up to leave.

"Wait," he said.

She fidgeted, unable to stand still. Tears formed in her eyes. "Yes, Mr. Chairman?"

"It's time you know. Your husband is already dead. I killed him. I liked it."

"Why do you tell me this now?" she cried.

"Aren't you going to do something about it?"

She shook her head. "I... I don't want to—die." She wiped her face, trying to regain her composure.

Vance got to his feet and winced with pain. With the back of his hand he slapped her.

She stood there not moving.

He slapped her again, and again.

"Stop that!" she shrieked.

He smiled.

She hit him back. Over and over again they slapped each other until he grabbed both her arms and threw her on the bed.

Kicking and screaming, she cursed at him.

"You may take this body—but it won't be me! It won't be me!" She continued to kick and wail and hit Vance with a hatred deep in her heart. And he liked it—fed off of her hatred. If she could kill him she would've. He could see it in her eyes.

He laughed. "Welcome to hell." He took her.

***

Her face bloody and body covered in bruises, she tried to use her hands to cover up. Vance sat on the end of the bed buttoning up his shirt. He looked down at his foot and removed the dressing. Nothing. No pus. No green. No pain.

"Thank you," he told Kathy and got up.

The hatred in her eyes pierced through him, bringing comfort. Grabbing her by the hair, he dragged her off the bed.

Again she kicked and screamed, calling him names that almost made him blush. She bounced off the marble flooring. She tore and scratched at his arm, drawing blood. He marched her down the stairs. Each step she cried out for his death.

"Open those doors!" he ordered one of the guards. The guard obeyed and Vance stormed out to the back patio and headed for the four foot retaining wall.

Kathy stopped screaming.

"No, no, wait, no," she repeated. Realizing his plan, she put everything she had into breaking free from him. It was to no avail.

With the strength of a thousand demons Vance lifted her up with one hand. The howl of many voices escaped him as he hurled her over the side of the wall, her screams echoing downward.

He wiped his hands. Inhaling deeply, he took in the pleasant aroma of pine and enjoyed the slight chill in the air. "What a wonderful view."

He could no longer hear her screams. The next order of business was to locate the special guest his Master wanted to see on the show.

"Simpson?" he called out.

"Yes, Mr. Chairman," the thin-faced Simpson with red in his eyes answered.

"We need to locate John Watters."

Using a stylus on a tablet he produced from a pocket,

Simpson wrote down the name.

"And we need to find me a new intern."

Simpson bowed and ran off.

Perfect, Vance thought, *having the beloved mentor of Lazarus on the show will bring out the worst in him.*

***

"Is this what's left of Pasadena?" Lazarus asked. The skyline held a brownish film over the area. The site was filled with broken pieces of pavement and freeways that led to nowhere. In the distance, damaged structures made it look like a scene from Pompeii.

No one answered.

Jonas touched his shoulder and pointed. "That was once the Rose Bowl."

Lazarus remembered seeing a game there once. His father was a big UCLA fan. Lazarus always figured his dad was disappointed he had never played the game.

To the east was a forest Zack said where they would be camping tonight.

Lazarus peeked back to see the ruins of that once great American city. The bland apartment buildings and the dark clouds of smoke from the factories showed the only signs of life. A life completely void of hope, of love, of God. He wondered what this journey had in store for him.

More death. More destruction. What difference could he make? Was *peace* really the answer?

He could see a white powder sprinkled on the ground up ahead. A large ditch was carved in the ground just before the forest. They all stepped up on the ridge and looked down. No one made a sound. Lazarus looked over at Jonas and could see he was upset. The smell of death still absconded around the white stuff there to hide it. Bodies filled the hole for over a mile. The mound of flesh was stacked three high. The bodies covered in white reminded Lazarus of pictures he had seen of the holocaust.

But a photograph doesn't quite have the effect of seeing it live. How does someone convince others this is okay?

How did this kind of death reach a nation once so proud of liberty? Apparently this type of horror is easier than loving our fellow man.

They walked alongside the ditch and over a mound into the forest. The amount of bodies went on for miles.

"Lord," Zack's voice was but a whisper, "please welcome these poor souls into your kingdom." He looked up at the sky. "Thank you, Lord. Your will, not mine, be done."

The camp was not far from the edge of the forest. The night's air had a bite to it. Lazarus couldn't sleep. Zack took the first watch.

The place was well-kept. The small area they laid in was obviously manmade. Each had a little dugout to sleep in. The design was perfect for keeping rain out or providing protection from the elements. The dirt area made a perfect circle. A fishing wire surrounded the spot. The wire was used as a simple warning system. If someone or something hit it the alarm would sound.

Lazarus tried to dream about the future since the past was filled with darkness. Just about the time he entered dreamland Zack woke him up. He nodded. Lazarus crawled out of his cubby hole and grabbed the shotgun from him.

Zack pointed over at the coffee. "It tastes like shit, but it'll keep you awake." Zack made his way over to his pit, signed the cross, and began to pray. How strange for a man his size. When he was finished he told Lazarus when to wake the next one on watch.

Lazarus poured a cup of steaming coffee into a tin cup that might've been made back when America was first discovered.

Coffee was made to be hot. He hated those pretentious bastards that used to order ice coffee. What the hell is iced coffee? He took a sip and immediately spit it out. Using the canteen Zack gave him, he poured water in his hand and splashed it on his face.

He checked to make sure the other three were fast asleep. "God keep me awake," he said from his knees.

He ran in place hoping to get his blood moving. The idea that these men trusted him with their lives was overwhelming.

195

Each of them a world away in their dreams—or nightmares, would they be ready if he sounded the alarm?

He peered out in the darkness trying to stay vigilant. The dim glow of the lantern next to the fire pit was the only light that illuminated the circle.

He stopped at Zack's hole. *Where does that kind of faith come from?* His mom had that kind of faith. She used to do the cross thing over her chest also. Lazarus always thought she was the only one to do that until he went to a Catholic wedding. The whole church had done it! He had been young and remembered thinking how cool it was that his mom taught them how. They had gone to a Methodist church for years every Sunday. His father stopped going at some point. Often he wondered why, but never asked. His dad still believed in God, and he prayed. But his parents were so different and yet it was easy to see how much they had loved each other.

He recalled hearing the words I love you spoken often in the house he grew up in. His father was raised in a white neighborhood somewhere in Orange County. His mom grew up in a poor neighborhood just outside of Detroit. Both of them had very similar values, even though his mom was a Democrat and his dad was a Republican. His mother would say the Dems were the only party that cared about the regular people and his father would usually get angry and tell him, "The Republicans are the party of freedom."

Lazarus suspected, however, that his father voted for Obama in 2008 even though he was a Democrat. That year he didn't go on his usual diatribe about the 'party of Lincoln.' His dad cried the night of *that* election. It was the only time Lazarus ever saw him cry. His mom cried too, but *that* was par for the course for her. Lazarus wondered if Americans would ever have the right to vote again for a president they wanted in office, and if they would ever defeat Vance.

A chair had been hand-carved out of rock where Lazarus sat, waiting. He still reflected on the past. The moon was missing only a sliver above, and the night was a dead calm. Nothing moved. It was almost creepy.

The alarm bushes sounded. Lazarus racked the shotgun and fired. The three men came to arms in unison.

"Talk Parker! Where is it?" yelled Zack.

"Hell if I know. The bushes…sounded."

"Thorn, what do you got?"

"Nothing here."

"Talk to me, Bey," Jonas said.

"Nothing here."

The trees fell silent and the dust settled. Thorn moved backwards toward the lantern and picked it up, creating a bigger circle of light.

"Clear!"

"Clear!"

"Clear?"

"Wait," Jonas said standing straight up and putting down his gun. "I found the culprit." He picked up a rabbit by the back of his neck and showed the other two. He broke the rabbit's neck in a snap. "Breakfast. Thanks, Lazarus."

He wouldn't have to make a life or death decision tonight. Minus, of course, deciding on trying rabbit for the first time in the morning. But he could feel, he could sense, that Chairman Vance would have something up his sleeve.

Resolved to follow the voice in his head, he still felt somewhat apprehensive. Doubt lingered all around. It was in the men who had saved him; it was within. Maybe he was just plain crazy.

Peace, Lazarus, peace. But the words or the voice or the idea did not bring comfort. A test lay ahead.

***

The morning came with the sizzle of meat cooking. It stank of wet grass mixed with burning hay. Rabbit. Lazarus figured anything was better than another can of cold pork and beans. He missed his mac-n-cheese.

The three were already up.

"Morning Lazarus," Jonas looked over and smiled. "Ready to eat?"

Lazarus walked over and Miles handed him a plate. The

wet grass smelling meat with a side of beans. Tentatively, Lazarus took a bite of the rabbit.

"Not bad."

"First time having rabbit, Parker?" Zack asked.

He nodded and continued to shovel the food in his mouth.

A thumping sound entered the camp. The thunderous stomping continued to get closer. Suddenly it stopped.

"Our ride has arrived," Miles said.

Four absolutely beautiful creatures appeared. The horses looked chiseled to perfection, stood about five feet tall and had a gorgeous chestnut-colored coat. Their long, black tails stood high on their backends.

"Stunning. What kind are they?" Lazarus asked Jonas.

"Arabian," he answered. "Legend has it that Muhammad chose these horses because of their courage and loyalty. *Al Khamsa, the five.* Supposedly five horses returned to Muhammad on his command even though they were dying of thirst. We're talking the desert so to turn back from the oasis was a pretty big deal."

"Are you Muslim?" Lazarus wasn't too fond of them. His father's brother had been radicalized. They had never talked about it, but he knew it hurt his father deeply. His lack of love for the religion was certainly passed on to Lazarus.

"No, just want to understand all people, friend or foe," Jonas answered.

"Yeah, but those bastards killed a lot of people."

"Not all of them. What some of those people did was pure evil, and pure evil should be destroyed."

"I have no use for any of them."

"Hey, I'm not going to defend their actions, but the God I believe in today—Jesus—tells me I have to forgive, I have to love my enemy. He tells me it's easy to love my brother. The idea is pretty radical and not easy to do." He turned to Lazarus and continued, "That's why I haven't completely discounted your idea of not killing."

Jonas paused. "Lazarus, why didn't you stand up to Vance before? Why now, after all these years? Was life so precious that watching people die, be taken in the middle of the night, appear on that God forsaken show—be *his* slave—why was all that okay?"

Jonas walked away.

The same prejudice Lazarus complained about for years had smacked him right in the face.

Jonas continued, "How do you like being judged by the color of your skin? How many sleepless nights did you have back when they were rounding up Muslims? Or Christians? Or what Vance called, 'enemies of the state?'"

"I guess I hit a nerve," Lazarus said under his breath.

"You're damn right you hit a nerve!"

Lazarus couldn't escape his feelings. He knew they were wrong, but a lifetime of calamity could not be overturned in a night.

Jonas took in a breath, exhaled and finished. "Look, the only way to win this fight, Lazarus, is to be better. Do you understand that? I want to believe saving you will be worth the risk."

Great, he thought, *I have pissed off the only ally I have here*.

Supplies packed, Lazarus slid on his horse. The last time he rode was with his mentor, John Watters. He remembered that part of his training well. 'You have to be ready for anything,' Watters told him. 'Horse, car, diesel, chariot, or an airplane, it is vital you have a working knowledge of them all.'

Reflecting back, he still could use a few more hours in the air. Flying an airplane proved much more difficult than he had anticipated during his training. He prayed and asked God to watch over him. John was the last person alive Lazarus cared about. Everyone else was dead.

The four of them rode out.

"Where the hell are we going?" he asked.

"The Black Hills of South Dakota," Miles answered. "That's where we plan to mount our attack on the bastard."

Lazarus smirked knowing that was a slight jab. He realized these guys were starting to grow on him. Perhaps it was time to reenter life. To unbind and live again. In time, there would be more to care about. It was dangerous. But there was also hope. He became conscious of the idea that peace started with that one word, hope.

It was at that moment he understood this trip would be his last. He felt it deep inside. He was going home.

***

The trip to a settlement on the eastern end of Nevada lasted just over four days. The small town of Mesquite had been turned into a small fort. The hotels had become barracks. Most of the gambling tables were used as firewood. The fanatical religious types would 'praise the Lord' each time another green felt was fed into a fire. Others would cry remembering a time filled with sleepless nights, overconsumption of booze, and the excitement of a *winner seven*. Regardless of what camp you leaned towards, everyone was welcomed.

"Over this way; we made it just in time for lunch," Jonas said leading them over to the stable.

The stable didn't have any other horses in it, but on the far side was a black tarp that covered a large object. They put their horses away and walked into a former casino building.

The fountain in the middle of the lobby had a Greek God with wings in a beautiful white marble. The growing blackness inside the fountain told how long it had been without water. The red-colored design in the carpet made Lazarus anxious. Guards were everywhere. It was a military zone.

"Why is there so much—security?" Lazarus asked Zack.

"They just made an attack on the droneport in Vegas. Just prepared for the worst here."

They made it to the entrance of a restaurant that was still operating. 'The Giddy Up Café' was the name carved in wood above the concave.

"Howdy all. How ya' been Jonas? Seems like a coons age since I last saw ya'," a southern man with a slight limp said. "Y'all have a sit at one them there booths and we'll getcha some chow." He nodded towards the other side of the room then disappeared into the kitchen.

The aromas coming from the kitchen made all of their

mouths water. Four days of road kill just didn't cut it. They sat down at a booth, waiting patiently.

The southern man, Samuel Buford, brought out plates and set them down. He returned to the kitchen and came out with two bowls full of food. One of them was homemade mac-and-cheese with a layer of bread crumb crust on top. Lazarus was in heaven. The other bowl was filled with fried chicken. Now he *knew* he was in heaven; a soul food heaven.

If he brings out hush puppies I'll ask him to marry me.

Lazarus dug into the mac-and-cheese and put a healthy portion on his plate. The crust was to die for. The final bowl had corn on the cob.

I still might ask him to marry me. Lazarus lathered up the corn cob with butter. The fried chicken was better than his mom's had been. The smell of the perfect amount of grease mixed with a golden brown coating brought back memories. She was the only one who could beat the flavor of the Colonel's original recipe. The Parkers were terrible cooks. Mac-and-cheese was all they had. Not they needed anything else.

But the Floods, his mom's side of the family, were incredible cooks. Even as a teenager when they would travel back to Michigan, he would get excited. It had been all about the food.

There was not a crumb left after the men finished eating. Miles talked endlessly about Abigail and the set up at Mount Rushmore. Zack and Jonas hadn't been back there in over a year. This trip was a sort of homecoming for them. They couldn't believe what their leader had accomplished. The ammunition factory was up and running, almost all the flags of each state were waving, and she had put together a plan of attack which had started here just in the last week. The conversation was vibrant and full of laughter. Lazarus had spent his entire life craving this type of fellowship.

"In a couple of hours we will be back on the road," Jonas informed the group.

Lazarus was not excited to get back on a horse. After four days he could no longer feel his ass or legs. Sex would be out of the question for a while even after all these years of living the life of a monk.

On the second floor they were escorted to a room that had a bed and bathroom.

"The water don't work, toilet don't flush, you gotta' go you go outside in the outhouse. You need anything let me know, name's Buford," the man said.

The bed was comfortable. He slipped his jeans and t-shirt off and fell into it. He wrapped the sheet and comforter around him like a burrito. He was still covered in dust, but didn't care. He closed his eyes. All efforts to think were useless. An image of a silhouette shaped like a man started off his first dream. Within minutes he fell asleep.

He awoke just before nightfall. From his open air room he could see dark storm clouds gathering in the distance. They were creating havoc somewhere straight north of the town. The clouds weren't far off.

The door flew open and in popped Miles. "Lazarus, we need to get going, now."

Lazarus jumped out of bed and put his Levis and t-shirt back on. Flying out of the room, he realized the entire place was in chaos.

"They will attack soon." He heard Buford tell Zack.

"Shit." Zack shook his head and placed his hands on his hips. "What do you need from us?"

"We need y'all to get your asses back to headquarters. I know you have doubts that *he* is the one but I gotta tell ya, Zack, there's somethin' about him." Buford smiled at Zack, chuckled and said, "Hell, maybe it's just cuz he loves my cookin'."

Zack gave a smirk and put his arms around Buford.

Lazarus was struck by how genuine the affection between the men was.

Everywhere people barked orders. The calmness and order was impressive. It was obvious they had drilled for possible attacks in the past. Rifles were handed out. Men and women took their places, prepared to fight.

Once downstairs, they were led to the stables and told to wait. Lazarus was still in a fog. Zack turned around and started to talk to himself. The words were clear but the message incoherent. He kicked dirt and waved his hands up and down.

Did I cause all this? Lazarus wasn't sure. "Is the government still after me?" he asked aloud.

"No, this has to do with the operation last week. They attacked and destroyed a large number of drones in Vegas. Needless to say, Vance was not pleased," Jonas answered.

"Tell them not to shoot back, it just makes him stronger."

"What the hell— Jonas? Is this guy for real?" Miles put his finger in Lazarus' face. "These people are gonna die! Don't you get that? And they want us to get away so *YOU WILL BE SAFE.*" He put his hands on his hips and shook his head.

"Look—" Lazarus started.

The building rattled from the blast. Dirt sprinkled down on them from the cracks in the roof. The lamp hanging from above flickered off, on, off—then on again. They all crouched down and looked up as if waiting for the whole barn to crash down.

The pounding of Lazarus' heart thumped hard in his temples. The pressure built up and made his brain feel like it was oozing out of his skull. The tension spread to his shoulders, down his back and in his legs. His hands shook. He wanted to pray but knew it would prove useless.

Run. I should run. But where? There was something on his shoulder.

"What the hell?" and then he noticed it was Buford's hand.

"What was that blast?" Miles asked.

"A rocket. Good thing none of 'em know how to aim. Don't any of you worry now, none of em' can hit the broad side of a barn standin'—"

A loud blast.

Once again the barn shook, dust fell on their heads, and the light flickered off then on again.

Buford chuckled and walked over to the black tarp and balled it up. He uncovered a black 2027 Vision Motors Champion. It was advertised to be the last and only car ever needed. The original didn't even come with a gas tank and according to the manufacturer it could go over 300 miles on one charge. The makers created a half-mooned shaped vehicle with doors that lifted up like a 1980s sports car. The plastic used on the body looked like a hefty bag covering a *Rent Me* dumpster shaped like an old Volkswagen bug. The idea was very confusing. Everyone knew the car was over ten years in the making. The designer in charge changed about six times; each one coming in with a new vision but working off the old one. The final design and results made the famous story about the demise of the Edsel look like a dream car. The idea of one charge that could go over 300 miles was a bit misleading.

To Lazarus the sight of Motor Vision's answer to climate change was a welcomed sight to the saddle.

Zack was handed the keys followed by another hug. Jonas and Miles embraced him as well.

"Lazarus. This is all pretty crazy, huh?" Zack made a dramatic gesture.

Lazarus was grateful, and not only for the mac-and-cheese with the golden crust. In the distance he could hear another blast. No shaking. No dust. No lights flickering. Much farther away than the other two.

Lazarus offered his hand to Buford.

"What are you kidding me?" Buford opened his arms wide. "I'm a hugger!" The grin grew bigger.

He surrendered and opened his arms to him. He did the short, soft three-pat on the back keeping his waist area in another area code. The typical man hug.

"Who am I?" he asked Buford.

The guys started to pile into the Champion.

"That's for you to find out," Buford grinned.

"No, not *philosophically*, I mean, to you, to them…" He pointed. "To—"

Another blast. This one much closer. The stable went dark. The next explosion knocked him to the ground. His heart was beating so fast he couldn't breathe. He heard footsteps.

The engine started. Headlights killed the darkness and he slid inside the car. The Champion sounded like a muscle car from the 1970s. There was an option to have a button installed that would make certain car engine sounds. The most popular among men was the 'Rev the Engine' button. Apparently this one had it and Miles loved it. Jonas told him to stop.

Then all that could be heard was the faint hissing sound of the LT4-Ion aluminum battery of the Champion. The back seat was a bit cramped for a big man like Lazarus, but anything was better than riding on those damn horses again.

The Champion sped off through the open door. Buford stood waving to them as they drove by. Miles slowed down to navigate through the rubble. There was a large hole in the building across the street. Pieces of metal frame were deformed by the blast and small fires burned. The debris on the ground had fallen on some unsuspecting soldiers. A woman was partially buried under a large section of the wall. A small boy, maybe ten or eleven, put his hand on her forehead. His mouth began to move and his eyes closed as they drove by. Lazarus had seen tears streaming down the boy's face. The boy had used his fingers to close the woman's eyes, made the sign of the cross, picked up a rifle, and ran towards the road.

Another blast. This time the casino took a direct hit.

The car made its way onto the gravel street where dead bodies were scattered everywhere. In the final glimmer of sunlight Lazarus could see a pack of drones headed towards the town. He remembered the destruction of Pasadena. These nice people would all be dead soon. Another mass grave.

He closed his eyes and could see the white powder covering the dead. The vision made him sick.

"We've got to help these people," he cried.

"We have a higher purpose," Zack responded.

The Champion made its way along the gravel road. Another blast rattled the car. On the edge of town Lazarus could see a graveyard. A real graveyard like he remembered seeing as a child. Mass graves or cremation were all Vance had to offer. He had kept his parent's ashes for a couple of years, but had finally decided to dump them in the ocean.

It certainly wasn't their idea or wish, but he couldn't stand staring at the urn any longer. He had been drunk when he did it. Not even the gin could make him forget how he had stuffed them in the back of his closet.

There had been nothing he could do for Angie and his son. *Are they in heaven?* He hoped so.

"What is this higher purpose?" he asked.

"It would be best for Abigail to tell you about it," Jonas answered.

"That's bullshit! I need to know. All you've given me is crap since we started this journey." He crossed his arms. "Stop the car!"

The three of them looked at each other.

"Look—" Miles said.

"Stop the damn car, now!" Blood flowed into his face. He trembled. He needed to get out of the vehicle. He calmed down and took a deep breath. "Miles, stop the damn car."

Miles' mouth opened.

"Now Miles, not another word out of you. Now!"

"Okay, okay, just—"

"Now!" The car stopped and Lazarus pushed his way out. He ran as fast as he could into the graveyard. He read the names on the tombstones. Each one had a message. One of the captions stopped him dead in his tracks.

Theodore Durnam, A Loving Son Who Will Always Be Remembered For What He Sacrificed. We Love You, Mom And Dad.

He dropped down, "NO!"

"Um, Lazarus. Just thought—" Zack interrupted his thoughts.

A loud blast.

"Just thought— Well, we should get going cause like, well, they're dropping bombs," Zack said.

A loud *boom* thundered and shook every cross, every gravestone. Not one of them fell. Lazarus got up and turned around. They were staring at him. Each of the men wore a look of confusion. He walked between them and started to head back to the Champion. None of them followed.

He shrugged. "Are we going, or what?" And continued

towards the car, popped the door open, and climbed into the back. Crossing his arms, he stared out the window at the graveyard. The chaos of war just a short distance away didn't faze him. He welcomed death, if that was what today had in store.

Behind his little hissy fit a fear of what these freedom fighters wanted from him stuck in his gut. Death seemed to be an easier way out. He might've bit off more than he could chew.

Peace, Lazarus, peace. The voice again. Louder this time.

"Look, Lazarus," Miles started.

"Just go, forget it," he said abruptly.

The car didn't move; Miles just stared straight ahead. A series of blasts rocked the earth below as balls of fire lit up the night sky in the rearview mirror.

"Look, I don't know about you, but being barbequed on Main Street with you three bastards doesn't sound like fun," Lazarus said.

The Champion crept forward, Miles keeping the lights off. He found his way onto Interstate 15; the highway in much better condition here than it was going into Mesquite. The stars lit up the night. Clouds covered the moon and shined in the distance. More and more stars appeared as they traveled farther from the fires of the small Nevada town. The area around them was flat for miles. The only sound was the hiss of the Champion.

Lazarus wondered if Abigail Payne was the teen's mother. And he wondered what that dead son at the graveyard had done for his parents. He wondered what message would be written on his gravestone.

The car ride was silent.

***

No one wanted to leave the townsfolk behind. But Jonas knew there was something much bigger at stake. He didn't understand it. He didn't have to. He was following his gut. And his gut told him that Lazarus was the answer. Now if he could only convince Miles and Zack of that his part of the mission would be complete.

***

"Hi John," Vance said with fake enthusiasm in his voice.

"I wondered if I would ever see you again." John Watters walked in scanning the large house. "Nice place," he added. The red-eye took off the handcuffs and John rubbed his wrists.

"I have to admit, I figured it would be you to lead the resistance. I mean, after what we've been through," Vance said.

"I gave it some thought. I wondered why you kept me alive," John headed towards Vance.

The Chairman put up his hand, letting the guards know not to worry.

"And then, it dawned on me. The very violence we the people create, the stronger you get. Am I right?"

"You were always the one I feared most, I have to admit. But after I learned it was you that led Payne to his daughter I knew you could be trusted to create the most turmoil." Vance stepped up to him. He slapped him.

John snapped his head back with a stinging pain, making no attempt to retaliate. He was slapped again. No reaction.

"I know what you want, Vance," John said, "you can't have my soul."

"Very well, then." Vance turned, keeping his back to John hoping for an attack. His foot began to ache. The tide was turning. All he could hope for was little moments of soul catching. This would not be one. The resistance was busy attacking right now, but his Master was warning him of the coming storm. A storm of calm that could very well end their reign.

This new tactic by the devil himself was buried deep in the nature of man. It was so easy to get people to hate than it was to get them to love. There would be no stopping him this time. The world would be his. Every soul would bow down to him and forget about the Enemy above. It was flawless—or so Vance thought.

Neither Vance nor his Master planned on someone like John Watters or his student, Lazarus. How ironic it was that it was *them* that sent Lazarus to this so-called weapons expert. It was the only time Watters was used to train. Vance didn't like his focus on healing and crap like that, so he only used him the one time. It was a mistake he wouldn't make again.

"Take him away!" he shouted. "Know this, John Watters, I will use you to get that bastard trainee of yours. I will destroy you, and I will destroy him."

Two red-eyes approached him and John put his arms behind his back. There was no need to resist. He could see Vance was afraid. For the first time during his rise to the top, he was afraid. It was much easier to get what you want than to keep it.

"Forrest—"

"It's Chairman Vance."

"So that's what this is about, Lazarus. He won't come for me."

"I don't care if he does or not. I need him to hate, deeply, or fear deeply once again. And for a broken man like that, the push back to submission will not take much. Your death will more than do it. You will suffer, and he will watch it happen."

***

The Champion putted along the highway not too far from what used to be Casper, Wyoming. They spent the night before in what was called the 'Y' which was a Mormon camp setup on the old BYU campus. They met good people who fed them, recharged the car, and gave them mini-canisters to make sure they could make it all the way to the Black Hills. The 'Y' was part of the resistance.

Miles told the story of how Abigail knew the ideal of religious freedom would grow into the wanting of other freedoms. It was what she believed to be at the very center of what made the former United States a great nation.

She was fond of repeating the words her father taught her

that were said by a preacher of the Black Robe Regiment. "There is a time to pray, there is a time to preach." It started the battle call, "And there is a time to fight!" According to legend, the preacher took off his robe and wore a military uniform underneath. That day 300 men joined the fight for freedom.

Abigail prayed each night that her radio addresses had reached some. Perhaps many. But she knew the real fight would be led by Lazarus. His coming was the new life of the resistance.

Lazarus silently listened to the story. He would have done anything to change the subject. First, it was overwhelming to hear he was supposed to lead some kind of rebellion, and second he wasn't quite sure she would welcome him with open arms once she realized who he really was.

Sure, he saved her from those red-eyes, but it was his plan and his men that uncovered the real Barker Wilson. The betrayal, it must have left a scar.

Plus, as Miles told the story he could hear in his voice the need to 'convince' Lazarus of the need to fight. And fight with weapons. The idea of ordering death and killing didn't sit well in his gut.

"My dad talked endlessly about the Black Robe Regiment," Lazarus said.

"Oh yeah?" Miles asked.

"He learned about them after 9/11. That day changed him. That was the day he became a Republican, or at least more conservative. He told me, since I was too young to remember, that watching those planes hit the Twin Towers caused so many mixed emotions. Our talks are probably why I said what I did about Muslims. My dad wondered why the supposedly moderate ones didn't stand up and condemn the radical ones. I had to agree with him. I don't hate them, I just don't trust them.

"Anyway, his conversion was very profound. He read and read and read after that. I remember my mom telling me how, although she wasn't very fond of his new political leanings, that he had become a better man. I asked my dad about it. He told me he wasn't a very good husband or father in his younger days. I wanted to know more but I didn't, you know what I mean?"

Jonas and Zack shook their heads. Miles turned and looked forward.

"Look, guys, I realize you have no idea who I am. I guess I was 'chosen' because when I was young I studied Martin Luther King and the ideas he stole from Gandhi."

"Oh, so this is a black thing," Miles said dismissively.

"No, I also studied Bonhoeffer. He was the Lutheran minister that not only opposed Hitler, but also tried to kill him. My mom became a Lutheran and I remember going to church with her one day and hearing about this man. I read a few books about him.

"First, when it came to King and Gandhi they were able to use peaceful methods because the governments they were fighting were not inherently evil. Good people will make the right choice when faced with the truth. When it is up to *we the people* we will only watch injustice for so long before we demand change. At least that was my father's explanation.

"Now in the case of Bonhoeffer, well, he *was* fighting pure evil."

"Yeah, and so are we. Can't you see that? I don't trust you. You worked for Vance," Miles said pointing at Lazarus. "You're trying to get us all killed, my sis told me about you."

"Yeah, I did work for him. Once. A long time ago when I didn't know who he really was. When I found out, I walked away. He didn't kill me. Why? I don't know. That has haunted me every day since."

Emotion flowed into Lazarus like a freight train. "Vance also has worked hard to fill my life with misery. He took my wife, my child, and my mother and father. So don't sit there and tell me I can't see what the son-ova-bitch is doing." Lazarus trembled.

"This guy's full of shit, Jonas," Miles said.

"Okay gentlemen," Jonas said calmly. "I still don't get it either, Lazarus. Why, if Vance is so evil, do you think we should use non-violent tactics?"

"I know it doesn't sound right. It's…just a feeling. Like

it came from—" He stopped. The next word was one he couldn't believe had almost come out of his mouth.

"Came from—*God?* Were you going to say God?" Zack said and chuckled.

"Actually—well, yes, that's what I was going to say."

They all laughed.

"But really, to my point. This guy is different. Vance feeds off of hate and violence. Like I said, I have racked my brain trying to figure out why he would tell me he killed my parents and then, let me walk away. It doesn't make any sense to me. Except—"

"Except what?" Jonas asked.

"Except for…*that* day. Well, the last time I saw Vance he handed me a gun and told me to shoot Frank Trippy, a guy Jack Payne served with."

Lazarus paused taking a moment to reflect not only on that day, but on the man himself. The buildup of emotion was traveling up his stomach into his throat. He tried to clear it. The feeling remained.

"Anyway," he cleared his throat again, "after I refused to shoot Trippy he told me to shoot *him*. Vance himself. There was a… Look, I can't explain it other than a yearning or desire, for me to do it. It was as if by me killing him *he* became more powerful."

The car remained silent.

Miles wondered what the hell Lazarus was talking about.

Jonas thought about his friend, Frank Trippy. He wasn't quite sure how he felt now he knew Lazarus had been there that day, and didn't stop Vance.

Zack wasn't convinced, but wanted to keep an open mind.

The three men struggled with the heinous crimes committed by Chairman Vance. A violent response seemed the only appropriate way of handling him.

How could Vance understand anything but fighting fire with fire?

The sandwiches Rachel, a woman they met, had packed for the four of them at the Mormon compound were passed out and devoured in minutes. The smell of homemade peanut butter and grape jelly filled the inside of the car.

Miles had spent all night hitting on her. It was embarrassing to the rest of them, but they let it go, chalking it up to his age. Plus, they got a pretty good meal out of it. According to Jonas, Miles would hit on any woman with a pulse.

Lazarus had been grateful he was able to bathe. The brownish milky water at the end of the bath was gross, but he felt refreshed again. He was able to shave his head and face, and yank out the ingrown hairs that had started to grow once again.

"What's that?" Miles pointed up ahead.

They had just entered the town of Casper. Casper had become a ghost town. No irony there. Very few structures still stood and those that did didn't look stable. The destruction wasn't from drones or an army, but from abandonment. One day there were people here and the next day there wasn't. Lazarus wondered what would make people leave their homes so suddenly. One old building made of brick with remnants of sandstone looked sturdy enough to stand another hundred years. Weeds and brush grew wildly around it and even out of the walls. He figured it must've been a courthouse or government building of some sort. It reminded him of one of his father's favorite sayings, 'The nearest thing to immortality is a government program.' Perhaps that goes for their buildings as well.

Miles pulled the car over to the side of the road. "I have to take a piss," he cried. He circled the car around the back.

"Better let me out," Lazarus suggested.

Jonas opened the door and pulled up the seat. Something caught his eye off to the right.

"What is it?"

"Something's moving down there." He pointed, but Lazarus couldn't see anything. He kept his eyes peeled.

"Miles, I think we have company," Jonas said.

"Where?" Miles asked.

Jonas pointed down the hill. The Champion sat up on an overpass.

"What is it?" Lazarus asked again.

"It might be nothing, but I would swear I saw something down there by that old, brick building."

Lazarus looked down where Jonas pointed hoping for *nothing*.

"Let's just get back on the road," Miles suggested.

They both nodded and wasted no time piling back into the Champion. Jonas told Lazarus abandoned cities can be filled with danger. These places provided shelter for those with nothing more to lose. Vance knew the need to patrol these unpopulated areas wasn't necessary. And now with the crazy environmentalists at Yellowstone branching out, he wouldn't want to. They are called *The Wild Ones*.

Zack warned them to keep their eyes out for possible attacks, "These people only care about taking mankind back to the stone ages."

Even without their help that seems inevitable.

"Oh shit." Lazarus looked through the windshield and saw a small fire ahead. A half-ass version of a detour fence made of splintery wood and put together with God knows what engulfed with flames blocked the road.

Zack flinched when Jonas racked the shotgun, "Here," he said as he handed the gun to Lazarus.

He racked another one; another flinch. This time it was Lazarus. He laid it down on the console for Miles and picked up a third shotgun. The *clanging* sound of metal filled the car as Jonas searched in his bag. Each of them received a Glock and two magazines.

Lazarus put it behind his back. It was a little unsettling the thought of shooting another person. Lazarus tried to forget about the scene in the tunnels back in Centerville, but all those memories came rushing back now that he held a gun again. Even if shooting a man was done in self-defense he knew it would only benefit Vance. In the subway, when the man fell to his death after the gun went off, he knew he needed to be diligent about his stance on killing. Or face the unknown consequences. He wanted to pull the trigger. He wanted the easy way out. Using the weapon for self-defense is a God given right.

But— Peace, Lazarus, peace. And so the voice had other plans. *Was it really the voice of God?* Then, he knew, *just knew*, that his stance on killing had nothing to do with the rights offered to man by God. It was deeper. It was *different*. The battle between Good and Evil was at stake. The devil had new plans.

And yet, God was one step ahead of him as always. But He would not intercede, just guide, leaving free will intact. And Lazarus was the *one*. He had the answer, but was he strong enough to see it through? *Peace* was like what the Ark was to Noah. Or Goliath was to David. His shoulders fell; he exhaled, and prayed for strength.

Miles slowed the Champion down. "Why don't you just drive through the damn thing!" Zack yelled from the back.

"These road blocks usually have some nasty crap behind them. Hopefully the fact that we're armed will chase them away and we can continue on *with* transportation," Miles answered. Sweat poured down his face. They got out of the car.

From every direction figures began to circle them. The men, women, and children all carried a weapon ranging from a butcher knife to a machine gun. All of them wore green camouflage outfits. These people looked so out of place in this terrain. They were better suited for the forests of Vietnam than the flat desert-like land of the old Wyoming.

But none of them were shooting.

Jonas stood up, racked his shotgun and walked right at one of them. They stopped moving closer.

"Watch the right side," Miles said. He stood up and turned around, using the hood of the Champion as a tripod. Lazarus pointed his gun towards the five or six heading his way.

"Weapons down!" the voice was stern and belonged to a tall man in charge.

All of them stood straight up, guns and knives to their side and in unison the crowd said, "Yes, sir!"

Lazarus pointed the front of his shotgun down. He could feel his heart beat.

The man was a large figure wearing the same grey uniform with a much larger rank on his shoulder. On top of his head was one of those cowboy hats that looked like someone glued the rim to the side. The man even had a sword sheathed at his side and a Starr Revolver. He walked onto the potential field of battle with no fear.

"We want the car," he crossed his arms and stared at Jonas. The dust settled around him.

The silence created an uncomfortable tension that surrounded the area.

Jonas felt a lump in his throat and couldn't swallow.

"You may go in peace if we get the car," the man continued. "It is polluting our air and must be destroyed."

"You can't have it," Miles yelled from his ready position. "It's electric, not fossil fueled."

"Please don't insult my intelligence!" he roared angrily. "Those electric cars create a bigger footprint than the other ones. You people think you can drive around and suck Mother Earth dry and live."

The crowd made a grunt when he said Mother Earth.

"We are here for one purpose and one purpose only, to save *Mother Earth* (grunt) from the evils of man."

Lazarus was reminded of one of those fire and brimstone sermons that the crazy old white guy would deliver at his Grandma Parker's church long ago. He'd walk out thinking God was going to strike him down at any moment.

"Be ready," Jonas whispered to Lazarus.

"This guy's a real whack job," Miles said scratching his head.

"I'm hoping after I fire a couple of shots these guys will run. I have a feeling they don't have any ammunition," Jonas said.

"Why do you say that?" Lazarus asked.

"Cause we're not dead."

"Good point."

The leader moved towards Jonas. Jonas kept his gun on the man and finally back on the crowd in front of him. Lazarus was at a complete loss. He wanted to pray, but thought it would be a waste of time. The man crept closer. He pulled his gun.

The shot echoed.

Miles' mouth dropped open. The smoke filled the air around him. He could taste the unsettled dirt swirling around. "Shit, they have ammo."

Miles shot him in the leg. The man fell to the ground.

The rest of the bunch quickly started in towards the four of them.

"Stop!" Lazarus screamed.

The man cried out in pain on the ground. Nothing moved. The smell of gun powder still lingered.

Lazarus rose and set his shotgun on the roof of the Champion. Removing the gun from his waist he set that on the car as well. The crowd was stunned.

A glow outlined his body. He moved as if he was— floating. For Lazarus it was nothing more than a cautious amble towards the man in uniform. The Starr Revolver sat near him on the ground. A sword sheathed by his side. The man held his leg, but still eyed the pistol.

Lazarus kneeled down next to him.

The man lost his fear in an instant. "Are you—Lazarus?" he asked.

He answered yes and nodded.

"You have—he has—risen?"

The masses had regained their composure and moved towards Lazarus. Each of them held their weapon, ready to attack. Jonas, Zack, and Miles moved in to create a perimeter around the two men.

"I really wish you wouldn't have left your guns on top of the car!" Miles complained.

"Tell them I come in *peace*."

A breeze swept through the air.

"Back off!" The man yelled to his troops. Then, softly he said, "He means no harm," making eye contact with Lazarus once more. He was mesmerized.

Lazarus talked to him and knew his name; it was William O'Bannon.

He pulled out O'Bannon's IFAK and began to dress the bullet wound. Everyone, including the three, watched in awe as Lazarus worked to help someone that moments ago had pointed a gun at him.

Miles asked what the pouch was and Lazarus told him it was called the *Improved First Aid Kit* designed after the September 11th attacks.

"You served?"

"Yes, but not in the regular military. I was told by my mentor John Watters the most important thing I could learn was how to heal."

"How did you know my name?" the man asked Lazarus.

"I have no idea, it…just came to me. How did you know mine?"

"I thought you were wishful thinking on my part. I've been dreaming about you. Lazarus, unbound and back from the dead."

Lazarus did not react, but continued to bandage up the wound. "There, all done. Stay off of it for the next couple of days."

Zack watched a single rain drop hit the ground. A small, white flower sprouted up and the Earth dried. Quickly he scanned the area to see if he was the only one to see it. He was. He turned to Lazarus and lost all former reservations about the man. A fair amount of shame covered him from head to toe. Who was he to say this man was not sent by God? The feeling in his gut that told him something just wasn't right never happened with Lazarus. He called it God's way of pointing him in the right direction.

Silently Zack prayed. *I'm sorry, Lord, for not having more faith in you.* Gently he put his hand on Lazarus' shoulder, "I'm with you."

"I know."

Miles and Jonas moved around the area rounding up men, women and children. Miles kept his gun on the crowd as Jonas checked weapons for ammunition. All the other guns were empty.

"Put your weapons down. These people will not harm us," Lazarus told Miles and Jonas.

They obeyed.

"Listen up, we are all Americans. We are traveling to Mt. Rushmore where many of us are gathering to battle the evils of Forrest Vance. All of you are welcome to join us there."

And as if the wind that once lifted him escaped in the snap of a finger, Lazarus fell to the ground. He shook his head and found it hard to rise to his feet.

William limped over and offered his hand. He lifted Lazarus up, making an effort to ignore the pain.

"Whenever one of us falls, the other will carry him," William smiled and put his arm around his neck. "Now, today *you* need to do the walking." The two of them made their way to the Champion. At that very second Lazarus believed. The evidence was overwhelming.

"Nice sword."

"This was General Lee's sword." William's voice cracked like he was starting to cry. Lazarus hoped the tears weren't for Lee. It always made his skin crawl when people would say what a great general he was. Like that excused him from fighting for slavery. William pulled out the sword and handed it to him. The inscription read:

Gen. Robert E. Lee CSA from a Marylander, 1863

It was written in gold inside a design that had flowers on both ends. The rest of the blade was a bluish color that wasn't caused by age. The ivory handle was surrounded by what appeared to be a lion's head. It was stunning. He turned it over.

"Aide toi dieu l'aidera," William said in French, "it means *Help*—"

"*Help yourself and God will help you.*" Lazarus finished the translation for him. "I know." Lazarus knew this man had been on the wrong path. He could *see it* plain as day. If there was anything he could understand it was being on the wrong path. In his mom's church the pastor used to say that we had the power to change the world. Each of us. And it happened one person at a time.

"Here, it's yours." William offered it to him.

"I'm black, why would I want a Confederate sword owned by a racist general?"

"Because, in your hands, it will not be wielded to keep men in chains, but to free them. Because, in your hands, it will not be raised up to strike down another man, but instead to share strength in *peace*. Because, despite his shortcomings, General Lee was an honorable man, and it should remain in the hands of another who is just as, if not more, honorable than he was."

Lazarus took the sword and bowed.

He motioned for William to climb in the back. He wore a smile of genuine peace. Miles started up the car and they were off. The only sound was the subtle hum of the engine. William gave them directions on how to get around the flaming diversion in the road and soon they say the mountains up ahead capped with snow. Off to the right sat another set of mountains that nestled up to the former town of Casper. The crowd scattered behind them. Many followed the old interstate on their way to Mount Rushmore. There was concern on William's face for the people he left behind.

"They will be fine. Many of them have seen, and now they believe," Zack told him from the front seat.

It was crowded in the back with three. William took off his hat to expose his bright red, curly hair. Freckles covered his face. "I know."

They stopped to recharge the Champion after a while. It must've been more than a couple of hours without a word from anybody. Lazarus handed William his Starr Revolver.

"We will be stopping in Newcastle for the night," Miles said as they entered the town. Before entering, they had been stopped at a gate where Miles was greeted warmly. Miles drove down the quaint, narrow Main Street. The town was surrounded by mountains. Sandbags and armed guards were everywhere.

They entered the parking lot of a white church, Miles parked, and they got out of the car. On the outside the paint had chipped. A line of smoke danced out of the rear of the building. Ribs. Lazarus could smell ribs. The BBQ flavor mixed with cooked pork made his stomach rumble.

"Sounds like you're hungry," a smiling man coming out of the church said. "Good. We've got some good eats inside. Name's Jim Mason."

"Lazarus, Lazarus Parker, pleased to meet you."

Mason introduced himself to the others and led them to the potluck the church was having that night. Men and women armed with rifles and side arms shuffled through the line. The five stepped up and took their places. It had been dark for a couple of hours, but the town was lit up like Broadway.

Jonas told him they were prepared, but didn't really worry about Vance here. Not yet, anyway.

The five of them sat together and dug in. Some of the soldiers came over to pay their respects to Jonas and Zack. Jonas had been fighting Vance since day one, and Zack joined just before Jack Payne was murdered. They were well-known among the resistance. Even with the upheaval shortly after Jonas rescued Abigail, the two of them had remained loyal to Payne's cause. They had picked her to lead them because they knew she was the right person for the job. And he had been right.

Abigail was a natural born leader. She had showed it from the very beginning when she was challenged by an old friend of her father's. Jonas remembered the fiery speech she gave that day, and then, in pure Payne fashion, told the resistance—what was left of them—that she didn't want to be the leader. But there was no question, even in the mind of Jack's old friend, that it was her that would lead them to victory. She took the position reluctantly.

Inside the church, the TV was on. A voice spoke over the crowd: "Up next, catch a new episode of the number one show on television, Welcome to Utopia! We have a special one for you this evening, our very own Chairman Vance will be with us tonight."

"That's not good," said Jonas.

The whole table knew what Jonas meant. Usually Vance appeared on the TV show when he needed to make a point. When he felt his 'citizens' needed a lesson. The fear he stirred up on his guest appearances had a way of bringing order to the masses.

But Lazarus wondered if that was Vance's plan tonight. His brand of evil *needed* evil to survive. It fed off of violence and hatred. There was something more to it than his usual fear mongering.

The show started and the entire church watched with anticipation. The half-circle around the television set remained quiet, listening.

"Howdy folks! It's me, your friendly host Willy Randolph here with another exciting hour where we say—he points the microphone to the audience and they scream '*Welcome to Utopia!*' That's right, so let's get to it. Chairman Vance is with us tonight. Mr. Chairman."

"Thank you for having me here tonight, Willy. It is always a pleasure to help eliminate the evildoers of this world."

"Mr. Chairman, I was told you have a special guest this evening. Can we get an introduction?"

"By all means. Allow me to introduce John Watters."

Lazarus gasped. Everyone turned to him. Whispers were heard racing through the small church.

"Hey, Lazarus," William asked, "isn't that your mentor?"

"Yes, and so much more."

***

The bright red neon lights flashed, *Welcome to Utopia!* It was a new set for this season with a locking chair on each side. A gallows would come up from the stage right in the middle for those special hangings Vance would order, sometimes during the live telecast.

Willy Randolph had hosted every show to date. His grey hair was the product of dealing with the always volatile Chairman. The show ran five nights a week with reruns filling up the weekend broadcast.

Vance didn't make many guest appearances, but would call in from time to time. He liked to watch hangings, which is why the new gallows were brought in this season. There was one episode where the cast took a noose and ran it up in the rafters. It broke when some poor soul was in it. That was the first time the show used the glass pool. Watching a person drown was disturbing for anyone but Vance.

The beginning credits rolled, and Vance had been introduced. As he called for John Watters, the cast pushed him out onto the stage. Watters' hands were tied to the top of a large concrete stake, but he was able to move around it. He wore a white cotton kimono with a black belt.

"Hi John," Vance said cheerfully.

John didn't respond.

The Chairman went closer and whispered in his ear. It was rubbish. He was merely playing to the crowd. Keeping the people at home glued to their television set.

"So," he smoothed back his slick, black hair, "are you ready to swear allegiance to Jahannam?"

No response.

"Willy, bring out the coals," Vance ordered.

Willy was at the podium which was used to control all the gadgets on stage. The *Welcome to Utopia!* sign disappeared into the ceiling. From the ground making a perfect circle around Watters were glowing red coals. The steam floated up in the air and it was clear John could feel the heat.

The occasional flame flared in the circle seven feet away.

Willy pushed another button. The coals moved closer— now six feet from John.

John began to sweat. Breathing in and out, he tried to calm himself as his mentor had taught him and how he had taught others. Death was certain. It was how he checked out that would matter.

"One chance, that's all you get folks." Willy warned. "But now, because there are those who don't know how to obey; we get to watch how long it takes to roast a human being!"

The audience applauded.

Vance, using his cane to aid him, made his way over to the podium. He pushed a button. The coals moved closer— now five feet away.

The heat was intense. John prayed for strength. By the end of the day he would be with his Father in heaven. What a gift. But first, he had to endure the pain and suffering that was to come. He stood, hands forced in the air, and tried to make his short, stalky build appear bigger than life itself. Over and over again, he asked God to let him show Vance, Willy, the audience, the people at home, what it looked like to overcome evil.

"Any final words?" the Chairman asked. Then he laughed.

Willy laughed. And the audience laughed with him. It was considered an insult to not find what Vance found funny. Or not enjoy what he enjoyed. Or not to clap when appropriate. And he *was* watching. You only had to ask former contestants on the show if it was true; that is, if you could find any.

Vance pushed the button once again. The fiery coals leapt closer. Now four feet away. John could taste the salt in the sweat pouring out of him. The stench of roasting flesh made some in the audience visibly sick.

And then he heard a voice. *Tell Him Peace.* And he came to life. Watters was in disbelief. Had he really heard that? *Who am I telling this to?*

Lazarus. That was who he needed to tell.

Yet, still the idea that as death was coming he was only becoming delirious remained. *What if he's not watching? Maybe he won't get the message.* The heat was starting to become too much for him. His head bounced left to right and back again, as if it had become loose. His arms were tired. His feet were red and burning with pain. The blood inside beginning to boil.

Vance pushed—the coals moved—three feet away. The kimono began to mold to his body.

Peace. Tell Him Peace.

Again the coals moved closer.

"We only have an hour show! Hurry up and die already." *Laughter.* Two feet away.

Hard to breath. "God—help…me," John said softly. Then with his final breath he yelled, "Peace!"

As his head dropped and his soul started its journey to eternal life, John felt something come over him. It was as if a fire-proof blanket had stopped the burning and carried him home. The battle was lost, but victory was still possible. It was not enough to wish God was on their side; they needed to be on *His* side.

The body left behind wore a smile. Lazarus had heard his message. And he had understood.

***

A sharp pain ran up Vance's left leg. He knew the gangrene

was back. His Master was not pleased. His Master was not forgiving. The lust for souls was an all-or-nothing proposition. His leg ached. The smell of burning flesh didn't have the same appeal it usually did for the Chairman. He hated disappointing his Master, but figured they couldn't win them all.

That thought grew the wound. He balled up his fists and *took* it.

I WANT THEM ALL!

Forrest Vance bowed his head too afraid to question the deal he had made.

***

The microphone reminded her of something Orson Wells would have used to spread the tale, *War of the Worlds*. Many in the community offered to steal a better one, but Abigail enjoyed it, claiming it had the *idea* of the United States of America written all over it: creative, innovative, entertaining, liberty. The set up inside the hidden cave had taken years to build. Mount Rushmore worked perfectly for the setting because it allowed the antenna to reach out hundreds of miles. Many people who worked for the resistance died finding ways to get the broadcast to reach the big cities on the coast.

"The time has come. Freedom is not a theory. We once had it here. The 5000 year leap our founding fathers took in 1776 has been dragged back to a God forsaken time of evil tyrants and ruthless leaders. Chairman Vance has spread nothing but death and despair to every corner of the world. He dipped us into a fire and renamed us Jahannam. I say we fight fire *with* fire. The time has long past for a peaceful solution. Or for *we the people* to trust that this tyrannical leader has good intentions. He took away our Constitution and we said nothing; he told us the problem was our guns and so we handed them over; then he bombed our cities and towns and we stood by as our fellow citizens were murdered, starved, and forgotten. Our time has to come to fight, or perish in a sea of despair.

"Remember, as many of you have learned, *you are not alone*. Search—and you will find the resistance. *We... surround...them*." Abigail stood and paced, walking back and forth in the small cave passionately calling for the American people to stand and be proud once again. She was especially zealous today knowing *he* was coming.

She raged on about the daily killings and the mass graves and the evils of Vance. She thundered on, waving her other hand in the air longing to bring back freedom and dignity to the new United States.

"Just the other night," she continued, "we watched as Vance roasted a man alive. May we all be damned if we stay standing and do nothing."

And that was exactly what Vance wanted. A silent rage meant a deep hate.

She railed on, torn between the desire to personally kill the Chairman herself and what she had been taught about forgiveness and love and service to others. She often wondered, *what would her father do*? and then Abigail would think, *perhaps I should be asking what would Jesus do?*

Not once did it dawn on her that Vance thrived on the conflict within her, within Lazarus, within each human being.

But she did think about what the day would bring. A new friend. Maybe some fresh ideas. Was she capable of looking at it from an entirely different angle? She couldn't answer that question. The answer was to fight not only with words and ideas, but with guns and bombs. Her hope, her desire, her prayers were filled with what tactical and military options Lazarus would bring that could help win the war. And it was anything but a Cold War.

She couldn't hear the voice. All He did was allow her to *see* who was chosen. Nothing more. It was up to Lazarus to convince her. Not an easy road to hoe.

Yet, she didn't know about Lazarus and his vision of *peace*. But she knew from her visions not even Lazarus fully understood how it would work—at times he thought he was just as crazy. The back and forth on what to believe and how to move forward still ping ponged within his own mind. It had been so long since he thought about fighting that maybe he could no longer stomach it.

Still, she raged on telling the American people to stand, to fight, to join.

Vance's leg healed oh so slightly with each word. With each citizen that started to hate.

Sticks and stones may break bones, but words, words *can* hurt. But then again—words can heal.

"America! Wake up! You have been deceived. Take. Back. Your. Country." She nodded to the booth and the broadcast ended.

Abigail continued to pace and breathed in deeply. It was time to meet *him*. She smiled. Picking up a towel she wiped off her face and dried her hands.

Reports flooded into the resistance. In the streets of many big cities crowds began to form. Riots ensued. The people picked up shovels and kitchen knives and baseball bats and began to fight the red-eyes. There were instances of neighbors looting and attacking each other. The newly formed Ministries of Government were set on fire in some of the bigger towns. The red of fire could be seen across the nation, some could feel the heat, and many could taste the ashes.

The battles in the streets were fought with the full force of the Jahannam military. The pus-filled sore on Vance's leg receded with each body that fell. America burned. His Master was pleased.

***

Abigail stepped out of the hidden cave and into the forest, hiked up past the newly built living quarters, and up towards the chow hall. She stopped and turned, admiring the four faces on Mt. Rushmore. The sun was setting; her favorite part of the day to look up at the wise faces—one of the few landmarks that hadn't been defaced. There was a perfect amount of light and shadow that defined the expression the sculptor wanted to capture of the first president. The stare of Lincoln made Abigail wonder what moment in his presidency was reflected here. And then there was Theodore Roosevelt standing proud with his 'big stick' and peace through strength. Finally, she envisioned the same sculptor capturing the essence of Thomas Jefferson's words in the Declaration of Independence and how we needed to *live* his words now more than ever. Each one of the greats would have marched into battle if necessary, but it was her generation that had been called to fight.

Often she felt it a lost cause. The dream had become a nightmare. That the chains of slavery had shackled the entire world. Evil was having its day, and there was nothing anyone could do about it. Often she had these thoughts and used prayer to keep it from lingering in her mind too long. Prayer worked. At least for now.

Today she didn't have those frightening contemplations. *He* was coming. Finally. She smiled up at the men on the mountain. "I'm trying, boys, I'm trying."

She turned and opened the tinted glass door to join the growing community of freedom fighters for dinner. The chatter was lively. The bouquet of fried chicken and buttery mashed potatoes was inescapable. She nodded over at Franklin O'Leary. He was the reason for the dinner on this particular evening. Franklin had turned hijacking government trucks into an art. There was a bunch of small farms the resistance ran, but the need of the community, especially during the winter months, was more than they could handle. Plus it pissed off Vance.

A rush of people came running in from the other side. "They're here! They're here!"

Abigail's heart jumped into her throat. Casually she made her way over to the other side of the chow hall towards the library. A circle of tall bookcases enclosed an area used for people who would spend quiet time reading. The shelves were not filled. It was difficult finding books after the burnings of 2030.

He walked in the glass door following Jonas, Miles, Zack and some other guy she had never seen before. He wore a pair of faded, stained blue jeans and a black t-shirt that had *Newcastle* embroidered in red cursive on it. His brown Red Wing boots had little life left in them. A number of paint stains had become permanent. His face and head were recently shaved.

***

Lazarus entered the camp still in awe of the gigantic carving on the side of Mt. Rushmore. It was one thing to see it on a postcard and quite another to see it in person. Abigail Payne wore a pair of tan Capris that appeared to be from the 90s and a turquoise blouse. Her tennis shoes were white with pink striping. Choices were quite limited. Her auburn hair was shoulder length but she was taller than most women.

The two of them made eye contact and stopped in their tracks. There was no doubt they recognized each other. There was a spark. Both of them decided right then and there to let it go no further. There was work to do.

At that moment Abigail and Lazarus laid the foundation of the wall they would build to keep the other out. Any feelings between them would be highly dangerous.

Frozen by the inability to know what to do next, Miles approached Abigail.

"Your boy's got issues," he said putting his hand on her shoulder. "We need to talk." He walked into the chow hall.

Zack strolled over. "He's the real deal." He had followed Miles in.

Jonas waved his hand in front of her face, "Abs? You with us?"

She broke the contact and looked over at Jonas.

"I've got nothing." He shrugged and made his way in towards the food.

There's already tension amongst the ranks.

"Hi, I'm Lazarus, Lazarus Parker," Lazarus said to Abigail.

"I know. Abigail Payne."

"I know."

"Welcome to the resistance. Are you hungry?" She led him into the hall.

William O'Bannon looked down at his arms and his legs, checking to see if he was invisible. "What am I? Chopped liver?" he joked.

***

Vance picked at the sore on his face. His Master still fumed about losing Watters' soul to the Enemy. It had been almost two months, and even though violence had ruled, the devil wouldn't let it go. Each time Vance would steal another soul the voices in his head would berate him, torment him, blame him for being too weak to score a true victory.

Still, he didn't dare question the deal he had made.

Using the cane to navigate the newly built spiral staircase at the mansion in Kingman he made his way down to breakfast. The smell of bacon lingered throughout the palace. A plate fit for a king was placed in front of him. He wasn't hungry. Vance longed to know what he could do; how he could make up for his failure. He *needed* to hear from the voices.

Give us your body.

What did that mean? Vance shook his head and pushed the plate of food away. His servant stopped by to remove it. Vance pulled the blade from his cane and ran it through the man. Nothing. He didn't feel better. Killing had always worked in the past. What was different? What more could he possibly give up? His body? Hadn't he already done that?

No. The voices informed him.

A two-handed broad sword made its way out of the ground. A gift. But strings were attached. Vance knew it was useless to resist. His vain attachment to his appearance was all that was left of a man who died years ago.

A moan. It was the servant. Using his boot he pressed down on the man's neck. The servant's eyes bulged in disbelief. Vance thought, *how could a man be surprised by his death when working for evil?* The man's facial expression angered him.

Vance released his foot oh so slightly; just enough to keep the man breathing a bit longer. Then, with the force of a freight train, he stood up and crushed the man's throat. The final gasp brought little comfort. But it did peak his appetite, and with his left hand he grabbed a piece of bacon. It was cold, yet the greasy crunch of meat still exploded with flavor.

It's time.

Vance nodded. He knew what he had to do next.

Bending down on one knee Vance asked for the final transformation. He screamed. His legs extended and his arms began to grow. The pain was excruciating. Blood escaped each of his finger nails; his eyes turned red, and his hair fell to the floor in clumps. A fire began to swell up around him. Slowly, he was changing. Vance was becoming the beast. His final fall from grace would last for eternity.

***

"Ms. Payne, news from Nevada," the stalky man handed Abigail an envelope.

All she could think about was Lazarus, just a few feet away. The last couple of months had been difficult. The tension between the two of them growing. On one hand he kept repeating over and over again the need to fight Vance with peace. She hated it. Abigail didn't understand it. Evil needed to be defeated, wiped out, destroyed. And yet, that's exactly what he kept pointing out—that through peace Vance would be eliminated. It was a tough sell.

Abigail opened the letter. "Damn it!" she cried.

"What is it?" asked Lazarus.

She threw the paper on the ground, "Another defeat." The large room used for planning the attacks closed in on Abigail. She leaned on the long, pinewood table and bowed her head. Finally the people had taken it upon themselves to rise up to the tyrannical Forrest Vance only to experience more death and destruction than before.

At first she pointed to Washington, a man who lost more battles than he won. A sign, at least in her world, that the resistance was on the right track. Now she would have to do something she didn't want to do…admit she was wrong.

231

The small crowd of military advisors were leaving the room. Miles put his arm around her shoulder, hoping to comfort her but followed the rest of them to the chow hall. It was almost time for lunch. Lazarus stayed behind.

"So, are you ready to listen, Abby?" Lazarus asked once everyone had left the room.

"Oh great, this again. Are you ever going to stop?"

"I know it sounds crazy, but, you have to believe me. This peace thing will work, I just know it." Lazarus moved closer using his hand motions to make his point.

Abigail motioned with her head, "Those guys will crucify me. This just—it sounds so—"

"Stop it!" the anger of the past two months of his idea falling on deaf ears came to fruition, "I am so sick and tired of all those bastards advising this and that. What the hell do they know? So far all we have seen is defeat after defeat. I'm sick of it." Lazarus turned and crossed his arms.

"Oh yeah? How about you? Peace? Really? Most of those guys have risked their lives in this struggle." She pointed right at Lazarus, "What have you done? Nothing, that's what. You watched as my friends were killed right in front of you. Your pathetic excuses killed my father!" Abigail was now inches away, screaming in his face.

"I can't believe you said that. What do you want me to do, leave?"

"Well?" Abigail flung her arms in the air.

"Fine," Lazarus said storming off towards the door.

"No, wait!" she cried.

Lazarus stopped. He turned around. The silence was deafening.

Abigail trembled. "I want you."

"WELL IF YOU WOULD—wait, what?" Lazarus put his hands on his hips.

Abigail held her breath still filled with disbelief in the words she just muttered. The two of them gazed into each other's eyes. Neither one of them knew what to do…not yet. The tension could have been cut with a knife.

Abigail rushed towards him.

Lazarus rushed towards her.

They embraced. They kissed. And kissed. And kept on kissing.

"You don't even know," she told him. Even his breath was sweet.

"Know what?"

"How long I've wanted to do this." They kissed again. She melted in his arms. The warmth of Lazarus' soft touch and uncanny ability to caress her in a way Abby never knew could happen filled her with joy. The moment lasted forever. And yet, Abigail knew it needed to end.

She backed off. Then went back for more. She loved it. Abigail was able to *give in*.

Finally, she pushed him away, straightened her blouse and dried her wet palms on her jeans. Wiping her forehead she said, "Okay, okay, we can't do *that* again. Ever."

"You're right," Lazarus agreed.

His answer crushed her. Abigail was hoping for a fight. Maybe he didn't have it in him. Maybe Lazarus wasn't into her. It was all she could do to let it go. What choice did she have? There was no way he couldn't have seen the disappointment in her face. Abigail's shoulders fell. But she knew it was the right move. Especially since she would have to sell his idea of peace. The military option wasn't working. It'd be much easier to convince others of his idea if she wasn't sleeping with the guy.

Still, no matter what her head continued to tell her, Abigail longed to kiss him once more.

17

Miles walked into the abandoned shed on the outskirts of Hermosa, a former small town used as an outpost for the resistance. He put his hand on the holstered gun that hung off his right side. Gently he rubbed it. It had been months since he last used it. The idea of peace was working. Abigail, went with the new tactic. Lazarus wrote the words and she spoke them. The message was simple: share *God's peace* with each other.

At first many had died. It was like sending lambs to the slaughter. But then it happened, a miracle. Vance put an end to the mass killings and went into hiding. Miles couldn't remember the last time the Chairman made a public appearances. The show, *Welcome to Utopia*, was canceled. The last show ended with the forced suicide of Willy Randolph.

Miles was upset. He wondered when his time to lead would come. His sis continued to tell him there would be no need to lead a resistance. That with the peace plan put together by Lazarus, all of them would once again enjoy the liberties once afforded to every American. She told him he was still young. He hated that. The condescending tone was clear. She denied it.

And then there was *him*. That bastard, Lazarus, had invaded and taken over like he owned the place. She was closer with him now than with her own brother. It was as if he wasn't there in the planning meetings. But that would all change. The meeting he set up would make him important once again.

He had wandered off the Hermosa outpost over an hour ago. He had to be careful. Certainly he didn't want to be considered a traitor. But Lazarus had to go. The entire community was excited about how *peace* was working. But Miles knew it was just a ruse. It was more like a band-aid than a solution.

Sure, at the moment all seemed to be going well, but soon it would change and things would be worse. It was as if they had let the devil in and allowed him to call the shots. So Miles had to do something.

The meeting was set up in good faith. He could feel it. The voice that spoke to him led him here. It had taken him this far with little to no resistance. Sure, he had to keep it secret. But secrets are necessary sometimes. The truth has a funny way of diverting us from the right path. This wasn't treason; it was diplomacy.

"Hello, Miles," Vance said in a raspy voice, "how can I help you?"

Vance no longer looked human. The gangrene covered his legs, his arms, his chest, his face, and probably the inside of his body. Miles thought he had been turned inside out. It was hideous. A small fire burned on his face turning the torn flesh into a black char. Black burns mixed in with the dried blood of flesh that had been ripped off. He grunted with each breath. The smell of burning flesh nauseated Miles. It did not mix well with the odor of human waste.

"Mr. Chairman, I come in peace."

Vance screamed in agony, "Don't say that!"

"Sorry, what I am mean to say is—" Miles contemplated his next words carefully. He didn't want to give him the impression that this was about betraying his sister. "We seem to have the same problem."

"You're talking of Lazarus. What is your beef with the man?" Vance lost some of the gravel in his voice. He could feel the hate brewing within Miles.

"Well, I want to get back to fighting. I hate all this peace and love, not war crap. I figured it was time to get back to fighting our battles the old-fashioned way, with gun powder. Plus, Lazarus and, well, my sis—"

"You don't want a nigger screwing her."

"No. No, it's not—I mean, I'm not, like a racist or anything." Miles stopped and began to pace. Leave it to the devil's advocate to be brutally honest. "There's something about it. It's not right." Miles reflected back on peering through the window of the conference room back at Mt. Rushmore. He saw the kiss. It made him sick to his stomach.

Vance's face began to clear. How wonderful it would be to have an insider. Not someone working *for* him, but unknowingly taking this world on the same path. All in the name of 'God.' He chuckled. Miles didn't like it. The Chairman didn't care. This man's prejudice was the perfect kind. The Dark One had begun to seek those who hide their hate within.

"Say no more. There could be some casualties."

Miles nodded. "I understand." He had his own vision of who that casualty might be.

"We will start with Lazarus."

Miles quickly sat up.

"But I need him alive! Do you understand me?"

"That shouldn't be a problem."

"Good. Then we have an accord." Vance motioned for him to leave. The new aide for Chairman Vance walked Miles out. They talked about the plan. Miles gave him information about the fort at Mt. Rushmore and where to find Lazarus. Soon his one and only problem would be removed. Together with his sister and Jonas, they would battle Vance to get Lazarus back. Only—by the time they got there—it would be too late. The so-called hero would be dead. But the sacrifice of one would save many. The resistance would stop acting like a bunch of pussies and fight for a true victory.

There were times when we all needed to make a deal with the devil. Miles knew this was one of those times. Sure they had seen peace for a couple of months. But by the looks of that hideous thing calling himself the Chairman it wouldn't be long before he unleashed the full power of Jahannam— or, whatever Miles thought was the United States.

He strolled down what was once called Highway 79 towards the fort at Hermosa. It was a beautiful June day without a cloud in the sky. The thunderstorms would come later in the afternoon or in the middle of the night.

This was Miles' fifth summer living here. He and Abigail had bounced around a lot after the fire in the Smokey Mountains before settling in the Black Hills. He had to admit it was perfect since most of the Dakotas, parts of Wyoming and all of Montana had been deserted by Americans. The need for food, water and shelter forced them into big cites mainly on the two coasts. Places like Denver and St. Louis grew by leaps and bounds. The drone attacks and the lack of supplies to remote areas chased everybody out.

Vance figured it was easier to find them if they were in a few designated areas, as for the rest, he used the drones to help hone the skills of his pilots or let the citizens starve to death. Some survived and became radicalized like the Wild Ones, yet others made it to the fort at Mt. Rushmore.

When they first arrived it was a safe place to rebuild the resistance from, but, now that was no longer true. Vance knew everything. And it was Miles, the son of Jack Payne, who was responsible.

A small hill led up to an abandoned gas station. The rains had made everything green. The smell of the wet grass was much more pleasant than the attacking mosquitos. Miles wore a black pair of shorts with a t-shirt that had *Mount Rushmore* written on it. His fair skin was brutally attacked by the blood-sucking bugs in the air. He slapped at his skin and itched, but for the most part he worked at ignoring it.

One of the men up at the community had developed an insect repellent out of natural ingredients, but Miles refused to use it. Somewhere along the lines he picked up that *real men don't cry* mentality. Abigail knew it didn't come from their father. The man practically cried at everything. Maybe some men are born with it.

On the other side of the gas station was a drive-in theater. The screens had been torn down. The small building was used as the headquarters where scouts reported in from all different locations.

Finding, stealing and creating batteries for the walkie-talkies were the biggest issue for all the resistance outposts around the country. Each day a new location would sprout up. In most big cities they were used to coordinate the peace movements. The red-eyes tried hard to break them up, but had been ordered not to kill anyone. The use of fire hoses and night sticks became common at the rallies. The resistance would use methods to protect them, but were told not to engage in a hateful or violent way. Abigail told the people how these red-eyes had been drugged and were not at fault. She told the people they could be saved, perhaps, by love.

Up ahead Miles could see three men briskly walking towards him. The one in the middle was Zack. Miles waved. Zack did not. Miles stopped. Two men moved around him to each side, but Zack stayed in front with anger in his eyes.

"Arrest him," he told the two men. Before Miles could make a case or say anything he was in handcuffs.

"What the hell are you doing? She won't stand for this!" Zack said.

Zack turned around and led them back to the small building.

Miles wondered how he found out. The idea that Vance double-crossed him didn't make any sense. But, then again, he was dealing with the devil. Maybe they were just guessing. It must be Lazarus sending in the orders all the way from the streets of Denver. Even with the black bastard gone, he still controlled what his sister did. *Pathetic*. Miles' stomach turned thinking about her with him. Then, realizing his predicament, he felt shame.

Did I really make a deal with the enemy? What was I thinking? He put his head down. *Can she ever forgive me? I'm so sorry, Abby.*

***

Locked arm-in-arm leading a group of thousands down a once-crowded street of Denver, Lazarus thought about his mentor. He thought about how he kept his feelings for Abigail at bay. The battle of a fear he could not fully comprehend and keeping his ego in check was no easy feat. Studying the face and eyes of Martin Luther King in pictures from King's freedom marches in the 1960s Lazarus often thought about what was going on in his mind. Now he wondered if what he was feeling is what King was feeling then.

Lazarus struggled to keep a meal down. At night he would suffer from panic attacks. Then the ego would flare up. He would tell himself all the good *he* was doing. But he trudged on getting little moments of comfort from God—even when he asked for it.

The riot squad was less than a mile up the empty street. On the left Lazarus could see remnants of Mile High Stadium. Memories of him and his father watching their beloved Raiders play the Broncos came storming back. Quickly he would come back to reality seeing the red-eyes dressed in all black carrying batons and shields and wearing helmets.

Lazarus once thought how cool it would have been to march for civil rights back in the 60s. It's not that cool now that it has become reality. This time it's not to convince free people to be true to their words *that all men are created equal*. This time it's for the God-given right of all people to experience what no longer is true for anyone. Freedom.

Lazarus still held on to the old ideas that a black man marching for a couple pieces of paper written by rich white folks was more than ironic. But the words and ideas of men like King, like Fredrick Douglass, came rushing back. They *knew* the ideas were profound—all they asked was for the words and ideas be followed. The problem now was all the bickering.

Lazarus hoped this coming together, regardless of religion or skin color, would be the final fight the United States would need so all could enjoy the liberty Thomas Jefferson once wrote so passionately about.

But some work still needed to be done. They were winning the fight through peace. But it was fragile. It wouldn't take much to turn the people that had followed him faithfully for the past few months. Hate and violence was so easy to fall back on. Each night he prayed for every soul in America to understand what they were up against. Not only was freedom at stake, but their very souls. The devil wanted it. God wanted it. But the two had very different ideas of what that meant. Love versus hate. When EVIL was spelled backwards it became LIVE. And Lazarus wanted to live.

The ensuing clash of peace versus violence marched closer. On his right was Jonas. Jonas had taught him all about Jesus. The two of them had become the best of friends. Lazarus may have turned thirty-five the week before, but Jonas was ten years older. The two of them had spent each night discussing having another 'five' birthday. Jonas told him it was a time of reflection.

He said he remembered struggling with having Abs as his leader five years ago when he turned forty. How through prayer he came to humble himself enough to follow a woman into battle.

"Her ability to fight didn't hurt," he told Lazarus, "but I had to walk through my own misconceptions about women in general."

Lazarus could understand that. He still battled over his ideas of Muslims even though the soldier currently marching on his left was one. Jonas told him he needed to acknowledge his prejudice and pray that God will remove it. It didn't help that the man's name was Osama. He also talked with an accent, but Lazarus had spent time with him. He was a good man fighting the same fight for liberty, for peace, for his very soul. It was so much easier to demonize what he didn't understand.

"No matter what happens to me, don't let it derail you from our ultimate mission." Lazarus yelled to the marching resistance. The symbol he had become especially in the Midwest was both good and dangerous. He was shocked Vance hadn't already killed him.

The smell of sweat and fear swirled over both sides. The blazing summer heat gave the marchers a preview of what hell might be like. Each man and woman prayed for strength as Lazarus had taught them to do right before the clubbing began. A memory of John Watters flashed before him.

"How do I know what to believe in?" he asked his mentor. He was so young, so lost in the idealistic world he thought he shared with then Congressman Forrest Vance.

"You will know," John said. "For starters, you're more than welcomed to steal what I started with many years ago. I just figured my Creator was loving and caring. It has grown since then, but that's where it started." Lazarus had no use for that advice back then, but was so grateful he could lean on it now. He also understood how in the last few months that he had grown.

Jesus had saved him. No matter what happened today he knew that deep in his heart, and the idea that his faith had led others to be saved as well. The true battle didn't happen in the streets, it happened within.

Within each man, woman and child was the fundamental idea they had a choice to make. The true battle was for their very souls.

The first batons hit. Lazarus was taken by surprise and fell to one knee. The left side of his head began to throb. He looked up. The baton was on its way back for another blow. There was no way he could get his hands up in time.

But the guard was kicked in the chest before he could finish the swing, and went flying back. It was Osama. Irony was a bitch.

Lazarus stood up. All around there was chaos. The crowd had dispersed, and the Denver Guard clubbed the marchers in an all-out frenzy.

Lazarus felt something wet on the side of his face. He wiped. Blood was coming out of his ear. His head ached. From his right came a clubbing guard. He dodged the baton, grabbed the man's arm, and flipped him. He landed a roundhouse kick to another man Osama was defending himself from in what was slowly becoming a losing battle. Osama nodded and went back to work.

About twenty yards away Lazarus could see a man being beaten continuously by an overzealous red-eye. He ran over to help.

Once he stepped up ready to knock the guard off of the man he heard the crack of his skull. The man's body went completely limp. The Guard hit once more and stopped. As if the entire crowd could hear the splitting head open and begin to ooze blood, they all froze. No one defended themselves. No guard used his baton. All of them turned and stared at the offending guard. The body on the ground suddenly squirmed a couple of times. It was the first death on either side since just after Abigail implemented the peace plan.

The guard squealed. He dropped his shield and baton. His head jerked from side to side and he clawed at his arms and face. Scratches caused bleeding, but his real scream of pain came from inside his body. The man's feet were on fire.

The cry grew louder. The flames climbed up his legs and circle his midsection. The scream was unbearable. Lazarus stood there stunned. He couldn't even feel the heat. It was as if only *this* man could experience the hell growing around him. And hell it was. The flames engulfed him. The size of the fire was six feet tall. The crowd watched in horror. Even the red-eyes didn't want to watch, but did out of loyalty to their Dark Master. The intensity of the man size flame began to shrink. It became a huge ball quickly dissipating taking the body with it. A final *poof*. Nothing was left. Not even an ash.

The Denver Guard dropped their shields and batons in front of them. They walked away. The marchers cheered. The city was free.

As they rambled away, many of the red-eyes started to *come to* not remembering anything. Others curled up being taken by the flame that dragged them down. Their hell had just begun. The rest of the Denver Guard lay down and slept. Each one took a final breath. The crowd watched as a white smoke danced its way up to heaven. Souls were saved that day. But some were lost.

"Mr. Parker, Mr. Parker!" a young man came running up to him. He wore a frightful look.

"What is it, Ray?" Lazarus asked. Jonas and Osama came up to hear the news.

"It's Miss Payne, they took her. The fort at Mt. Rushmore is gone."

***

It was midnight by the time they made it to the outpost in Hermosa. Lazarus and Jonas pulled the Champion into the old drive-in theater and parked at headquarters. The two of them walked in. Zack sat in a maroon office chair behind a small desk. Streaks of red streamed down each side of his face. Lazarus knew he had been crying.

"How you doing?" he asked.

"It's a horror show up there. I—I don't know what we're going to do." He never looked up to meet their eyes.

"Where's Miles? Is he okay?" Jonas asked.

Zack shook his head, "He doesn't know, he's…well, locked up."

"What? Why?" Lazarus' voice rose. He wasn't the biggest fan of Miles, but it was Abigail's brother. That boy was always on her mind. Lazarus knew the guilt she felt. They had talked about it for hours. He would discuss his parents and Angie and the child. They had many scars.

"He…betrayed us."

Jonas couldn't believe it. He yelled at Zack and demanded to see the kid.

Lazarus knew it was true. Miles was jealous of the relationship between his sister and him. The dirty looks, the snide comments, all of it pointed to a man so filled with pride and anger that he was the easiest target for Vance. Confusion was the devil's greatest weapon. Some people would say doubt, but Lazarus knew better.

"Jonas, stop, where is he?"

"In the back."

Lazarus walked over to Zack and put his hand on his shoulder. He said a silent prayer. The prayer was for him as much as it was for Zack. Lazarus had fallen in love with Abigail. He worked hard to hide it. It was obvious the chemistry between them, but both he and Abigail denied it. Not only to others, but themselves as well. The kiss still lingered each time they were together. At this moment, faced with the idea of never seeing her again, the wall Lazarus had built up had come crashing down. It would be different if he got her back.

God wants me to be happy. God wants everybody to be happy.

"Don't lose hope, my friend, victory is within our grasp."

He whispered to Zack, his soul struggling with doubt. Zack nodded fighting back more tears.

The three of them made their way into a back room where Miles was sleeping in a bed. He was handcuffed to a metal ring on the ground. Jonas kicked him.

He awoke. "Holy shit, when did you guys get back?"

"Just now, where is she?" Lazarus' voice was stern and distant.

"Wha—who?"

"Your sister, they took her."

"That son-ova-bitch! It…well, that wasn't supposed to happen."

"What does that mean?" Jonas kicked him again. The anger in his eyes was brewing. Miles was visibly shaking.

Miles rubbed his eyes. "Look, I screwed up. I… I went to Vance, yes, but not to betray you guys, just so, we…well, could fight again."

Lazarus faced away from him and rubbed his head. It was time to shave again. A struggle fermented within.

Peace, Lazarus, peace.

"I know, damn it, I know," he yelled out. Then shame overcame him. The other three guys stared at him. Lazarus turned around, started to say something, then laughed. "Look, Miles, what can you tell us? Anything?"

"Not really, he was…well…"

"Spit it out!" Jonas exclaimed.

"He was supposed to grab Lazarus. He wants him. I figured with you out of the picture we could go back to the way things were. He was going to take you to Kingman, you know, Pike's Peak. That's where he is at. I'm sorry, Lazarus. I just—" He put his head in his hands and cried. "I didn't know he was going to hurt *Abs*." Miles sobbed. "I'm sorry."

The three of them headed out to the front. Zack was so angry his first thought was execution. Jonas didn't think they needed to go *that* far, but a punishment was in order. The two of them bickered back and forth.

"Jonas, Zack, we need to forgive," Lazarus said wearily. They went at it again, baiting Lazarus to join them. Lazarus wished Abigail was here to quiet the disturbance. She was the voice of reason. When she spoke, they listened. Sure it was his words that had been transmitted around the country, but it was her *voice*. The problem was now he was the one that needed to lead.

Abigail and he had spent endless nights talking about when the day would come and he would lead the resistance. She told him it was her vision, that he would make the final blow to Vance. That he must lead the final charge. It scared Lazarus. He was no leader of men. That was her department. But like all the other fires he had been through, it was time for him to walk through yet another. The time to lead had come.

"Gentlemen!" he cried.

Jonas and Zack turned.

"Now is the time. Vance has set up camp at Pikes Peak. That's where he is holding Abigail. And that is where the final battle will take place." He paused putting a hand on each of them. "We need him to come with us. We need to forgive him for all the atrocities."

Jonas immediately countered, "I think that may be dangerous. What if—"

"No 'what ifs,' Jonas. A clean slate. That's what you taught me, we all get a clean slate. I can't look into somebody's heart, but it appears to me that Miles is asking for our forgiveness. We have to give it to him; we need him to come along, for our hearts must remain pure."

"The student becomes the teacher," Jonas said with a tremble in his voice. The three of them embraced.

They released Miles and piled into the Champion. The first stop would be Mt. Rushmore. Lazarus sat in the back next to Miles. They did not speak. He thought about Abigail and what he needed to tell her, if given the chance.

Love was a funny thing. It came in all shapes and sizes. He loved the men in the car. They had saved him in more ways than he could count. He loved the community at Rushmore. They had taught him how to coexist and live peacefully, even in the eye of the storm. He still loved his parents, Angie, his unborn son; they would always hold a special place in his heart. He was now able to forgive himself, but it had been a tough road.

And he loved Abigail.

What he had denied himself since the moment they made eye contact in the chow hall seemed so silly now. Jonas pulled the car in to what was left of the parking garage at Mt. Rushmore and stopped.

When they got the first look at the damage, the mood was somber. The four of them stumbled through a mess. It was two in the morning and able bodied people were still cleaning up the rubble. The presidents' faces were gone. Erased from the mountain like a drawing on a chalkboard. The tattered flags of each state laid flat in the dead calm. The chow hall had turned into a makeshift hospital.

William O'Bannon ran up to them. "Lazarus, we have hundreds injured, and hundreds are dead. We have no idea. I have no idea when we will get an accurate count. Bodies— they're everywhere. I... I don't know what happened, it was...so quick. Drones, ground troops, how did they get by our outposts?"

"This is my fault. I told Vance. I can't tell you how sorry I am," Miles said.

"What?" William looked at Miles, realizing he had betrayed them. "You bastard." Tears streamed down his face. "Children were killed. I don't care how sorry you are."

"We have to forgive, William," Lazarus said softly.

"I don't think I can do that," he trudged off.

The cleanup continued. Miles, Jonas, Zack and Lazarus jumped in to help. It was almost noon by the time the people slowed down long enough to take in what had happened. Many sat down in circles, silently hoping to wake from this nightmare. The kitchen had fried up chislic. The skewers of meat lightly seasoned with garlic salt were a welcomed sight for the hungry mourners.

The crowd that circled together just outside of the chow hall was just over sixty strong. A far cry from the thousands the resistance numbered just a few days prior.

Lazarus thought back to the radio address he heard Abigail give. *Summer soldiers and Sunshine patriots.* The words of Thomas Paine that sparked a nation. Here in front of him sat those unwilling to *shrink from the service of their country. The celestial article of freedom* is and should be *highly rated*. Here Lazarus was not faced with defeat, but instead could proudly stand with those who would stand up and oppose tyranny. These were the people that deserved *the love and thanks of man and woman*.

He got up on his feet and spoke loudly, "My fellow Americans." The quiet chatter ceased. "We are but a step away from taking back this country from what we thought was an unimaginable evil. Forrest Vance tricked us with his promises and charm. By the time he took off the mask it was too late, or so we thought. But *our* time has come. Just like our countrymen who fought the tyranny of King George, those who stood up for freedom and kept our Union together, and those who marched in our streets to make the words in our Constitution and Declaration a reality for all, it is *our* time to fight so others can be free. To fight for our own liberty. To fight for the loved ones lost here and over the past decade. To do everything in our power to bring back our fearless leader, Abigail Payne. There will be a time to mourn, but we must stand together now."

The crowd rose, each of them lost in the moment.

"We must stand up to Vance and his evil. I cannot promise all of us will live to see his demise, but those left behind will have the opportunity to rebuild, giving thanks to our Creator, a new covenant. A chance to live by those founding words of this great nation. There will be no need to spill any more blood. Our children, and their children, will be able to live where freedom is not just on their lips, but in their veins. Our generation is blessed to have a cause worth dying for."

The audience erupted in applause and cried freedom.

Lazarus sat down with Jonas, Zack and Miles and started to go over the plans. A crew would need to stay behind to finish up the work here. Some would need to travel to Kingman with them. Were there enough Champions around? How many were needed? What do we tell those left behind if they didn't return?

Time was of the essence. They would leave the day after

tomorrow. Today they would plan, they would rest, and then the battle for the soul of America would be decided.

***

Abigail sat in her prison cell in the basement of the castle at Pikes Peak. She had been here before: Vance upstairs plotting what to do with her; playing God with the ability to manage other people's lives. It was sad, really. There was no fear for Abigail. Live or die, she knew her life had made a difference. That wasn't true over eight years ago when her life with Barker came to a sudden end. Never did she think that the man responsible for crashing her wedding would be the man she would fall in love with.

Regret. There was one. Lazarus. They allowed the scars they carried to keep them apart. Foolish. If they weren't fighting for the freedom to be together, then what is *this* all for? Lazarus endlessly talked about God's love and our love for each other, but deep down both of them were afraid to love each other.

"If I get out of this one," she scanned the sixteen by sixteen cell, "I'll tell him."

She smiled remembering the last time she made a promise to herself. It was that day Lazarus and her first met. He came in and went all kung fu on those two guards. Even then she was impressed, even a bit attracted to him, but she had Barker. *Boy, was my picker broken.*

Abigail reflected back on their last meeting together before he left for Denver. It was all business. Or at least that's what the two of them strived for. Miles told her after that he didn't like what was going on between her and Lazarus. She figured he was jealous.

Lazarus' hand had lightly brushed across hers; it was magic. They gazed at each other. Locked in a stare of eternity, yet it only lasted but a minute. The kiss weighed heavy on her mind. There was nothing more frustrating than finally finding something real to live for only to realize you're at the end.

Two guards appeared and opened the door. They motioned

for her to turn around. She hadn't seen the Chairman since she had been abducted. She prayed for the strength to stay strong. She had been exposed to his disgusting ways in the past and she didn't want to relive it. But now, in a way, she felt sorry for him. His need to take what he wanted had fear and loathing written all over it. That kind of anger and hate and need to control must be exhausting.

"Thank you for the simple life, Lord," she said looking up. The two guards put on her restraints and led her up the stairs to the living quarters.

***

The place was in complete disarray. Dust settled everywhere. The project to redesign the house had come to a screeching halt. Vance had bigger fish to fry he told the foreman. He was so angry at the time. Grabbing the foreman by the collar, he stole a glance into the man's soul. He couldn't kill him. The man was not ready for hell. He threw him aside and pouted.

"Abigail, how are you?" he said in a raspy voice she could hardly understand. His face was so disfigured it looked as if his lips were sideways. The blood and pus spit out of his body from every pore. He wasn't easy to look at. She felt ill.

He grunted in pain. Vance no longer had the use of his right arm. Pointing with his left he continued, "I can't tell you how much I would love to kill you."

"So why don't you?" she turned her face away.

Vance knew his Master would kill him for it. No way would her soul be collected by the devil. He had no desire to tell Abigail this, for if he did she probably would sacrifice her own life for others. The ultimate in unselfishness. It made him sick just thinking about it. Plus his Master would have a whole different place in hell for a demon to allow something like *that* to happen. No, he knew what he had to do, it had to be Lazarus. The final blow needed to set up the next one. The sense of loss for Abigail and the rest of those fools would lead many to the dark side. It was his last and only play. She was the bait. But he wouldn't mind if the collateral damage ended up killing the bitch.

"In time, my dear, in time." He cracked a crooked smile.

"I see you can't get it up anymore. Looks like the devil cut it off. A fate worse than death for a rapist piece of shit like you."

Abigail started to shake. Memories of the white house with the white carpet and white sheets flooded every thought. Conjuring up the past, she hoped to get him to strike her down. She knew his game. The *peace* Lazarus talked about was as clear as day. If Vance killed her she would be in heaven with her Father enjoying eternal life. He would be just another failure to his Master.

Vance showed his teeth. Sharp, pointy. A swirling fire enveloped his left hand as he tried to reach out to strangle the life out of Abigail. He screamed in pain and retracted. "You bitch," he said.

From behind him he pulled out a long-sword with a ruby handle. The blade was black and forty three inches long. He wielded it easily with one hand. He stepped up to Abigail and hissed. His breath smelled of rotting flesh.

She gaged.

***

The time has come.

Lazarus wasn't quite sure what the voice was trying to tell him. All he could do was pray for its understanding.

The past day was busy. Clean up still went on as he planned the trip to Kingman. They could bring only three Champions; at most fifteen men could go. The word went out on who would make the trip.

"Osama—" he said to the man, as he realized he no longer held on to his old ideas. Lazarus was now free of the prejudice. He owed *that* to God. It had taken no effort on his part, only to *let go*. Jonas had been a great spiritual teacher to Lazarus. The Word was clear. Lazarus would not hate Osama based on his religious beliefs. It was no easy feat, but his heart was now clean—thanks to the power of the Creator.

"Osama, I need you to go with us. You will help Zack and Jonas on the ground gathering up people for the final peace march." He put his arm around him, "I trust you."

Night was beginning to fall. It was almost nine and still work needed to be done. The cars were equipped with additional canisters. The work stopped for a religious service. God's meal was prepared and those who were saved by Jesus ate of His body and drank of His blood. Everyone joined in prayer. Even the few who did not believe were not offended, and showed their respect. When it was done the community had a feast. Leftovers were packed for those leaving the next morning.

The time has come. Again, the voice.

Lazarus kept moving knowing more would be revealed. Rifling through his clothes, he stumbled upon the sword O'Bannon had given him. He didn't know why but there was a strong tug for him to take it. He sheathed it and wrapped it around his waist.

"Lazarus? Can I talk to you?" William asked.

"What is it?"

"I was wondering why I'm not going with you. I mean, I'm sorry for what I said to Miles. At the time I had seen so much—death."

"William, my friend, there is a time to fight and there is a time to heal. It is my time to fight. It is your time to heal. You need to put the pieces back together. A much more important job for you is here, than those of us who are going to fight. You need to *heal* their wounds." The words poured out.

It was then that Lazarus knew why he needed to bring the sword.

And seeing the sword at his side O'Bannon knew he may never see his friend again. "This isn't because of Miles?"

"No. You're staying because I cannot think of a better man to help these people rebuild their lives. You are tasked with continuing the resistance if we are to fail."

William O'Bannon gulped. His eyes grew big.

Lazarus gave him a hug.

In his embrace William felt a comfort he would never be

able to explain.

"I trust you," Lazarus whispered into his ear. The two of them walked up to the chow hall where most of the people had started to gather.

Lazarus walked up to Jonas and Zack, "Where is Miles?"

They shrugged.

"I'm here," he said. Miles was coming from the direction of where the faces once looked down from.

"Where you been?" William questioned.

Lazarus glared at him. He knew O'Bannon asked because of his distrust and dislike of Miles. He prayed the two of them could let it go.

"Just helping out." He turned and pointed at a group still removing debris from the lookout. "Lazarus, can we talk?"

"Sure. Guys, can you give us a minute?" The other three scattered. "What can I do for you, Miles?" Lazarus folded his arms over his chest.

"I know we've had our differences. I just want you to know I'm here now. I wasn't for a long time, but I'm here now." He appeared forlorn. "I just want to get her back."

Lazarus stepped up and gave Miles a tight hug. "That's the plan, my friend. I need you pure on this one. The two of us will be there with Vance, but I need you to keep that gun in its holster. Your job is to get her out of there. Mine is to fight. This is your time to heal." He pushed Miles away from him but still kept a firm grip on his shoulder. He peered into his eyes. "Do you know what I'm talking about?"

"Yeah, you won't be coming back, will you?"

"I certainly hope that's not the case, but it is a possibility." The voice was directing him to fight for the first time. He wasn't even sure if that's what he was supposed to do, but in his gut it felt right. The time was ripe for this final confrontation.

Miles looked upset by the news. He nodded with his head down and walked away.

Lazarus didn't know how much he could trust a man that just two days prior caused so much heartache. And yet he had to. He didn't have a choice. Forgiveness was the main ingredient needed to save America from the clutches of Satan and his agents. Lazarus knew peace, forgiveness, tolerance, love, were all important, but the devil was always finding a way to twist one more than the others.

He strolled over to the chow hall and took in a deep breath. It may be his last one here in the beautiful Black Hills. Just about the time he had finally understood what he was meant to do in this life, that's when God comes calling.

"I guess it makes sense," he whispered to himself. "When the student is ready the teacher appears." It was an old tale. All he could comprehend was the human in him. There was a quiet disappointment deep down for all he would miss in life. And still the idea of meeting his Maker was exciting. He prayed for the strength to walk through *this* fire and be willing to make the ultimate sacrifice, if that was His will.

***

The three Champions stopped on Briar Street in Kingman. The time had come for Miles and Lazarus to depart. They sped off towards Pikes Peak. The others discussed how they would divide up the town to get the people to rise. Then, Osama pointed.

In the streets the red-eyes had already started to gather. It was too late to call on the good people of Kingman. The resistance numbered ten. The Guard numbered in the hundreds.

"We need to hold them off as long as we can. We have to give Lazarus time," Jonas told the others. He fell to his knees and put in a word with the Man Upstairs. He stood up—and the fight began.

The red-eyes slithered up to the overpass the small band of rebels decided to make their last stand. They were in full riot gear marching to the beat of their own batons.

"It was a pleasure serving with you, Jonas," Zack said.

Jonas ran up, grabbed a soldier's baton, and flipped the man stealing his weapon. He grabbed the shield off the ground, turned and said, "I'm not ready to say goodbye quite yet, Zack!" and pounced on the enemy.

Zack laughed and took another guard as his prey. The

rest of the resistance started in, but the numbers were too overwhelming. Slowly the resistance became consumed by the guard.

And then… Jonas noticed from all over citizens of the community came to the rescue of the freedom fighters. The red-eyes turned to concentrate on the much larger force. For miles the men could see people leaving their homes to come to the aid of their countrymen.

"I'll be damned," Osama said, "you Americans really are crazy."

"You keep fighting like that and we'll have to make you one of us."

"Jonas, I will always be one of you."

Zack ran up, "Hey, Jonas, I have to go. Don't ask me why because I can't explain it, but I need to be with Lazarus."

Jonas shrugged, "Out of all the crazy shit I've heard lately this one doesn't rate. Go, and God be with you. As for the rest of us, let's kick some red-eye butt!"

Zack jumped into one of the Champions and sped off. The rest of the rebels joined the thousands in the streets taking the guard down.

It wasn't long before the red-eyes *came to* as had happened in other parts of the country. A fire swirled and took away those with hate in their hearts. Others became the white puff of smoke that danced all the way up to heaven. The people cheered, yet there still was a sadness to the day.

Jonas knew this was the easy part. Up on the mountaintop the real fight would begin any minute now. They had done all that was asked of them. He knew it was selfish, but he prayed asking that Lazarus and Abigail come home with them. It was a tall order. He was willing to trade places with either of them, or one of them. Whatever it took.

***

On Pikes Peak the door had come crashing down. Miles, Zack and Lazarus stormed in.

"Lazarus!" Abigail called out. Vance laughed and started his long blade towards her.

She ducked just in time. Another swing at her, but Lazarus had arrived to defend the killing blow. The clash of metal rang out. Lazarus did everything he could just to hold on to the blade. Vance asked for more and more power from his Master below. He released and went to strike again.

"Where is Miles?" Lazarus asked Zack.

"Here," and there he was using a key to unlock his sister's chains.

The swords met once again.

Vance was powerful. Too powerful. Lazarus could smell the blood of others on the Chairman's blade. The room grew hotter and sweat dripped from every pore. A slip of the blade caught Lazarus in his gut. The cut was two inches deep. Blood had been spilled.

He wiped the sweat from his forehead, then held onto his side. Another strike by the Chairman. Lazarus held his ground. A kick to Vance's elbow loosened his grip, but he regained it. Another blow; the Civil War sword went flying across the room. Lazarus was unarmed. He stood straight up accepting his fate.

"This will be my sweetest kill," Vance brought the blade down.

"NO!" Zack shrieked. Rushing in from the front Zack jumped in front of the sword. The cut sliced him in two. Death was immediate.

Vance brought back the weapon and laughed. What could that possibly do but kill the both of them. He loved it. The chance to leave this world more hopeless than when he arrived.

Again Vance lifted the blade, ready to strike.

A whisper in his ear. The air escaped him. He knew what he had to do. The sacrifice of Zack was not the resistance's final blow, but instead it was *His* final blow. Unselfishness. Damn Him. The voices wanted him to do it. *God abhors suicide.*

Vance knew what had to be done, and never had he felt more alone, so empty. Only a hole remained. It would remain for eternity—a hell in its own right.

Vance propped up the sword preparing to fall on it. The

devil would find no honor in his sacrifice. A brief thought that maybe he shouldn't do it entered his mind.

Do it! The voices demanded.

"But, can I kill Lazarus?" he asked. The voices wanted him to end his own life, yet Vance still held on to the hate for Lazarus. And Vance knew it wouldn't end there. Abigail would be next. Then Miles. Then Jonas. Ad infinitum.

Vance turned the sword back on Lazarus who still stood there stunned by the cries and pleas and screams of the beast before him. Snapping back into reality Lazarus turned to locate his sword. It was gone. Lazarus held on to his side realizing his life would soon end.

"AHHHHH!" Vance shrieked. Looking down he saw Miles, sword in hand. He had been run through. Blood spit out of his gut. Miles pushed in. Another screech. Vance dropped his blade.

With both hands Miles pulled out the sword. He lifted it up. Closing his eyes he pulled back and with all his might he swung lodging the sword in Vance's neck. He held on to life as long as he could. The gasps for air raised the hair on Mile's arms. He coughed up blood and screamed. The body twitched. The final breath came when he realized it was useless to try and shed a tear for his life lost. His Master would never let him. Forrest Vance went limp and his soul made its way to the very pits of hell.

Lazarus and Abigail stared at each other.

"Well, say something to each other," Miles said.

Abigail ran into Lazarus' arms. Lazarus held on to her tight. They kissed.

"I love you. I never want to let go," Lazarus confessed.

"You know, these things don't usually last," Abigail said.

"I know, but let's enjoy it until then."

Abigail and Lazarus walked hand in hand out the front door. Miles smiled. Across the moat came a Champion. It stopped and out jumped Jonas and Osama.

"What happened?" asked Jonas.

"It's over," Lazarus answered.

Jonas looked down at their hands and up at God. He couldn't believe it. His prayer had been answered. Then he realized Zack was not there. He was with God now. Victory could be so bitter sweet.

The crew sat down on the stairs leading to the front door. Abigail bandaged up Lazarus. A word or two would be exchanged, but none of them knew how to feel. Zack was gone. Each of them talked a little about the man and what he had meant to them. Tears were shed. Vance was gone. Relief. But it was hard to say the killing of a man, even one as evil as Chairman Vance, was something to celebrate. At least not yet. The time had finally come for the resistance to return home.

"Now what?" Miles put his arms in the air.

"Now we rebuild," Osama said and turned to Lazarus.

"That's right. America is reborn."

18

Lazarus sat at the microphone not knowing how to begin. He loved the old-fashioned look of it, of everything. Miles and Abigail watched from the other side of the cave, realizing they were witnessing history.

The metal felt cold in his hands. Lazarus stood up and started to pace. It was as if he knew exactly how to act, yet the words had not come. All over the country the red-eyes had been defeated. The future was bright. Still, there needed to be a unifying voice. And here at Mt. Rushmore the community had picked Lazarus. Her dream had come full circle; it had come true.

It was five minutes to air time and all that Lazarus could think about was *her*. Two weeks after Pikes Peak they married in the auditorium at Mt. Rushmore. Jonas was his best man. Miles led the service. It could not have been more perfect. Since Zack was the reason they could have a life together, they promised to name their first son after him, if God blessed them so. A memorial was planned at the site of his death. The people of Kingman renamed the town Thorn Springs to remind them of the past, the present, and the future.

Two minutes to broadcast. The words still were not there. What to do? It had been two months since the final battle was won. The pieces needed to be put back together. Lazarus knew an entire nation sat by their radio to hear his message. It was the new fireside chat. And he was about to deliver the first.

Thirty seconds. He had to come up with something. Then, like a bolt of lightning it came. He had been searching for *his* words. What he needed was *hers*. The red light flashed:

"*You are not alone*," he started. "*You are not alone!*"

258

And throughout the country there was the cry of freedom. Love, tolerance, understanding, all came down on the people like a soft rain that day. The impossible road ahead felt possible.

"The time has come for our nation to heal. Out of the depths of hell we have risen to live once more to claim our unalienable rights of life, liberty, and the pursuit of happiness. What an exciting time God has chosen us to live in. We have endured the greatest threat to our liberty and proved once again that man is capable of governing himself. It will not be an easy road, but it will be one that we can travel together. The self-evident ideas our founders wrote down over two hundred and fifty years ago can once again live and breathe in each one of us."

Miles put his hand around his sister. They gave each other a smile. He whispered it was time for him to go. She nodded and he walked out of the cave up to the chow hall. The words of Lazarus blared throughout the community. Crowds circled in bunches and hung on his every syllable. In silence Miles walked up the hill, giving a nod to those who caught his eye. He grinned from ear to ear. What a glorious time to be alive, he thought.

The blank spot where four presidents once towered over the hills already had men hard at work dedicated to sculpting it once more. But today nobody worked. It was a day to remember; it was a day to reflect on what the future held for America. Lazarus' healing words echoed in the background.

Walking past the chow hall and down towards the amphitheater Miles continued on. The aroma of soul food danced in the air. The words God had given to Lazarus on this day played a beautiful beat. Miles was filled with gratitude. He traveled down the presidential path that still made its way to where the faces once shined so bright. Past the first turn he trudged into a small section of the forest. The smell of pine filled his nose.

"What a wonderful time to be alive," he said to himself.

Just on the other side of a large tree to his right he found the entrance to an abandoned shed. The splintered wood showed signs of neglect. Once inside he strolled over to a step, kneeled down, and bowed his head.

Are you ready? the voices asked.

"Yes, Master."

You will be my greatest disciple yet.

Miles rose. His mouth had gone dry. He licked his lips, "Where do you want me to start?" he asked.

The devil wanted his soul. Miles gave it to him.

Acknowledgments

I am grateful for a loving wife who has supported me through the trials and tribulations it took to get this book to you. She drove thousands of miles as I wrote and read this novel to her on many long trips across the great state of South Dakota. Without her this would not have been possible.

I am grateful to a loving daughter for spending two summers watching me turn a dream into reality. For a host of friends and family that have been rooting me on since I started this venture over five years ago. I also want to thank those who took the time to read the earlier versions of this novel.

I want to thank Fred Mastison for taking the time to share with me and answer all my questions. I would like to thank Brittiany Koren and Denise Kirchmayer for their guidance and support through the editing and publishing phase of this book, and Eddie Vincent for creating a kickass cover.

I want to acknowledge the principal and staff at St. Thomas More Middle School for the opportunity to teach 7th and 8th graders the importance of writing in their lives. I want to thank them not only for their support in my writing career, but for their loving guidance and direction during my first year as a teacher.

To Matt Galbraith who always believed this book would happen. And for being a great guy to work with and work for.

To all my students—my life is richer because I had the opportunity to know each and every one of you.

To my father, John, who passed away in June of 2009. I miss you and pray that you can see me now. I did it, dad! I did it!

To my mom because not to mention her would be a crime. Her undying loyalty and unconditional love has kept me going even in the toughest of times.

And finally, for a loving God that without Him none of this would have been possible.

About the Author

Anthony D. Flores lives in Rapid City, South Dakota with his wife, youngest daughter, and two dogs. Born and raised in California, he moved to the beautiful Black Hills in 2004. He dreamed as a kid about becoming a teacher and writer. In 2006 he went back to college to make those dreams come true. Anthony earned his degree in Writing and Literature from Union Institute & University before attending Black Hills State University to achieve his teaching credentials. Currently he teaches 8th grade Social Studies and Writing at St. Thomas More Middle School. *Lazarus Rising* fulfills the other half of his dream and is his debut novel. He spends his down time in the summer studying American history, reading historical and science fiction, and working on his next book. To learn more about Anthony and his books, visit his website and blog at www.anthonydflores.com or follow him on twitter: @ FloresFreedom or on his Facebook page.